AWARD-WINNING
WINNING

TALES

MOONLIGHT MESA
ASSOCIATES

AWARD-WINNING TALES

©2011 MOONLIGHT MESA ASSOCIATES, INC.

ALL RIGHTS RESERVED

PRINTED IN THE UNITED STATES OF AMERICA

PUBLISHED BY:

Moonlight Mesa Associates, Inc.
18620 Moonlight Mesa Rd.
Wickenburg, Arizona, 85390
928-684-5235/5231
www.moonlightmesaassociates.com
orders@moonlightmesaassociates.com

Dealer Inquiries Welcome

ISBN: 978-0-9827585-1-9

LCCN: 2011900117

Cover and Gun Illustration by Vin Libassi

Dedicated to the Western writers
who freely contributed their stories to this book.

Joe Kilgore
Jon Adams
M. Carolyn Steele
Drew Davis
Robert Walton
Melissa Embry
Michael Fishman
Paula L. Silici
Simon Lake
Mark Redmond
T.A. Uner
James O'Brien
Paul Conn
Loree Westron
M. Edward Wyatt
Harold Miller
Arthur Kerns
Lane Thibodeaux
Barbara Marshak
Jerry Guin

Publisher's Note

Every story in this anthology is an award-winning Western tale, or at the very least a finalist in a short story writing competition. A brief biography follows each tale so that readers who enjoy an author's work can follow up with that writer.

As the editor/publisher of this work, I again want to thank every writer who so graciously and enthusiastically granted Moonlight Mesa Associates permission to include his/her story in this anthology. A portion of the proceeds of the sale of this book will be donated to a charitable cause.

The twenty-six stories contained herein are in no particular order. The reader will find olden-day Western stories intermixed with modern-day tales, and romances mingled with murders. Finding it very difficult to decide which story should go in what order, I did what any logical person would do and simply placed the stories in the book in the order in which they were drawn from a hat (a cowboy hat, of course). We regret that several stories arrived too late to be used in this collection.

As the publisher, I want to thank you, the reader, for your interest in this publication. Each reader, as well as each writer, along with all of us here at Moonlight Mesa Associates, are helping to KEEP THE SPIRIT OF THE WEST ALIVE.

Now, it's time to mount on up!

Becky (R.L.) Coffield, Publisher
January 2011

CONTENTS

Ned…..Joe Kilgore…..1

The Wild Ones…Jonathon Adams…11

Waiting for a Friend…M. Carolyn Steele…19

The Spittoon…Mark Redmond…31

The Dead Rope…James O'Brien…39

The Taming of Jump Off Joe…Becky Coffield…49

Indio…Robert Walton…57

Navidad…Robert Walton…67

Maniac…Drew Davis…77

Showdown at Diablo Flat…Michael Fishman…87

The Gesture…Joe Kilgore…97

Coahuila Captive…Drew Davis…109

Old Outlaw…M. Edward Wyatt…121

Llano Estacado…Lane Thibodeaux…133

The Bard of Stockman Flat…Harold Miller…141

The Best Things…Paula L. Silici…151

Eight Seconds…Melissa Embry…165

The Mystery of Fire Opal Mine…R.L. Coffield…177

Hostage to Fortune…Simon Lake…187

All the Water You Want…Jerry Guin…195

Lost Letters…Barbara Marshak…207

The Difference Between Cowboys and Clowns
Loree Westron…219

The Banker's Wife…T.A. Uner…229

Bull Pen…Paul Conn…239

Grabbing the Reins…Arthur Kerns…249

State of Grace…Becky Coffield…257

Award-
Winning

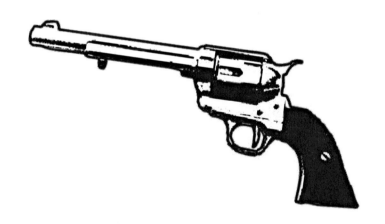

Tales

NED

Joe Kilgore

(2nd Place Winner 2009 Cowboy Up Contest)

In 1877, hard men came out of the Sonoran Desert. Those who weren't hard enough became carrion for coyotes and turkey vultures. Their bones bleached white beneath the Arizona sun.

Ned Ashford was one of the hardest. He had just done a year in Yuma for gutting a Mexican intent, from Ned's perspective, on giving him a new navel. The vaquero was cut stomach to spleen before his gun hand ever gripped pearl. Witnesses were divided on whether the Mex was going for his hogleg or merely trying to get the hell out of harm's way. That lack of consensus proved to be Ned's good fortune. It motivated the judge to substitute manslaughter for murder. A decision which kept Ned's neck from getting stretched. But it still cost him a year spent mostly in dark cells for conduct infractions and general orneriness. He even picked up a few extra weeks ball and chain time for telling guards that if given half a chance he'd bolt quicker than a mare could swat a horsefly off her ass. That pronouncement was deemed vainglorious insubordination rather than a bona fide escape attempt. So an additional year wasn't added to his sentence. But it wouldn't have mattered to Ned if it had been. He thought it was only right his jailers be aware of his intentions.

For better or worse, that's the way Ned was. The way he had been reared. His old man had instilled Ned with independence, backbone and absolute intolerance for anything but the truth. Liars were lower than pond scum, the boy was taught. And truth, no matter how harsh, was to be spoken straight out. A code his mother felt was taken to extreme when Ned's father told his son he couldn't take care of him anymore and the lad would have to make his own way in the world. She couldn't deny years of drought had taken its toll on their farm and livestock. And just having enough to put on the table at breakfast and supper was becoming virtually impossible. Still, in her view, for a fifteen year old it seemed cold. But her husband said he had imparted all the wisdom, character, riding and shooting skills he could. And he'd be damned if he was going to watch the fruit of his loins dry up and blow away on this same dirt graveyard that was laying claim to him and her.

So Ned left home with ten dollars in his pocket. Fully one-half his parent's life savings. He never saw his mother or father again. But over the next ten years he saw a war that spilled blood on both gray and blue uniforms.

He ate dust and drove cattle from Texas to Kansas. He played cards on riverboats, drank whiskey in saloons, spilled his seed in whore houses, knifed a man who turned out to be a lying cheat and a slow draw, and spent a year in Yuma Territorial Prison. Now he was out of jail and heading west toward the type of destiny fate enjoys doling out every now and then.

The tired roan Ned was riding snorted, shook her long neck and came to an abrupt halt that woke him. He had been drifting in and out of sleep for the past half hour. For an instant, he thought he might still be dreaming. But a quick rub of knuckles over swollen eyes convinced him otherwise. That and the flies buzzing round the body.

Slowly, Ned swung down from the saddle. With reins in one hand and his Colt in the other, he led his horse the few remaining feet to the lump of humanity crumpled face down near the base of an eight-foot saguaro.

A horned lizard perched on the downed body's backside. When Ned's boot came up to brush the critter away, blood shot from its eyes before it scampered off.

This wasn't the work of Apaches Ned decided quickly. No signs of mutilation. He used his right foot on the man's hip to roll him over which produced a groan he wasn't expecting. A guttural noise approaching speech escaped with scant breath through his parched, torn lips.

"Save…me."

Ned's inability to tell anything but the truth involuntarily kicked in. "No chance of that. You're gut shot. Can't believe you're still drawin' breath."

The fellow whose insides had already spilled out into the rock, sand and dust was inexplicably still forming words.

"Are you…God?"

The answer came back without hesitation. "No. I'm Ned."

"It…burns…bad," the weakening voice panted.

Ned's curiosity trumped his compassion. "Who did this to you?"

The cracked lips moved almost imperceptibly, but the sound came out. "Lar…Larson."

Ned knew he wouldn't last. In fact, he was flabbergasted the man could still speak. He said the only comforting thing he could think of. "I'll move my horse between you and the sun. So you can die in the shade." In the midst of unbearable despair, it seemed a kindness to the dying man.

But there was more on the doomed man's mind. "Don't let him get my wife."

Other men might have humored him. To make his last seconds

on earth more bearable. But Ned wasn't like other men.

"Not my concern," Ned said flatly.

But the mortally wounded man wasn't done yet. "Or…my…money."

Ned's eyebrows went up. "What money?"

His tongue was bloated in his mouth. He could barely form words. "Money…under porch. Buried…under porch," he whispered.

Ned leaned in close. Disregarding the stench of bowels and death and innards cooking in the heat, he asked, "What's your name?"

"O…only…if you save…my wife…from Larson," he spat, along with blood, mucus, and peeled lip.

Ned paused before replying. He chose his words carefully. "I'll look into it. Now tell me your name."

"Ches…Chester," he mouthed. "Hen…Henry Chester." He was about to say something else. But he never got the chance. His eyes locked on Ned's. Then he went stone dead.

"Adios, Henry Chester," Ned said dryly. "Thanks for the tip."

He carried no spade, pick or axe. Nothing to facilitate the digging of a grave. He gave no thought to taking the body with him. Hot sun and rotting corpses don't mix. So Ned gathered whatever sizable stones he could find and piled them around the deceased. The desert had a way of taking care of its dead. It wasn't pretty. But he figured Henry Chester was beyond giving a damn.

The following morning Ned and his plodding mare were a couple miles outside Gila Bend. Ned assumed that Henry Chester and this Larson were probably from the town closest to where he found the dying man. Gila Bend was it. That assumption was pure conjecture of course, but it was the only idea Ned had. So he played it out.

They looked a sight. The roan's head was down so far she nibbled grass while she walked. Ned slumped in the saddle, hat pulled low on his head. But his eyes peered out from under the brim and he didn't miss a single shack. Saw four in fact. Not one with a porch.

By the time they reached what Ned took to be Gila Bend's main street, he had formulated his plan. He would make inquiries. Subtle ones to be sure. Last thing he wanted was attention. If anyone was curious as to why he was asking after Henry Chester, well, they'd just have to stay that way.

Amid the pedestrians and horsemen, buckboards and freight wagons, Ned spotted an old man sitting outside a wood-framed, two-story building with a sign on its overhang that read Prickly Pear Saloon. Perfect, Ned thought. Codgers like that old coot always know everyone.

He reined the mare near to where the elderly man sat and said to him, "Got a question if you don't mind."

"Don't mind a bit," the old timer responded.

"Wouldn't happen to know where I might find the Chester place, would you? Henry Chester's place?"

"Yep. Due west. 'Bout two and a half miles. You'll come to this Ironwood tree. Biggest one you've ever seen. Twice as tall as your mount, I guess. Don't like to keep her head up, does she? Anyway, there you take the trail that leads toward the butte. Henry's place is 'bout half way to the mountain."

"Much obliged," Ned said.

"Course, you won't find Henry there," the old man added.

"Oh yeah?" Ned replied, wondering how much the geezer knew. "Why's that?"

"He lit out 'bout two days ago. After taking the strongbox from the overland stage."

Hmmm, Ned said to himself. Then he probed a bit more. "Don't say? How'd they know it was Henry?"

"Driver recognized him. Said his bandana slipped when he was pickin' up the box he had em' throw down. Man gets desperate…then nervous…then careless, I guess."

The old fellow was wound up now and kept rattling. "He'd been worryin' the bank was gonna foreclose for some time. Decided to take the bull by the horns, I guess. Hell of it is, now he's gonna lose his freedom as well as his place."

Ned said, "Sound awful sure he'll be caught."

"Oh, he'll get caught, all right," the old man chuckled. "No doubt about it. Constable John Larson's on his trail."

The sun was high in the sky and what little wind there was felt like hot breath on Ned's grimy neck as he leaned on his pommel and eyed what he believed to be the home of one recently deceased Henry Chester. It was little more than a ramshackle cabin. A blight on the open land surrounding it. But it did have one particularly interesting architectural feature. A front porch that ran the width of the house and cleared the ground by three to four feet.

Ned envisioned Henry Chester sitting on his porch at the end of the day gazing out at the sun's last light. He saw him standing there in the morning finishing a smoke before beginning his chores. But most of all, Ned's mind's eye saw Henry Chester, sweaty, scared and frantic, scurrying beneath that porch with a short-handled spade and burying a strongbox heavy laden with coin of the realm.

Ned's reveries were not without angst, however. The chief cause of which was a gelding hitched to the post at the front of the house. He was a big horse. The kind that would carry a big man. A Winchester protruded from the rifle scabbard tied to the saddle. Ned figured neither the horse nor the weapon belonged to the widow Chester.

Sneaking up on the place was out of the question. The ground was too open. Waiting out the situation didn't appeal to Ned either. What if the rider of that horse already knew where the money was?

Ned got down off the mare and walked her toward the cabin. He thought he'd look less threatening that way. He stopped a few feet short of the porch. There were windows in the front but they were shuttered. So he assumed no one had seen him yet. Nobody came to the door. He dropped the reins and let the mare graze, knowing she wouldn't run off. Then he got down on his hands and knees and looked under the porch. Two feet behind and three feet right of the front steps he saw what appeared to be recently upturned earth. The flat of the spade had patted it back down, but digging had definitely gone on there.

Decision time. He got up and walked to the gelding. Stroking him gently on the rump, he looked at the saddle. The initials J. L. were carved in the leather. He remembered the old man calling him Constable John Larson. He remembered the dying man asking him to save his wife. He remembered saying *"I'll look into it."*

Ned slipped his Colt from its holster and held it at his side. He stepped up onto the porch. Still, no one came to the door. But he heard something. Not words. Sounds. Sounds he recognized. Copulating sounds.

"By God, I gave that man my word," Ned told himself.

So he stepped back to the edge of the porch then put everything he had into rushing forward and kicking the living shit out of the front door. It flew off its hinges and he burst in.

"Stop that fornication," Ned yelled.

A frenzy of uncoupling began as man and woman scrambled for covering simultaneously.

Ned didn't mince words. "I'm gonna kill you, Larson, for raping Henry Chester's widow. So put on your pants if you don't want to be shot naked."

"Let me get em'," Larson said. But instead of reaching for his trousers on the bedpost, he pulled his Peacemaker from under a pillow.

Ned swiftly shot Larson in his hairy chest. Then concerned that more lead might be required to finish the job, he methodically put two more bullets into the constable's torso.

As he sent Larson to the fires of hell, Ned felt he was keeping his word with a dying man, upholding the honor of a married woman and earning the money he would soon be recovering from its shallow grave. So intent was he on dispatching the lecherous lawman that he failed to notice the widow Chester pulling a double barrel 20-gauge from underneath the bed.

The initial blast blew Ned back through the door from whence he'd entered. Moments later, his shock was such that it took Ned a few seconds to realize he was now supine on the hard ground back out in front of the cabin. He made what he thought was an attempt to move but none of his parts, even the ones that weren't riddled with buckshot, seemed to respond. He couldn't move anything at all, or even raise his head, which may have been a blessing. For he knew he definitely did not want to get a look at what had formerly been his chest.

NED

In the time it took the widow Chester to throw a sheet around her nakedness and walk to him, Ned realized he could at least speak. As she stood over him, still cradling the shotgun under her arm, he said, "Your husband…asked me to save you."

"Didn't need saving."

"Planned to use that scatter gun on the lawman…didn't you?"

"He told me he killed Henry before he took me. He deserved it."

"Then you planned…to keep all the money."

"I deserved it."

"Then I bust in."

"You surely did."

Ned didn't plead for his life. He knew it wouldn't do any good. So, true to his upbringing, he simply said, "Any minute now, I'm gonna start to hurt somethin' awful. Hope you won't let that happen."

"I won't," was the last thing Ned heard before she emptied the other barrel into him.

In 1877 hard men came out of the Sonoran Desert. Hard women too.

JOE KILGORE: Before turning to fiction, Joe Kilgore was an award-winning advertising writer who plied his trade around the world. He has had one novel published, *The Blunder*, and his short stories have appeared in numerous publications. Joe currently resides in Austin, Texas, where he lives with his wife and a houseful of pets. A lover of the west, Joe and his wife maintain a presence in Sedona, Arizona, and plan to build a home there. He can be reached at www.joekilgore.com.

THE WILD ONES

Jonathon Adams

(1ˢᵗ Place Winner 2009 Cowboy Up Contest)

When he headed for the barn the day was only a bloodstain over charcoal hills. He stopped twice in the starlit yard to rest his leg and then continued smoothly with his back straight and his gait flawless and his teeth clenched and his stare straight ahead. He lit the kerosene lamp on the wall just inside the door and the eyes of the horses glowed bright as they turned to watch him in the amber pall. He took the small bridle and the easy bit from the tack room and after brushing Lucy down he threw the weathered old cavalry saddle over a woven Mexican blanket spread on her back and led her outside. He dropped her reins and watched Buck snort his dejection, glaring out from his stall as the big doors swung to and the crossbar fell into place. He heard the mare blow behind him so he cinched her up, then tightened the gun belt around his own waist. The well-oiled, scrollwork strap he had peeled from an *unteroffizier* lying dead on the Norman highland. The double holsters he had taken to Boise for retooling, to hold the old blue Colt .45's and bear the Rafter A under eagle claws where a swastika had been.

With a grimace he stood to the stirrup on his good leg and eased the other over. He walked Lucy down to the edge of the back pasture, more at home on four feet now than two. Leaning forward, he undid the gate and let it fall and the sturdy grey mare clopped on through. Now that he was set he felt the chill and shuddered under his canvas jacket. As the sky grew lighter he could see Lucy's breath hanging in the still air and he could smell pine needles and snow off the mountains.

They crossed the river at a shallow place above the falls with the sun well up and shining through frost-gilded leaves, the forest ablaze and sparkling while limbs tossed gently and great blue ravens boomed down in the canyon. Far upstream he could hear cattle calls and the bell cow clanging as the herds grazed down slope to the clear runoff water at the flint-rock bend. He felt the old autumn thrill that meant it was almost time to bring them in and he thought about how much there was to do and how excited Buck would be. Lucy wove quietly through the aspens with her head up, carefully probing the thin air. He watched her close. A mile in she stopped dead and tossed, and an instant later he heard an angry, pounding clatter. He slipped down out of the saddle and hooked the reins over a low-hanging branch.

He felt the hair standing on the back of his neck like in the old days, and as he moved along the deer path in a crouch toward the clearing he drew one of the pistols and thumbed back the hammer. He kept a stout poplar between himself and the trap and peered around to look at the bear.

It filled the whole expanded steel box with rippling muscle under silver-tipped and matted fur and it was the biggest grizzly he had seen or heard talk of since he was a boy. It did not see him or scent him because the imperceptible wind was in his favor. He watched as it gathered itself back on enormous haunches and slammed its great wide head into the solid door like a bull, ringing the spring gate like a bell, skull on steel. The trap sat up high on wheels, and with each concussive blow he was sure the whole thing was going over, but it stayed erect and swaying even

12

as the bear smashed into the door again and again. He took a moment to admire the incredible breadth of the scarred head and the longer he looked the less he could believe its size. After a while he worked his way back through the trees to where Lucy stood patiently.

Wanda had a steak sandwich and coffee waiting for him when he came up from the barn. He said grace silently and started lunch and shuffled through the mail while she watched him eat.

"You must've got him. You still have your hat on."

He looked up. She stood by with the carafe and refilled his mug when he set it down, like she used to do when she had waited tables at Rose's in town.

"Sorry," he said, his voice rough. The first word he had spoken all day. He took his hat and hooked it on his knee. "We got him. That is surely the biggest old bear I've seen in a long time."

He thanked Wanda for lunch and was on the phone to the Fish and Game office in Coeur d'Alene before noon. He asked to be transferred over to Matt.

"Officer Jurek," came the short answer. His young voice was tired and there was paper shuffling in the background.

"Matt, this is Dale Allen out at the Rafter A."

The kid's tone picked right up. "Dale, tell me you've got some good news." He sounded excited and the paperwork stopped. Like he'd been waiting for this call all his life.

"Well, he's a big one for sure. We caught him on what was left of that calf carcass in the clearing on the other side of the river. He doesn't look too happy about it, either."

"I don't imagine he does. You have time today to help me haul him up toward the border? If he's in there too long he might hurt himself, and everybody else is out for deer opener."

Dale leaned against the kitchen wall. He had wanted retribution and he was disappointed. "I'd just as soon shoot him now and save someone else the hassle."

Matt sighed. "Dale, don't--"

"Calm down. I promised I wouldn't. I'll give you a hand."

It was a sore subject but Matt let it go. "I'll see you later, Dale."

When the big green diesel pulled into the yard, Dale walked to the passenger door and climbed in, dragging that leg after him. He leaned the lever gun against the front of the seat with the muzzle against the floor and shoved a wad of dip into his cheek. He put the tin back in his shirt pocket and wiped his fingers on his jeans.

"You planning on needing those six-shooters?" Matt asked. He said nothing about the rifle.

"A man ought to be prepared," Dale replied as they bounced along through the pasture.

Matt was quiet for a minute. "That's some gun belt anyway."

"Yes it is," Dale said, spitting into an empty aluminum can from the cup holder. "It's some belt."

They crossed the river in the same shallow place but drove along the shoal until they found a clear cut the loggers had left many years before. Matt was a good driver and deftly negotiated the grapple of fallen timbers and uneven ground in the big truck. The sun was just barely turning west and it had warmed much and the sky was clear as it is only on a fall day in the mountains. Dale was relaxed and enjoying the rare opportunity to leave the responsibility of driving to someone else. He took the time to appreciate the beauty of his own familiar grazing land; with Wanda's health, he hadn't had the chance to ride out enough lately and it ate at him.

The grizzly exploded when he saw the pickup coming down to the clearing. They could see the whole green metal contraption rocking back and forth, alive with force and defiance. Matt backed up to the hitch on the trap and Dale stood off a little with the rifle cradled in the crook of his arm. He watched the young man crank the jack down until the back end of the truck sagged with the weight of the bear. As soon as the truck was joined to the trailer, it too awakened with the violent shuddering protests of the enraged animal. They climbed back in and crawled off down the mountain toward the access road and the highway.

"I've never seen a bear so big," said Matt once they were on the blacktop. He had strapped a tarp down over the whole trailer and checked the safety locks on the steel gate before they came out of the woods. Standing next to the giant banging away at the cage had made Matt feel quite small.

"I have, once. It was dead, though. When I was a kid before the war we lived up by Bonners Ferry. My father called old Hank in on another calf killer and they baited for him for about two months. They finally set up on him at night and had eight rounds into him before he went down. When they dragged him up into the yard with the horses balking we went out with lanterns and I just couldn't believe it. I guess everything looks bigger when you're a kid, but that bear was something else."

"I hear old Hank was something else. A lot of folks up here still haven't gotten quite used to me replacing him." Matt kept his eyes on the road as they drove north.

Dale watched him for a minute. "Well," he said, "I would imagine it can be difficult standing in for a legend like that. The old man was up here nigh on forty years. His grandfather fought in the Indian wars, a real cowboy legend himself. Old Hank volunteered for the second big one too, even though he didn't have to, and a lot of us respected that. We all got to know him pretty well over the years. That was before it all changed. It's hard to get to liking somebody when the animals he protects seem more important than the people in a country. It's not your fault, though. I guess policy is what changed."

Matt colored some and they rolled up the highway for a while, saying nothing. The bear thumped sporadically in the back but the hum of the road had lulled him into a kind of swoon.

"It's hard for the animals too," Matt said. "There's less and less room for them now, with people encroaching on their natural habitat." He pointed his thumb toward the back. "This guy probably came down from Canada where his original range was all logged off. It's too bad about the cows, but we have to consider the wild ones while they're still around. That's why we relocate instead of exterminate. You know, for posterity's sake."

Dale was silent but didn't feel like he had encroached on anything in his life. Maybe farmhouses in France, but that was under orders. He figured he had a right to raise calves on his own land without something coming along and eating them. But he said nothing. Matt was a good kid, handsome and likeable, and was just living what he had learned at school. He deserved a chance, and in a few years he would better understand things up here.

For an hour they bumped up an old logging road near the Canadian border that looked like it had been abandoned forever. On one side a mountain flank climbed to impossible wooded heights, on the other plummeting emptily away to nothingness and leaving Dale with a hollow feeling in his gut. The bear was silent and the men were silent and the sun was headed down and the temperature was dropping. They came up to the top of a cliff where the road opened wide into a flat, graveled span. Matt turned the truck around and parked. They got out and Dale helped roll the tarp back.

The bear lay on his side, breathing steadily but with a kind of sick look on his face. There was a puddle of putrid vomit near his snout. He still looked monstrous.

Dale climbed into the bed of the truck with the rifle while Matt undid the pins in the gate until there was one left. He attached a nylon cord to it with a carabineer and clambered up on top of the expanded steel box. He spoke quietly.

"The bear seems relaxed, so it's a good time to open up. I'm going to pop it and we'll wait for him to come out. They usually make for the woods after a minute, but if he starts back for us, shoot into the ground or something to scare him off." He swallowed. "You ready?"

There was a heartbreaking sunset over the mountains. The air was cold and still. Stately pines stood silent vigil, white fog coiling among them, the spirit of the ageless world.

Dale nodded and gripped the rifle. He had a round chambered and his finger on the trigger. He felt a sudden chill and his body tightened, like when they could hear the planes coming or the thunder of a shelling before it came whistling down. He hoped he was wrong.

He wasn't. When the pin plinked free, the bear rammed the door and it flapped open with a loud clank. He poured out fast as lightning, all wrath and indignation. Dale fired into the dirt but the bear hammered the trap from the outside now for revenge, and Matt tumbled over into huge, waiting, open jaws. The bear caught him at the shoulder and shook him back and forth, limp and flailing, too fast to see. There was a tearing sound and screaming from the kid and then the resounding shot of the rifle. Dale levered in another and drove it between the bear's eyes as that colossal head swung over to face him. The bear went down hard against the fender of the truck and died there. Dale was over the side and on the ground next to the boy with two limping steps and he still gripped the rifle even as he knelt to see.

Matt lay on the ground gasping for air in dry rattles. He had his eyes shut tight against the torn up feeling. His whole arm was coming apart at the shoulder while blood bubbled down into the gravel. Dale tried to apply pressure but he didn't know where because it came from all of it. He kept saying it would be fine but he knew better and he choked on the words. The kid began to calm down as life soaked quickly away and he opened his eyes slowly and looked up at Dale's stubbled face. The sun was down behind the looming hills now and night was coming fast.

"I didn't know a bear would do that," Matt rasped, his eyes wide and strained.

"Me neither, kid," Dale lied through welling tears. "I guess everything is still just the same as it's always been."

JONATHON ADAMS is a young American fiction writer from North Dakota. He is an avid outdoorsman and a dedicated reader. He has lived and traveled throughout the United States, northern Canada, and Mexico, and enjoys using the places and characters he has known as inspiration for his work. He was the winner of Moonlight Mesa's first annual "Cowboy Up" short story contest, and continues work on several other pending fiction projects. His appetite for the adventurous promises a steady supply of fresh material, as does his recent marriage to his wife, Belen.

WAITIN' FOR A FRIEND

M. Carolyn Steele

(1ˢᵗ Place Winner 2010 Cowboy Up Contest)

A bitter January wind whipped long hair about the half-man's face. With a crutch tucked under the stump of his left arm, he stood defiantly on one leg, waving a branch in the air.

"Ye be thinkin' to rob me valuables, ye'll be talkin' to the devil."

Crockett stared at the apparition before him and sputtered, "Tarnation, mister, why would I want to rob you?"

A cough rumbled through the grizzled Irishman. "There be some scallywags think to find an easy mark in a cripple. By the saints, I ain't gonna be caught unsuspectin' again."

"Well, I ain't no bushwhacker. Name's Crockett. I never robbed nobody." He ran a palm along the neck of his grey-muzzled roan. "Old Boozer throwed a shoe and less'n he sprouts wings, I reckon we'll wait out the night under this hickory. Don't reckon to cross the river into the Territories with night comin'."

"Where ye headin'?"

"Nowhere special. Maybe Missouri, maybe not. Seems I'm not much good for herdin' cattle since the army turned me out with lung disease."

"Humph," the Irishman scratched his whiskers, "The army does that once you're no use to 'em." He took a deep rattling breath and looked down as if visualizing his missing limbs.

"Well, ye and the horse are welcome to me fire providin' ye have vittles to share. Name's Mike."

Tugging the reins for the roan to follow, Crockett pointed to the sling around the Irishman's neck. "I can shoulder that wood for you."

"I nay ask for help, Lad." Mike's brows met in a frown over sunken eyes. "I welcome yer company, but I nay want yer pity." He grimaced as he shifted his crutch and continued along the river bank.

The Irishman led into a shallow cave nearly hidden by scrubby willows. Charcoal slogans scribbled along the limestone interior attested to its frequent use as a refuge for those waiting to cross the Red River. Long-ago phrases, "No rebs here," and "Giv them unionists hell, Genral Lee," battled for space on the wall. Wood smoke clung to the blackened ceiling.

Mike dropped the branches and lowered himself next to a campfire.

"What're you doin' out here?" Crockett slid the saddle from the horse's back. "You waitin' to cross the river?"

"Nay, just waitin' on a friend to take me home." Mike worked his pant leg up and exposed a soiled bandage. A bright red spot bloomed along the stump end of his leg. "Got left behind by a travelin' show."

Crockett sucked air through his teeth. "Mister, you need a doctor. You can ride Boozer to the ferry tomorrow."

The veteran stared at his leg and shook his head. "Thanks, Lad. Reckon I'll just wait here for my friend. He'll be along to fetch me soon enough."

Mike stirred a small pail of butter beans. "Be there any salt pork about ye to flavor the beans?"

"That depends on how you feel about used bacon." Crockett

held his hands over the campfire.

"Used, ye say?" The Irishman tilted his head. "Well now, a lot o' things come to mind about used bacon. None o' which I care to speculate on."

"Aw, ain't such a mystery 'bout used bacon." Crockett slipped his boot and sock off and peeled away a thick rasher of bacon sculpted around his reddened heel. "Applied fresh this mornin' to cushion these blisters."

"Ah," Mike grinned and reached with two fingers for the dangling bacon, "'tis only a bit used, and mightily seasoned."

The cave cozied with the arrival of tree-whipping wind and rain outside. Crockett watched bacon pieces shrivel in the bubbling pot, watched Mike's hand shake as he spooned beans onto a tin plate.

How a cripple came to be living in a cave burned to be known, but since the war, it wasn't wise to ask questions. Crockett took the plate, settled back, savoring the hot food. It wasn't his cave. Maybe the Irishman didn't want conversation.

Mike ate from the pot, scrapping it clean, then wiped his whiskers along his sleeve. He tilted his head. "Ye didna' say which army."

There it was. The question. The war over nearly a year and people still touchy. The right answer was never a sure bet.

Crockett fished in his knapsack and produced a can of peaches. "Union," he said and held the can up. "Make a difference?"

Mike smiled, shook his head. "Figures. Confederates were down to beardless boys. They'd not turn ye out less ye was missin' somethin'."

"Never shouldered a rifle. Caught measles instead." Heat flushed Crockett's face. "Pa didn't want me joinin' up, so couldn't go home after the war. We had a place north of St. Joe. Figured to prove myself a man down Texas-way." He jabbed a stick into the flames stirring a column of sparks. "Not much call for a man can't breathe dust."

The Irishman frowned. "Well, Lad, ye think whoopin' and fightin' like a banshee makes a man of ye? Nay. Nigh on to anythin', whether man or animal, will fight when survival be at stake. Gettin' up each mornin' fair weather or foul, workin' and providin' for family even when the spirit wishes for more, that's bein' a man.

"Yer pa nay wanted ye in the war. Well, me Annie Laurie nay wanted me to go marchin' off. Now she has but half a man what can't drive a railroad spike no more." Mike studied the spot of ground where his leg should be.

"Ever since I got over the surprise o' livin' and not dyin', I've pondered the chore o' providin' for Annie. I can write me name, but not read nor sum figures." The Irishman arched his back and groaned. "I never worked indoors, and without the sun on me face and wind at me back, I'd dry up and die anyways.

"Bloody shame the Pony Express done expired. They could lash me to a horse and away we'd go. Without the weight o' me arm and leg, likely make the trip in half the time. Always wanted to see Californie." He scratched through his beard and a grin slowly appeared. "Course with limbs only on one side, I'd always be leanin' to the right and me poor horse might run in circles all day."

Crockett chuckled. "What say we open these peaches." He pierced the lid with his pocketknife and sawed around the edges.

The Irishman sat, caressing the stump of his left arm. "It was in a sad little place called Fort Pillow."

"What?" Crockett asked, pulling the lid back.

22

"Where I was wounded! On the Arkansie and Tennesse border. Fort Pillow sits on a bluff o' the Mississippi River." A touch of bitterness laced the Irishman's answer. "Me little brother, Liam, thought it fair situated, but it weren't. I went to Tennessee to join up with him. The Thirteenth Regiment West Tennessee, Company D. It were unlucky you know, the thirteenth. Only thing lucky were bein' a private. Most o' the officers were killed."

"Must'a been some battle."

"Rebels drove our pickets in soon as the sun was up. Our company were sent out as skirmishers." Mike took a deep rattling breath. "Even the trees were pure Rebel, a-spewin' bullets from their branches."

The Irishman narrowed his eyes as if trying to see the battle in the flames."Someone hollered 'retreat' and we started on a run, bein' picked off by them sharpshooters like flies on the wall. Bullets rainin' down so hard they popped back up at ye from the ground."

He shivered and glanced out at the rain. "Liam were next to me, runnin' and scramblin' through the bushes and over bodies. A ditch surroundin' the fort were twelve foot wide. That were the longest run we ever made.

"Them Secessionists were some o' the best marksmen I ever had the misfortune to encounter. Well, they was in the bluffs drawin' bead on us as we clawed our way back up the banked earth, looked a mile high. I dove over the breastworks and thanked the Blessed Mary for I weren't hurt more'n a few scratches. Then, I heard Liam screamin' me name."

Mike closed his eyes. "He were on the other side."

Several logs in the center of the fire collapsed sending sparks into the air.

"It were back into hell I went, for a man can nay leave his brother to suffer alone. It were in me thoughts this be me last day on earth and I nay wanted Saint Peter to ask where me brother be. The journey down were a lot faster than the climb up. Liam, impatient as he ever were, whispered in me ear. 'Michael Patrick O'Neal,' says he, 'what took ye so long?' I were a mite peeved at the seriousness o' the spot we were in. 'Liam,' says I, 'if'n ye nay stopped to pick daisies, we'd be havin' a cup o' tea now.'

"A waste o' breath to scold. Naught else to do but hug the underside of a log for shelter from the rain o' bullets. All the while blood bubbled up from Liam's shattered arm like a spring o' water burstin' from the ground. I gripped his arm tight, knowin' in me heart if I let go, I let go of his life."

Mike groaned and rocked back and forth. "Mary, Mother of God, I prayed, help me. The gun-boat, *New Era*, were sittin' out on the ol' Mississip', firin' her guns, shatterin' trees, and tremblin' the ground with each hit. Then, it went quiet. One of the boys hollered down that the Reb's General Forrest requested the fort's surrender."

Crockett glanced over at Mike. "A man fights hard, I reckon there's no dishonor in surrender when he can't do nothin' else."

"Surrender?" The Irishman snorted. "There'd be no surrender. You see, defendin' the fort with the Thirteenth Regiment were a detachment o' coloreds. Must o' been three hundred. Run-aways. Givin' up would mean their death.

"Nay, Liam and me lay in the sun waitin'. Him beggin' for water and me beggin' him to live. His life just kept seepin' away, soakin' into the ground, into me shirt, no matter how hard I gripped. I could see in his eyes his soul were leavin' and, too soon, it were gone and I were huggin' a dead man."

Tears streamed down the Irishman's face. Crockett swallowed

hard knowing no power on earth could hold back death. "I'm sorry, Mike. Ma would say it were the Lord's will, but I don't believe that. Old folks passin' on is the natural thing. Ain't natural to go before you live a score of years."

"Guess I ain't really cried for Liam before. Weren't no time then." Mike blew his nose into his fingers, then wiped his hand across his pant leg. "I no sooner closed me brother's eyes so's he wouldn't see naught but the gates o' heaven, when the awful'ist Sesech yell went up. Like howls from ol' Lucifer's hounds. I purely thought the devil had loosened his minions on us poor sinners.

"The smoke o' gun fire were so thick, a man could hardly breathe. I knew I'd be joinin' me brother soon when the boys come scramblin' over the breastworks. Once'd them Southern boys gained the fort, weren't no way to go but to the river. Them Rebs was breathin' hellfire and brimstone right down our necks."

Mike closed his eyes against the fresh torrent of tears. "Trapped. Trapped between the fort and the river."

"I confess wantin' to hear 'bout the fight," Crockett said, feeling like an intruder in the Irishman's agony, "but if'n the rememberin' brings pain, it ain't worth the knowin'."

"Lad, like we was trapped that horrid day, these tears been trapped inside o' me. Seems they been burstin' to get out and this be as good a time as any to let 'em go."

Crockett nodded. Sometimes a hurt needed airing. He focused on a hole in the knee of his pants, so's not to see another man's tears.

"Nothin' to do but run," Mike continued, voice husky. "Tryin' to outrun them bullets 'bout as useless as tryin' to outrun the wind, what with leapin' over logs and bodies. One boy grabbed me ankle, beggin' for help. In the blink o' me eye, I were squirmin' on the ground with the poor bloke, me legs screamin' for mercy. I were ready to disown 'em when I looked down and found they had a right to be complainin'."

Mike paused to ease his pantleg back over his bandages.

"All that were left were to roll into the bushes and wiggle like a snake for the river. But if the boys thought there be safety in the water, 'twas their undoin'. The Rebs turned the fort's guns on the *New Era*, and she steamed off around the bend leavin' all them boys in the Mississippi's grasp. Like a jealous woman, she claimed all them Secesh bullets missed.

"Oh, I cried then, for I knew certain there were no mercy in the heart o' the enemy." The Irishman shook his head, eyes closed at the memory. "Nothin' to do but wiggle away from the water's edge. I nay wanted to be spendin' eternity at the bottom o' that merciless river. Made me way up a ravine where a giant oak at the edge o' the creek, with a girth as big as a cow, had a delicate grip on the land. Most o' the soil washed out from underneath and her roots swayin' back and forth in the bit o' water beckoned me close. I crawled in under those roots and put me back against the earth."

Mike's voice grew weaker and took a bitter edge. "For the rest o' the day and into the night, them Rebs tramped about puttin' all those injured boys out o' their misery. Their screams still play the devil's music in me dreams. The oak saved me. Kept me wrapped in her embrace, she did. That night the black sky boiled red when they torched the fort and I feared me oak would blaze up, too."

Crockett stirred the campfire. Flames stretching and dying along the branches became agonized boys reaching out to him.

"The night be ever so long, filled with grown men cryin' for their mothers." Mike lifted a glowing twig and stared at it. "I still have the smell o' the burnin' in me nostrils. It were a surprise to see the sun come up and know I weren't in purgatory. Me right leg had but a flesh wound. I've had worse at the end o' a lash. But me left leg hurt powerful and she cursed me good for bein' in harm's way."

"How long you stay under that tree?"

"'Bout the time I figured mother tree would be me tombstone, the *Silver Cloud* come puffin' up the Mississippi. I could see the boys left alive crawlin' from under bushes and wavin' to her. I figured she'd just keep on goin', but she shelled the bluffs. While those Southerners kept their heads down, she sent a skiff in close to shore.

"I bid me oak goodbye and told me legs that it were up to them, and for once they listened to reason. I begged and cursed 'em all the way to the river's edge, crawlin' and limpin' along in the mud. But them Rebels weren't finished yet. The skiff were full o' bloody boys and them sharpshooters took to takin' pot shots at us again. That's when me arm got hit, but me legs pushed into the water and soon enough I were on board."

He shook his head. "I nay should have left me oak, and I'd have me arm. I nay should have left Annie Laurie and I'd have me leg."

Crockett sat the peach can in front of the Irishman. "I ain't the only one never went home, am I, Mike?"

"What would a young thing like Annie do with half a man? I sing fer pennies in saloons." Mike lifted a peach to his mouth with two fingers. "Pure fruit o' the angels," he said and reached for another peach. "Want to see a true angel?" He wiped his fingers dry and pulled a locket from his shirt, then popped it open, and handed it across the campfire. "Annie'll find someone better than the likes o' me. Lots o' blokes workin' the railroad up in Chillicothe."

A dark-eyed woman, curls framing her thin face peered somberly from the tarnished locket. "Real handsome lady," Crockett said, handing it back. "Does Annie know what happened to you?"

The Irishman stared at the picture. "Does your ma know what happened to you?"

"Ain't the same thing, Mike."

"Ain't it?" Mike closed his fist around the locket and sighed. "Didn't seem right, me bein' the only one knowin' what happened to Liam. T'was a burden. I'm obliged to ye fer listenin'." A liquid cough shook his shoulders, gagged him, robbed his breath. Gasping, he hunkered into his blanket, the shakes back on him. "Rememberin' be a tirin' thing."

***

The dull whack of stone against wood silenced the jabber of crows overhead. Crockett, huffing with the morning's exertion, leaned back on his heels to survey the stake he'd just planted. The rain had been a blessing, softening the soil like it did. Even a half-man takes a fair size hole dug with naught but a peach can.

"Guess you're done waitin' on your friend, Michael Patrick O'Neal." Crockett settled the can, upside down, over the stake and looked out across the river at the dreary landscape. Indian Territory. Missouri beyond.

"Don't seem right bein' the only one knowin' a man's end." He stood, thrust one hand in his coat pocket to finger the scrolled edges of Annie's locket and patted Boozer's soft muzzle with the other. "Best I recollect St. Joe and Chillicothe ain't too far apart."

M CAROLYN STEELE retired from a commercial art career to pursue a love of writing. Historical eras, specifically Civil War and Native American, capture her imagination. Nominated for a Pushcart Prize, she has won numerous writing awards, and has stories published in twelve anthologies. Combining her knowledge of storytelling and genealogy, she presents programs designed to inspire others to record their own family stories. She authored the book, *Preserving Family Legends for Future Generations*, a 2010 Heartland New Day Bookfest First Place winner. View her website at: www.mcarolynsteele.com.

THE SPITTOON

Mark Redmond

(Finalist 2010 Cowboy Up Contest)

I'm a private kind of man. I don't make a habit of poking my nose into other folks' business, and I'm obliged when they stay out of mine. I'm not unfriendly, and I try not to be unpleasant, but some people just don't know when to quit. When the loud man flung the batwing doors open and stomped into the saloon, I just knew he was one of those people.

I was sitting at a table in the back corner with my back to the wall. Less than half an hour earlier I had ridden into Bisbee, Arizona. After two weeks of riding from sunup to sundown to get there, I was tired of beans and jerky. I was tired of washing particles of sand from my mouth with the brackish water from my canteen. I was tired of sweating all day and sleeping on rocky ground. Almost thirty years as a cowboy, pony express rider, and Texas Ranger had accustomed me to discomfort; they had not made me fond of it.

On the table in front of me sat my supper: a large, juicy steak; four big, fluffy sourdough biscuits; a large, open tin of peaches; and a cup of the best coffee I had ever tasted. All I wanted was to be left alone to enjoy my meal. Now I was pretty sure that I was about to be interrupted. Keeping my attention on my plate, I decided to put away as much of my meal as I could. Besides, maybe the loud man wouldn't pay any mind to me.

"Hey, Grandpa!" he said. Ignoring him, I continued to eat.

"I guess the old man must be deaf!" he said. The two cowboys who had come in with him, smaller rags torn from the same bolt of cloth, laughed.

"Maybe you should speak up, big brother," one of them said.

"Or move a little closer, Del," the other added.

I poured a second cup of steaming coffee from the pot that the bartender had left for me. Still looking at my plate, I bit into a biscuit.

"I ain't getting any closer," said Del. That old man stinks bad enough from here." Again there was laughter.

He was right about one thing; I didn't smell very good. Riding straight through town to the livery stable, I had unsaddled Midnight and paid the stable boy to rub him down and give him a double helping of oats. I had stopped at the hotel, paid for a room, and left my gear there. On my way out I had asked the clerk to recommend an eating place and then ordered a bath to be ready in an hour. Then I had come here to enjoy my supper.

I ate another piece of steak so tender I could almost cut it with my fork. As I chewed, I closed my eyes and anticipated soaking my tired, aching body in a tub of hot water while smoking one of the stogies I had tucked away in my saddlebags.

"Shhhh -- I think Grandpa has dozed off," said Del. "Matt, he just might fall into his plate and smother hisself. Maybe you better wake him up."

I heard the distinct sound of someone cocking a Colt. A nearly deafening explosion followed; and I could feel the bullet smash into the floor inches from my feet, showering my pant leg with splinters. As I glanced in their direction, Matt, who appeared to be the youngest of the three, spun his six-shooter on his finger and slipped it smoothly into his holster.

"Grandpa," said Del, "I reckon you ought to thank Matt here for saving your life. I would have asked Tony to do it; but he's such a bad shot, he might have hit you."

I knew they weren't going to go away, but I wasn't about to give up my supper because these rowdy boys wanted some entertainment. They appeared to be more bored than bad. I took another bite of biscuit and washed it down with a swig of coffee. Saluting them with my cup, I smiled.

"I'm obliged, Matt, for keeping me awake. I'm mighty tired right now. I'm obliged to you, too, Del, for picking the best shot to do the honors. Why, who could tell by looking that he's the one that can shoot straight enough to hit the floor?"

I had another bite of steak while the brothers digested what I had said.

"I think that old man is making fun of us," said Tony, taking a step forward.

"Hold on," said Del, placing a hand on his brother's shoulder. "Old man, are you trying to make fools of us?"

"Now, that would be closing the corral gate after the horses were gone, wouldn't it?" I asked.

"What horses?" Matt whispered.

I buttered another biscuit, took a bite, and then cut off another piece of steak. Del was about to speak, but I cut him off. "I'm saying my dear, departed grandmother could have made that shot from twice as far away and without her spectacles. But then you weren't wearing yours either."

"Matt don't wear spectacles," Del said.

"Maybe he needs to," I said, sipping more coffee.

"Del, he is making fun of us," said Tony. "Can I--"

"I'll take care of this," said Del, his hand resting on the butt of his Colt. "You got some mouth on you, Grandpa," he said.

"Thank you," I said. I finished my biscuit and began to butter another one.

"Stand up!" Del said.

"Can't," I said.

"What did you say?" he asked.

"Can't!" I said, nearly shouting. Taking a bite of steak, I shook my head. "Matt's eyes are bad, and Del's hard of hearing. Is anything wrong with you, Tony?"

Leaning with his back against the bar and his thumbs hooked in his gun belt, Tony focused his attention on raking the floor with his spur. "Well, sometimes when the thunder and lightning gets real bad, I--"

"Shut up, Tony!" said Del. "Grandpa, I told you to stand up."

"Can't," I said.

"Why not -- are your knees knocking too bad?" Del asked.

"Nope," I said, chewing a large piece of steak and gesturing at the table with my fork. "I'm eating my supper, and I like to eat sitting down when I can."

Three explosions followed so quickly that they sounded more like one long roar in the room. A small cloud of smoke drifted toward the ceiling. Brushing splinters from my pants, I glanced at the bullet holes in the floor. I shook my head slowly and looked at Del, who was still holding his Colt.

"Granny shot like that one time," I said. "Shut herself in her cabin for a week -- wouldn't talk to anybody for the pure shame of it. Barkeep says he's got some dried apple pie in the kitchen. You wouldn't happen to know if it's any good, would you?"

"Yes, sir," said Matt. "I have a piece pretty near every time I'm in town --"

"Shut up!" Del said. "I hit what I'm aiming at, old man."

THE SPITTOON

I buttered my last biscuit, laid my knife across the edge of my plate, and then took a silver dollar from my vest pocket. Holding it up, I asked, "Del, are you a gambler?"

Del looked confused. "What are you getting at?"

I smiled and laid the dollar on the edge of the table. That dollar says you're not a good enough shot to move the spittoon at the end of the bar twice without putting a hole in it."

"I only get two shots?" he asked, squinting at the spittoon.

"Yep," I said. I drank what was left of my coffee and then refilled my cup. I put another piece of steak in my mouth and chewed slowly.

When Del's first slug hit the floor close enough to rock the spittoon slightly, I gave him a nod. His second shot was too far to the left. He holstered his Colt and flipped me a dollar, which I caught and laid on top of the first one. "Double or nothing, Matt?" I asked. "You get four shots to move it three times."

"I don't mind taking on old man's money," Matt said, smiling. "Let me get your dollar back for you, big brother." He drew smoothly and fired.

"Looks like one of us is going to be buying a new spittoon," I said.

"You talk too much, Grandpa," said Matt, taking deliberate aim and squeezing the trigger. The spittoon scooted two inches, nearly turning over. His third shot moved it again.

The barkeep, standing behind the bar at the same end as the brothers, had been silently polishing glasses and stacking them within easy reach, stopping occasionally to pour more whiskey for them. "Someone will have to pay for it," he mumbled.

"Loser pays for the spittoon," said Del smiling, I reckon, at the idea of getting his money back.

"Fair enough," I replied, brushing the two silver dollars off the table just as Matt fired. It wasn't much of a distraction, but it was enough. Matt's face reddened as he holstered his gun. "You did that on purpose, old man!"

"Sorry to be so clumsy," I said, stooping to retrieve the coins. "Tell you what I'll do though, boys; I'll call off that bet and make the same bet with Tony. All he has to do is hit the spittoon three of five times. It's ruined anyway. What do you say?"

Del and Matt looked at each other and then at Tony. "You got the two dollars?" Del asked.

"Come on, Del," said Tony, a trace of a whine in his voice. "I can do it -- I know I can! Just give me a chance!"

I used that last biscuit to soak up some of the juice from the steak. Wiping my mouth with a cloth napkin, I leaned back in my chair and smiled.

"You'd better hit the danged thing!" said Del, giving Tony a shove that put him two feet closer to the spittoon. I noticed that Tony's brothers stepped behind him as he drew his gun, and I wondered if I should move. I was, after all, only fifteen feet to the left of the spittoon. I had reckoned that Del had exaggerated about how bad Tony's shooting was, but he hadn't. The one time he did hit the spittoon, his thumb slipped on the hammer, causing him to fire before he had taken time to aim. Head hanging, Tony turned to the bar and finished his drink.

"Here, mister," he said, shuffling toward me and holding out a handful of coins. "You win."

"Wait a minute!" said Del, grabbing Tony's shoulder. "This old man has stole all the money from us he's going to -- in fact, I'm going to take back my dollar and his too." As he started toward me, each brother grabbed an arm.

"We agreed to the bet, Del," said Matt, "and we lost. Pay the man, Tony."

As Tony let go of his brother's arm and started toward me, Del's head drooped; and his shoulders sagged. He must have felt Matt's grip relax because suddenly Del tore free. Jumping to his left, the big man leveled his Colt at my chest.

Sipping coffee, I studied him over the rim of my cup. "Barkeep," I said, smiling, "I'm ready for pie."

"Don't get between us, Tony," said Del. "Just keep walking to the side, and get them two dollars. Bring them back here and give them to me."

"Del," said Tony, "I don't want no trouble. Why don't we --"

"Move!" Del said.

"Del," I said, "listen to Tony. You don't want trouble. I want to show you something very special, and then we'll see if you still want the money. May I? I'm going to move very slowly so you can see what I'm doing." With my thumb and forefinger, I pulled my own Colt from its holster and laid it on the table.

Matt's spurs jingled as he stepped to Del's side. The three stood in a rough semicircle in front of my table with Tony a step or two closer to me. "It looks like a plain old Colt to me," said Del. "What's so special about it?"

"It has something your guns don't have," I said. I picked it up with my right hand and cocked it, keeping the barrel pointed at the ceiling.

Instantly Matt and Tony drew their guns and pointed them at me. Del chuckled. "That Colt of yours is outnumbered three to one, Grandpa. What does it have that ours don't?"

I motioned to the barkeep, who started toward the kitchen. "Bullets, Del," I said with a smile. "You boys light a shuck. I have some pie to eat, a bath to take, and a cigar to smoke." I extended my left hand toward Tony for the coins. "I'm much obliged to you for the entertainment and for the supper which you have so generously provided. I'll be happy to recommend your hospitality to others if you wish; but if not, I'll never breathe a word of what happened here today."

They shuffled from the room without looking back. The barkeep set a huge piece of dried apple pie on the table in front of me. Holstering my Colt, I ate my pie in peace.

MARK REDMOND taught high school English for twenty-nine years. Redmond has had more than twenty-five short stories and articles published, but he is best known for his middle-grade series, *The Adventures of Arty Anderson.* He is a member of Western Writers of America and Single-Action Shooting Society. Redmond lives in Indiana with his wife Susie and children.

THE DEAD ROPE

James O'Brien

(2nd Place Winner 2010 Cowboy Up Contest)

A man doesn't think too much about the details of another man's gun. He just doesn't work that way. Well, that's not true. If a gun is pointed his way long enough, then the man begins to pick up on little things. He'll notice the way the sun catches in the curved metal of the barrel, or the way the etchings run along the steel just above the tan of the wood grip, dancing in the sun, barretted darkly by the heads of the pins that keep the parts attached.

When a pistol is pointed at a man long enough, a man looks into a black hole, a dark void of all life, and there is a nothingness that swells up inside him. A piano could drop from a tree, explode into ivory and splinters, and a man on the business end of a bulleted gun would be surprised to find the piano in pieces, if he made it that far, if he lived long enough to look. This nothingness that swells up in him, it contains everything, his whole life. Everything gets packed into that black hole.

"Wouldn't move, sheriff," Jayep Knudson said, bleeding on the raft just above the lip of Tattum Falls, holding the long bright gun on Coakley. "Got a good bead. Got a damn good bead."

Van Coakley didn't say so, but it didn't matter about the bead. It didn't really. If Knudson knuckled that trigger and the slug lifted Coakley's skullcap like it had the counter boy's, back in Ungerton, then the rope wrapped around the sheriff's fists would go slack. The Columbia River would take Knudson right over the falls. On the other hand, if Knudson waited too long, all the blood in him would run out through the hole in his right leg that Coakley had opened with one poorly placed shot, a half-mile back. Didn't matter whether he moved or not. These were the two ways things could unfold. Neither left either of them with much of an upper hand.

How the men came to be in that position went like this. Knudson robbed the Ungerton feed store, took about a hundred dollars, and killed the counter boy with a bullet to the forehead, spattering his brainy matter all over the shelves of worm treatments and hot-spot balms. So went that. Coakley knew it was Knudson from the beginning. Knew it, because he knew Knudson well, knew him since they were boys.

Knudson was Coakley's brother-in-law-- these days, unhappily -- but they'd grown up in the same part of the high country, one ranch next to the other. Coakley had been the older of the boys -- both of them were motherless. Knudson's ma had died of pneumonia, choked with it in the long yawn of an Ungerton winter. Coakley's mother had sighed and stopped breathing at the end of birthing sister Elizabeth. He'd watched this happen. He'd placed his palm on her cooling forehead, held it there until Pappy took him into another room. Next door to each other, in the wake of these things, the boys bonded for a time, but, in the years between boyhood and the feed-store shooting, Coakley watched Knudson go bad, bad for no real reason.

Knudson became the kind of kid who killed a kitten. A certain quantity of moons over a growing young man like that, and sufficient whiskey in the mix, well, things only got worse from there. Coakley certainly never liked it that sister Elizabeth took to Knudson, once Pappy was gone and he himself was away from the ranch most of the day, learning his ass from his elbow as Ungerton's deputy under Deke Posner. Coakley never thought of his neighbor as a man going crazy, at that point, but he'd seen a poor end for the two of them -- Knudson and Elizabeth.

In any case, Coakley warned Elizabeth off the courtship, but eventually he was sure she wouldn't listen. And then he did a secret thing, paying a few dollars of his salary every month to Carlson Wheelock, an attorney who kept his office above River Street, sitting at a big desk brought to Ungerton from back East. Elizabeth and Knudson got married. Coakley stepped up to sheriff when Deke retired. All the while, he kept Wheelock on that retainer.

The way it turned out, thanks to Wheelock, was that a certain agreement about the land shared between Elizabeth and Knudson eventually bore both his sister's and his brother-in-law's signatures. Not that both of them knew about the agreement, but then neither were ever asked to be a part of it. Nobody questions the signatures a sheriff delivers, not even lawyers. Especially not lawyers who liked having their practice above River Street in that sheriff's town. Especially not lawyers drawing a certain monthly retainer. As such, Knudson didn't know it, but when he started taking a hand to Elizabeth, he also guaranteed that she would get half of the Knudson property if a bad end came. When a bad end came. Shortly after that, Coakley saw Elizabeth packed off to Portland for the month. He told Knudson it was family business, an ailing cousin, and while it wasn't quite that, it was still family business. It took about a week, after she left. At the bottom of a bottle of bourbon, Knudson crossed the rest of the divide.

**

He laid backwards on the plank raft, which was inexorably drawn, but for Coakley's single rope, into the pull of the Columbia. And Coakley, still under the blank-dot barrel of Knudson's forty-five, held the rope as hard as he could. The sheriff's boots ground into the soft pine needles of the earth along the bank. His clothes, soaked from his splash into the edges of the river, clung to him in patches. The air was full of the roar of the falls, a white roar that never ceased, snatching words and swallowing them down.

"Decide what you got to do," Knudson said. "I kill you either way, sheriff."

Thinking about it, Coakley thought Knudson started to turn bad just after his daddy died in a dispute over a lame horse. Coakley had already lost Pappy by that time. Killing kittens, stealing sugar -- that was Knudson before his daddy dropped with a cracked skull. Following these things, the long, hot summer days in the fields along the Columbia turned sour in a way that maybe Knudson failed to understand, at the time.

As they started to turn, and Elizabeth took him in, Knudson did what lost men do when they are taken in: he lost track of whatever held him to a course in the first place.

"You gotta' decide," Knudson said, from the raft. "I got a hell of a good bead, you son of a bitch."

Knudson was a sharp shot, even if he was distracted by the bloody wound. It was funny how nature built a man so good at one thing, but so bad at anything good. Let the rope go, and Knudson wouldn't have a chance, but he would have a shot. Maybe two shots. Then he'd spin out to the middle of the river and speed towards the drop, a quarter-mile down. Meanwhile, Coakley's own gun lay useless on the ground. The scar from his brother-in-law's slug had cut into it, just in front of the cylinder.

The sheriff was lucky the piece hadn't blown apart in his grip, maybe eliminating a finger or two of the hand that held it. Or maybe he'd been unlucky, if you looked at it another way. Maybe if he hadn't had a second hand to grasp the rope, Knudson's raft would already have pulled free, and the man who held him at gunpoint would instead be down at the bottom of the Tattum drop.

Looking at the broken gun, he saw the way the sandalwood was worn where he liked to rest his palm on it, pressing it down into its holster as he stood on the fresh pine porch out on River Street. That's how he could stand for hours, a plug of tobacco stinging the inside of his lips, watching the ladies in their large hats, watching the men eat their lunch in the shade just outside Loftin's. They were tough men, in Ungerton, but they were basically hard workers. At the end of day, most days, they drank their fill inside and caused no trouble. Not Knudson, though. When a man starts drinking more than his fill, and does it too often, the bottle starts to drink back. It drinks a whole man down, in the end, sucking him into the same opening from which he draws.

With his bad hand, Coakley twisted the river-wet rope another width around his unhurt palm. Slivers of steel from the blown-apart gun sang hot inside his injured thumb, spearing deeper into the soft knob of flesh, just behind the main joint of his fist.

"You'll go over," Coakley said.

"What do you reckon?" Knudson said back.

Coakley reckoned the Columbia wanted that raft pretty badly. To Coakley's left, just a little up the slope along the river's edge, his horse stomped once. It had followed them down. It was a good horse. A half-mile upstream, where the falls weren't so loud, Knudson's horse lay dead: one of Coakley's bullets in its lung, blood draining out of the beast's mouth into the soil and water. It was sad to see that horse go down. Last remnant of the Knudson palominos, probably.

"Bet I get you twice, before I go over," said Knudson.

"Thought about that," Coakley said. "You're bleeding out, Jayep."

Knudson's horse had gone down with one shot, just as they'd come to the ford where the plank raft bobbed by its rope off. It was a deep crossing, only good for the largest horses, unless the summer had been especially dry. Knudson meant to drive his half-breed palomino right into the water, break for the other side. Maybe he would have made it. Coakley's horse was a lot smaller, not right for the river at this spot. Perhaps it would have worked for Knudson, but he never had the chance. Coakley had aimed for the man's middle, but the half-palomino reared. When Coakley's pistol barked, instead of a torso-hit, the slug opened a hole from one side of Knudson's boot to the other -- pulling with it skin, muscle, and bone -- and it exited into the middle of the horse's ribs. Lung or heart, whichever it hit, the horse went down and stayed there to die.

Knudson had toppled to the far side. He'd crawled from the heaving animal before Coakley could get new bearings in the confusion, flopping onto the square wooden raft, yanking its anchoring rope free. He'd rolled over, leveled his iron, and squeezed a blast in Coakley's direction. It was a sloppy, desperate business. Not even close. Coakley was already off his horse and into the water, going for the tie line, his own gun in one hand. The raft was already almost away. Knudson stopped shooting, rolled over, and tried to paddle for the thick hemp guide that was meant to let a man pull the raft to the opposite dock.

THE DEAD ROPE

Grasping the end of the tie rope, which was slick from the current, Coakley had tried to haul the raft back with him onto land. His legs found the hardscrabble shallows, as they moved downriver, and he pulled as hard as he could manage, falling backwards onto the needle-strewn shore, water running out of his every soaking fold. They made their way along the half-mile like that, all the time toward the falls. Knudson seemed panicked. He tried to paddle; he clutched his leg; finally he pointed his gun at Coakley -- Coakley still jogging and falling as he held the rope and kept up with his current-stolen quarry. Knudson couldn't hit him, still undone by the first wave of panic, and the Columbia's chop. The river swelled against the falls. Coakley heard the bumblebee of lead around him. When he tugged free his own gun, the rope sawing against the inadequacy of his single-handed grasp, a tongue of river leapt from its barrel.

The next bark of Knudson's revolver made it moot, anyways. The sheriff's iron flipped away, hot as a stove coal. By then, the rope was rail straight, almost gone from him. He should have let it go, but the reaction was pure instinct. Coakley fumbled for the end of it with his free, bleeding hand. Knudson scrambled on the raft, seeing his death in the curve of green-grey water as it went over the steaming edge, into oblivion.

***

Now here they were. Knudson had him at the end of that wide black barrel, calmer now, the aim of a man with nothing left to lose, while Coakley had Knudson at the end of the wet taught rope. The fiber of it felt cold against his hand. He thought about Elizabeth, on the coach back to Portland. If she took up secretarial school, she might make a go of it there. It would be dry work, but she wouldn't have to come back to Ungerton. She could maybe make a fresh start, before she was old enough that fresh starts stopped making any difference. There had been one other task to which Coakley had set the lawyer. It had been meant for later in life, in case things went wrong for Coakley before they went wrong for Elizabeth. A sheriff made too much money in these parts, when what he liked to do mostly was stand on his pine porch and watch River Street. This was a stupid way to end things, here on the river, if it turned out Knudson's way, but maybe it all made some kind of sense -- just a little sooner than Coakley had planned. He watched Knudson drain pale on the boards. The rope felt like something dead, like something that wanted to slip away at last, up and over that precipice swell.

"Okay, Jayep," he said.

As Coakley opened his hand, he heard Knudson's gun off. The raft whirled out into the foaming water. The punch came into him just over the collarbone, into the hard straight muscle that stretched back to his ear. The sound in his head was like a dog's bark. Coakley thought of his dog: Pounder, years distant. He saw the flash of maize fur in the tall grass along a summer's hillside, the dog leaping as he went. On the raft, Knudson's legs were straight up in the air, but they were also pumping in the waist-high grass next to Coakley, the two of them racing together for the pond behind the ranch, speeding towards a quick swim after church. With Pounder behind them, Coakley wasn't a sheriff, soaking his handprint into the wood of a gun. Knudson hadn't set his foggy sights on Elizabeth, yet. Elizabeth waved from the top of the hill. She knew nothing about her future; about coaches to Portland; about inheritances (maybe twice in one year). The two men were still boys, and they ran under an impossible sky. Coakley splashed into the black pond's surface. Knudson stopped short, afraid of the cold dunk. The dog's yellow coat turned white

46

in the sun. Coakley dove for the bottom then, leaving Knudson behind at the water's edge.

JAMES O'BRIEN was a finalist for the 2010 Santa Fe Writers Project Literary Award, commended in the 2010 Basil Bunting Poetry Award, and specially commended in the 2010 Aesthetica Creative Works Competition. His fiction has previously appeared in *Haunts.* His poetry has appeared in *Flatmancrooked's Slim Volume of Contemporary Poetics*, *Dark Sky Magazine,* and in *Tidal Basin Review.* O'Brien is a Ph.D. candidate at the Editorial Institute at Boston University, researching Bob Dylan's non-song writings — focusing on unpublished works and those writings given only limited distribution. He is a news correspondent for *The Boston Globe.*

THE TAMING OF JUMP OFF JOE

Becky Coffield

(2nd Place Arizona Author's Literary Contest 2009. A tale told by horse trainer Tom Siecrest inspired this story.)

From the moment I first laid eyes on that Tom Freeman, I figured he was a real cowboy and probably no darn good.

He wasn't my first choice by a long shot, but he was the only horse trainer available. Besides, he was affordable. I was desperate, and no one else would even consider my request after they took one look at my horse. I was stuck with Tom, but I needed him, and he needed a job, so maybe he was stuck with me. At any rate, we worked it out so he'd come every day for a month to break my horse. He said it would only take a few days, but I said I'd pay for a month. I didn't want there to be any doubt.

Before I continue, there's one thing I need to get out in the open. I'm fat, okay? I came out of the womb looking like the Pillsbury Dough Girl. I've never married, although I've had a few boyfriends. Gentlemen callers, my mother wistfully used to call them. But they weren't gentlemen. Not one bit. I've always been embarrassed about my weight, even though lots of people have said that my eyes and face are beautiful and that I should just develop a nice personality and nobody will notice how fat I am. They don't say it exactly like that, but that's what they mean. No one uses the "fat" word with me. They use words like "wholesome," "healthy," "a big boned gal," "a farm girl," "a full bodied woman." It's obvious what they mean. Kids at school used to call me "fatty." You know how kids can be. I think I gave up way back then, but anyway, that's neither here nor there. Let's just get on with things. I just needed to clear the air and get this part over with.

My mother died when I was thirty-two, and I inherited enough money to buy a tiny, older, ranch style house with a few acres that held a small orchard, an old barn and some rickety buildings. The entire place was fenced and suited me fine. I bought some furnishings, good used ones, and moved into my first home. I invested the rest of the money in CDs and started working online from a small home office. I may be fat, but I'm smart. Two dogs and a cat soon joined me. The dogs accompanied me on long walks along country roads and into town where I'd collect my mail, get my hair done from time to time and buy groceries. I felt good, almost smug in my quiet, orderly world, and then I bought Jump Off Joe.

I don't know what possessed me to buy that horse. Well, that's not entirely true. On every walk into town I passed by the field where that wild mustang grazed. I never really noticed him until one day I saw him fiercely munching the grass on the wrong side of the fence, the side I was on. I stopped to watch for a second, and then suddenly we were looking at each other, eyeball to eyeball, just like we knew what each other was thinking. From then on, every time I passed by that horse would come over, no matter what he was doing, and greet me with a friendly nicker. Feeling silly, I tried to neigh back, which made me sense that we were somehow connected.

A couple of months later a sign wired to the fence announced "Horse 4 Sale." I bought Joe that day and paid extra so the owner would deliver him. What did I know about leading a horse home? My impulsive purchase excited me, and I stopped at the library that afternoon and left hours later with a pile of books about horses stacked so high I could hardly carry them without one or two sliding off the top. When the owner delivered Joe, he gave me an old saddle and some other dirty horse gear. I think he felt bad about how much I paid for that wild thing. He brought a small load of hay too. Left his number in case I had any questions, but sternly repeated that the *sale was final*. I meekly replied, "Okay."

So, now I had two dogs, a cat and a horse named Jump Off Joe who ran wild about my property, even coming up on the back porch once and leaving a big pile of poop. Finally I put him in a large corral I paid a handyman to build.

I'm the indoor type probably because, well, you know, but things changed when I got Joe. I had to go out to feed him at least twice a day, and if I didn't go out regularly he'd stand out there and whinny and carry on like I was beating him. So out I'd go and he'd come up to the fence where we'd stand and I'd talk and he'd listen. Pretty soon I worked up my nerve and started patting him. I could tell he liked that. Finally, I bought some fancy grooming items. I squeezed through the rails of the fence and showed Joe the nifty new things I'd purchased for him. He sniffed them thoroughly, and then I started gently brushing him. I held firmly onto the fence in case I had to make a quick escape, but Joe just stood there, almost purring, as I combed his matted, snarled mane.

Soon I was reading newspaper articles aloud and playing the flute for him in the evenings. I spent so much time at the corral that I was having to work late into the night in my office. I often took my dinner out, and I'd sit in a chair that I'd wrestled out there and set under a barn eave, and Joe and I would dine together. Occasionally we shared watermelon, apples, and carrots. It was heart-warming to have a friend.

We spent a year together in this way, during which time I walked and brushed Joe daily. I came to love that horse as I have never loved another being. I loved him truly, deeply, and with all my heart. And, miraculously, Joe loved me. I think he was the first creature on God's earth that loved me exactly how I was. He whinnied whenever I came out the door. Sometimes he'd stand and stare at the house for hours, waiting for the sight of me, and he never disappointed me when I'd finally emerge. He'd greet me enthusiastically, with the ardent exuberance of a passionate beau. He would gently nuzzle me, licking my cheek or the back of my neck. Sometimes he'd breathe softly in my ear, his breath warming my lonely heart. I finally opened the corral gates and let him roam freely on the property. At least he kept my lawn neatly trimmed.

One day, as I gazed into Joe's warm, chocolate eyes, the idea of riding him leaped into my mind. I'd never ridden a horse before. I'd never even *imagined* riding a horse, but instantly I envisioned the two of us joyously roaming the public lands that abutted my property. Would I be too heavy? Finding scales depressing, I only weighed at clandestine moments when I was alone in the grain room at the local feed and tack store. Despite my having lost more than thirty pounds since Joe'd joined me, I still feared that I'd never be a pretty sight. Anyway, after this riding idea entered my head, I hired Tom.

The morning he showed up I could smell beer on his breath. I rolled my eyes and hoped I hadn't wasted $400. I told him what I wanted, and also what I didn't want, and I emphatically didn't want my horse hurt in any way. I told Tom all the details about

Joe, how loving he was, how I loved him, how clever and smart he was, how affectionate and caring. Tom stood on the porch during this time, dirty hands stuffed in his pockets, dusty hat pushed back on his head and said nothing. After fifteen minutes I stopped. "Well, you go on about your business now. I'll just stay here and work."

"Suit yourself, lady. Some of this may not be pretty, but you need to know that I don't hurt the horse. The horse hurts himself." With that he strode to the corral and stood for a long time watching Joe watch him.

I hid behind the kitchen curtains with binoculars pressed to my head, watching the two of them watch each other, waiting for something to happen. Nothing happened except the staring contest.

For several days Tom arrived early in the morning and did things with halters and a long looking whip. Joe got so he ran to the other side of the corral when Tom showed up, and my heart just broke to think he might be scared of that stubble-bearded, beery man. Finally, my waning patience was rewarded when Tom began saddling the horse. I couldn't watch after that, and it was all I could do not to run out there and put a stop to the whole horrible debacle. What with Joe snorting and bucking and looking all wild-eyed, and Tom yellin' and gee-hawin' I had to put a pillow over my head.

Several days later Tom mounted and I saw the wildest, most unimaginable, unbelievable rodeo in my own corral. That horse jumped from side to side, spun, bucked, threw his head violently every which direction, crow-hopped, bucked some more, screamed, kicked, spun again and then galloped madly, furiously, around and around, then repeated the whole process. He kept that up for the entire afternoon. I knew then I could never ride Joe.

No, he was too wild and wooly for this city girl. As I peeked from behind the curtain I began to cry. I'd been stupid to think I could ever ride a horse, particularly one like Jump Off Joe. I could see now why he was so named. I sank to the sofa and sobbed, feeling sorry for my pitiful, lonely life, my ridiculous dream to ride my horse, and every tiny, wretched, feeble detail from the last thirty years that popped into my self-pity-partying head. Who was I to think I could ride a horse all by myself? I was an idiot.

I cried for many hours, long after Tom Freeman left anyway. Sadly I walked to the barn that night to feed Joe. I couldn't even look him in the eye, I felt like such a fool. Joe whinnied softly, but my disappointment and despair were too great for me to greet my friend.

After that I stopped watching Tom train my horse. It was too painful, and I was too embarrassed to think about my excruciatingly stupid idea.

Three weeks later Tom Freeman knocked loudly. "Thought I'd let you know that your horse is ready to ride, ma'am," he drawled. I noticed his clean white shirt and freshly shaved face as he stood there in his levis, boots, and new hat rakishly set back on his head. "He's all saddled for you and waitin'."

I could feel my face burning in embarrassment. What the hell. I might as well get it out in the open. "Tom," I faltered, "I don't think I'll be riding Joe. I think I overestimated my…" I stopped as tears formed. Oh my god! Now I was going to humiliate myself further by crying in front of this man who would surely tell this story for laughs and free beer for years to come.

"I just don't think I'm suited for the horse," I finally finished.

"Well, ma'am. I think you might be surprised. It'd be nice if you tried. He's waitin' for you. I'll give you a hand."

For a moment time stood still as I groped for a response. The next thing I knew Tom stepped back and extended his hand to me. "Come on, now. Don't you be scared. That hell bastard is a fine horse."

My legs mechanically carried me to the corral. Every possible objection to riding I could think of raced through my feverish brain. I opened my mouth to spew them all, but the words caught in my throat.

"I made you a small mounting block, ma'am," Tom said rather proudly.

"My name is Laura," I heard a strange, tinny voice, surely not mine, answer.

"Laura, just climb up there and I'll bring him right on up to ya."

Suddenly, Joe stood beside me. He seemed gargantuan. I reached out stiffly, robot-like, to grab onto the saddle. One moment I was looking at the side of a gigantic horse; a moment later I was sitting on the tallest animal in the world. I saw the ground and Tom Freeman far below me as though they were in a distant galaxy. Tom spoke, yet I heard not a word as he placed the reins in my sweat drenched hands.

Then it happened. I felt the horse tense and draw himself together. I knew he'd buck and I'd be on the ground, a pile of blubbering lard. Suddenly, Joe's head swung around. He glared fiercely for several moments before his severe scowl faded and his eyes softened as if to say, "Oh, it's you. Okay."

I rode Joe around the corral for the rest of that brilliant, sun-kissed afternoon while Tom sat on the top rail giving helpful instruction. Soon we were laughing and talking like everything in the whole world was as it should be. We ate pizza that night – well, Tom ate pizza and I had a salad, no dressing – while we talked about Jump Off Joe and all the fine things horse people talk about. Tom winked and said his fee included teaching me to saddle up and ride, and then he asked if I'd seen the movie showing at the local theater. I said yes because I didn't realize he was trying to ask me out. Then I said no too quickly and we both laughed in that friendly way I'd seen others laugh.

So, that's my story about Jump Off Joe and cowboy Tom Freeman. For a year Tom and I rode our horses almost daily and spent our nights dreamily together. Even though I knew Tom'd never stay, I could not resist the love and tenderness he offered me. He moved on after a year or so to ride the rodeo circuit. I get a postcard now and then. Still and all, Tom Freeman and Jump Off Joe are the two best things that ever happened to me. They changed my life forever.

BECKY COFFIELD is an award-winning freelance writer, author, and publisher. Coffield writes under several pen names, including **R.L.COFFIELD**. Coffield is the author of the award-winning Ben Thomas suspense novel, *Northern Escape*, and the award-winning, humorous travel/memoir, *Life Was a Cabaret: A Tale of Two Fools, A Boat, and a Big-A** Ocean.* Becky is the head cook and bottle washer at Moonlight Mesa Associates, Inc., a Western book publisher located in Wickenburg, Arizona.

INDIO

Robert Walton

(3rd Place 2009 Cowboy Up Contest)

Indio smiled as a summer storm broke around him. Fat drops splattered on his pony's head, shattered on his shoulders. Lightning split red sandstone three hundred yards above and behind his left ear. Its thunder sounded like the crack of Satan's own whip. Indio did not flinch. His eyes were fixed on three canvas-covered wagons in the arroyo below him.

A skinny girl lay groaning in mud next to the last wagon's rear wheels. Her right leg was shattered above the knee. Thick blood flowed onto the ground beside her. Indio walked up to her, knelt, pulled out his long knife.

She looked up at him, her blue eyes already dark with death's shadows. She said, "Mister, please don't hurt me no more, please. You understand?"

Indio grinned. "I understand." He grasped her fine hair with his left hand, pulled it taut, touched her forehead with his knife.

***

Joaquin Murrieta gazed into a cloudless sky. Morning warmth was just becoming heat. The buzz of many flies floated on the desert's heavy silence. Sighing, he looked down at the pillaged wagons, the discarded bundles of clothing and flesh.

He dismounted and tied his horse, Gallito, in the shade of a cottonwood well away from the dead. His duty was clear. He walked to the nearest wagon. The spade was strapped to its side, handy in case a wheel should become mired. He removed it and turned to his work. Fortunately the soil was sandy.

The muted thump of horses' hooves sounded. Joaquin raised his eyes. Along the arroyo's sandy bottom a dozen dispirited horses walked. Their heads were low, their eyes half-closed. Heat radiated from their dark bodies in waves. Nine of the horses bore riders. Fine, ghost-white dust covered these men. They were soldiers.

Joaquin rose to his feet and moved from the shade of a boulder into sunlight. Heat fell on him like a landslide. He shrugged his shoulders against its invisible weight. He raised his right hand in greeting and addressed a soldier with stripes on his sleeve. "Sergeant, I am Joaquin Murrieta. I'm traveling to Yuma."

The Sergeant halted his column. He looked at the row of graves and then at Joaquin. At last, he cleared his throat and spoke, "Did you bury these folks?"

"Yes."

"I thank you."

Joaquin inclined his head.

The Sergeant went on, "We've been chasing the man who killed them."

Joaquin's eyes lifted. "Who is this man?"

"A renegade. Calls himself Indio. Might be part Ute. Who knows?"

Joaquin nodded. "Quien sabes?"

The Sergeant motioned toward a makeshift litter pulled by two of the riderless horses. "He ambushed us this morning, killed two men and wounded the Lieutenant."

Joaquin glanced toward the dust-covered litter. "Is he badly hurt?"

"Belly wound. If God is kind, he'll die before we reach the fort."

Joaquin nodded. "May God be kind."

The Sergeant said, "We'll keep moving, Mr. Murrieta. You watch yourself. This Indio's a killer."

Joaquin said, "Adios." He watched as the listless horses plodded down the arroyo and disappeared. He then turned and looked toward the badlands. He murmured, "Indio, it is time we met."

Joaquin eased his pistol into its holster. A Navy Model Colt .44, it was a heavy, long-barreled weapon, made for shooting accurately. He had killed with it. Extra cylinders, loaded and primed, weighted his coat pockets. He grasped the satin-smooth stock of his Winchester. The clean smell of gun oil momentarily overwhelmed the desert smell of heated dust. He rested the rifle on the saddle before him and glanced to the North.

Even Indio would need water soon. He would come down this draw, search out some lonely ranch. Then he would kill again. There was no reason for him to hold back.

A wren slanted from sunlight into shadow. Gallito's ears twitched. Joaquin lowered his rifle, concealed it along the animal's right flank. Movement pricked his eyes like a cholla thorn.

Mounted on a gray pony, Indio moved from behind a scatter of boulders. Joaquin breathed deeply, exhaled completely. More than three hundred yards, not an easy shot, he dared not let this man come closer.

He twitched his reins. Gallito moved out of shade into the center of the draw. Left side toward Indio, rifle hidden, Joaquin halted his horse.

Indio stopped. Heat prickled the back of Joaquin's neck. He could feel the intense pressure of the renegade's gaze.

Then Indio's mount paced forward. Indio raised his left hand, fingers wide. Joaquin could see the white gleam of his greeting smile.

Joaquin smiled. Then swifter and smoother than a scorpion's sting, he brought the rifle to his shoulder. He aimed. He fired.

Even as the bullet ripped from the barrel, Indio dove away. The heavy slug slammed into the gray pony, knocked it screaming and kicking to the arroyo bottom.

Joaquin's smile became wider, grimmer. Now Indio would come to him – was coming now. He turned Gallito and rode toward an isolated stand of boulders. He dismounted in open desert on the far side of the boulders. He removed his rope from the saddle and fashioned a large knot. He stooped, plucked up a flat stone and dug a deep, narrow hole in the sand. He dropped the knotted end of the rope into the hole and covered it over. Finally, he tied the horse's reins to the rope's other end.

Joaquin patted the horse's neck and murmured, "You must be the bait, old friend. He can't get away from here without you. To get you, he will have to kill me." He removed the full canteen and the saddlebag containing food and ammunition. The horse eyed him morosely, shook its head in a gesture of profound disquiet. He patted its neck once again and turned.

He looked west. Securing Gallito had taken something less than four minutes. Indio should have covered half the distance from the arroyo. Almost in range.

INDIO

Joaquin looked at the boulders carefully. He had studied them earlier when he had chosen this place for battle, but he again traced their shadows, again fit their shapes into the plan he'd made.

He nodded a silent confirmation to himself and walked to the place where he would wait. It was a cleft. Two great stones leaned together; a third capped them with an overhang. His back was protected completely, his flanks somewhat less so. Before him was a small breastwork of stones and sand. He crouched behind it and looked out over the desert.

It was possible that he could get in a long rifle shot. He doubted this, but could not ignore the possibility that Indio would make a mistake. Long minutes passed. Heat began to build around him. He was in shadow still, but a trickle of sweat slid down between his shoulder blades. The urge to rub his back was overpowering. Movement, though, would betray him. He remained frozen in the hunter's stillness, or the prey's.

A small stone suddenly clattered down the slope to his right. Joaquin smiled. This was his only movement. Indio tries beginner's tricks, he thought. Let him. Again a stone clicked and chattered among its bigger brothers. This time movement followed, just a flick, sixty yards away, behind a clump of sage.

Joaquin fired. The heavy crash of his Winchester echoed and re-echoed among the boulders, across the desert. He fired into the sage five times, swiftly – left side, right side, low middle, high middle, low middle again. One of the slugs should have struck home. Joaquin raised his head slightly, peered through gun smoke.

A bullet screamed off granite inches from his left ear. Splinters of rock tore into his head. He let himself slide down behind the breastwork.

"Fool!" he cursed himself, "Fool! Indio moved the sage with a tied rope. He was farther back. Fool! But you have no time for curses. Is he rushing? Or is he waiting?"

He lifted the saddlebag with the barrel of his rifle. Raising it slowly, he pushed it above the rim of the breastwork. A shot crashed into the sand just below it.

Joaquin whispered, "He is waiting." He touched his face where it was beginning to sting. His fingers came away sticky with blood. "The eyes, at least, are whole, no thanks to your intelligence, old man. What next? He knows I live. He knows where I am. I cannot return his fire until he attacks. It is your move, Indio."

A bullet screamed off the overhang above and thumped into the ground a few feet behind him. A moment passed. Another slug wailed off of granite a few inches from the scar made by the first. It crashed into the sand next to his boot heel.

"Ricochets. He tries to bounce the bullet onto my head. In ten shots, or fifteen, he will succeed. You must move, old man. You must move to your left. You knew this might happen, but you hoped it wouldn't. Hopes have nothing to do with what is real. You must move like a young man. Now!"

He threw his saddlebag over the breastwork to his right and dove to his left. The small distraction to Indio's eye might save him. Fountains of granite splashed around him, sprayed him with silver splinters. He rolled twice and slid behind a large stone. Two bullets followed him into its shadow.

Joaquin lay back against a warm slab of stone. The setting sun washed the desert around him with tincture of gold. His battle with Indio had lasted through the heat and weight of the desert afternoon.

INDIO

The lava-flow-ooze of blood from his shoulder stirred his memory of past battles, past wounds. The distant thuds of his heart, the haze of pain were almost pleasurable sensations. He suspected that he would not die.

Unless Indio came again.

All his skill had barely kept him alive through the hours of stalking, the seconds of shooting. Only luck had allowed him to survive Indio's last bullet. It had torn through his right shoulder instead of smashing his heart. A cold trickle of fear slid down his spine.

"Stop it, old man. You are too old to be afraid." But you are. "At least he thinks I am fifty yards from here. He thinks I am curled up in a hole, dying."

Joaquin smiled. "I'm lying in sunlight, dying."

He looked down at the heavy pistol resting against his belly. It had been years since his life had depended on shooting with his left hand. It did now.

"Indio, you will cross this open space before me. God willing, I will kill you." You talk big, old man, but can you shoot with your left hand?

Swift and silent as a sidewinder, Indio slid from behind a boulder. Joaquin raised his pistol and fired. As the hammer crashed down, Indio caught the motion and whirled. The heavy bullet shattered his right arm. His rifle spun away into sand.

Joaquin looked down the blue barrel of his Colt at Indio. Indio, blood streaming down his arm, eyes burning with black fire, stared back.

Joaquin had looked upon death's face many times. Never had death's face been so fearless, so fierce. Indio's left hand streaked for the knife at his belt. Joaquin fired.

Miss, above his left shoulder. He fired again. Miss. Indio's knife sang past his ear, screeched off stone behind him. He fired again. The bullet ripped into Indio's thigh. He made no sound, but his teeth flashed white in a snarl of pain and unholy rage. He staggered once and dove behind a clump of sage.

Joaquin lowered his pistol. "Two bullets left. That was poor shooting, old man."

Blue shadow suddenly engulfed the desert like a sea wave. A breeze stirred chamisa branches near. Joaquin lowered his pistol, nodded to himself. "It is time to leave."

He swayed, straightened. Pain rose like a wind through his body. Blue twilight became black for an instant.

"Stop this, old man. You can still die here. Indio will kill you with his thumbs if he returns."

He staggered slightly as he walked beyond the boulders to where Gallito still waited. The horse turned his head and eyed Joaquin calmly as he rested his cheek against the saddle's still-warm leather. "Well, old friend, you smell blood and it doesn't frighten you." He reached down and untied the reins. "But then you've smelled my blood before." With glacial slowness, Joaquin lifted his left foot to the stirrup and mounted. The horse stood still as stone.

Joaquin leaned forward, rested his forehead against the bristle of Gallito's mane. He murmured, "The desert will finish Indio. Or it won't. We've done what we could." He clucked to the horse. Gallito lowered his head, twitched his ears and paced toward twilight's last pale flags in the sky.

Like the dark, strong hand of God, desert night closed around them.

ROBERT WALTON is a life-long rock-climber and mountaineer who has made numerous ascents in the Sierra Nevada and Yosemite. Three of his short stories about climbing were published in the Sierra Club's *Ascent*. Other stories and poems have appeared in *High* magazine, *Loose Scree* and in *The Climbing Art*. Robert converted a story named "Three's a Crowd" into a radio play which was broadcast on KUSF on November 22nd, 2006. It was later broadcast several more times on PBS. Walton's short story "Don Francisco Rides to La Paz" won the 2008 Saturday Writers short story contest. Most recently, Walton's "Perfect Partner" was recognized in the Kendall Mountain Literature Competition.

Tom Coffield

NAVIDAD
Robert Walton

(Finalist 2010 Cowboy Up Contest)

Joaquin Murrieta looked down at three graves. Wooden crosses, simple, but finely carved, marked each. Their darkened wood and the long grass on the low mounds indicated that the graves were not new.

His horse stirred impatiently. Joaquin rubbed its nose and glanced up at the sun. It was late afternoon, though earlier than it seemed. December sunlight slanted down through pines, silvering needles, weaving delicate webs of light and shadow over the graves.

"You got business here, Mister?"

Joaquin started. He had spent his life anticipating, even savoring the unexpected, but this voice sounding suddenly from behind had caught him completely unaware. He turned slowly.

A thin man, gaunt as winter branches, stood perhaps five yards away. He wore blue jeans and a thick wool jacket. His black hat was pulled low and shaded his face. In the shadow, hard eyes glinted. A rifle rested in the crook of the man's left arm. It was pointed vaguely toward Joaquin.

Joaquin smiled. All his wits, at least, had not deserted him. The weight and power of the gun had been in the voice, the words. He had not needed to see it to know that it was there. He said, "I am a traveler. I mean no harm. My business is in Sonora."

The man considered this. "You won't make it there by nightfall."

"No. Near Chinese Camp there is the place where the stagecoaches change teams. I will spend the night there." He motioned with his open hand. "You move very quietly, my friend."

The man grinned humorlessly, his hawk's beak of a nose tilting slightly upwards. He said, "I know these woods. My cabin's a ways up the valley. Name's Hawkins, Frank Hawkins."

Joaquin glanced down at the graves again. "Who lies here?"

There was silence for some moments. Joaquin looked up. At last Hawkins spoke, his voice as rough as oak bark, "My children. My wife."

Joaquin looked down.

Hawkins continued, "The diphtheria took them, my girl and my boy. My wife -- died a few months later."

Joaquin, still looking down at the graves, made no answer. They stood in silence for some moments. Wind rose over the ridge and set the pines to swaying, sighing. Joaquin glanced up at Hawkins.

Hawkins stared down at the wooden crosses.

Joaquin took off his hat. Low sunlight shone in his silver-white hair. He bowed, not deeply, but with respect. Still holding his hat in his right hand, he turned and led his horse up the path to the main trial. Once on the trail, he mounted and looked back. Hawkins had not moved. Joaquin shook his head once and softly spoke, "Santa Maria, Madre de Dios…" He rode on.

He rode for two miles. Rounding a curve in the trail, he stopped. Dusk was deep now. Something stirred in the oak-shadow darkness ahead. A horse whinnied. Joaquin's horse shook its head and nickered an answer.

Suddenly the small sun of a kerosene lantern flared beneath the oaks. Joaquin saw a woman's face, golden in the light, staring intently down. Then the light was cut off by the square shape of a restless packhorse. He touched his mount's flanks gently with the rowels of his silver spurs.

He pulled on his reins and halted as he entered the circle of light. There were four horses. Two carried packs and two bore saddles. The woman, kneeling on dry oak leaves, held a silent baby. A man rose from beside her, peered briefly at him and stepped forward.

Joaquin said, "Good evening."

The man removed his wide-brimmed hat. He was young, though the lantern's light picked out fine lines of fatigue around his eyes. He spoke, "Name's Sam, Sam Whitney. Sarah's my wife."

Joaquin nodded politely to the woman.

"Mister," the man continued, not waiting for Joaquin's reply, "do you know of any ranches or cabins near?"

"It's our baby," Sarah broke in, "she's sick, very sick. We've got to get her someplace where we can help her."

Joaquin looked at Sarah. Her long, dark hair was drawn up high and held with a faded red ribbon. Her eyes shone with unreleased tears. She was not more than eighteen years old.

He nodded. "There is a cabin several miles from here. We can get help there. Follow me."

Sam took the blanket-wrapped child. Sarah quickly mounted. Sam handed the baby up to her. Joaquin glimpsed fever-red skin, a lock of hair, wispy gold in the lantern light. Sam lifted the lantern and blew out its flame. Darkness closed around them like a fist.

The muffled thump of horses' hooves on pine needles followed them. Joaquin found the branching of the trail with little difficulty. Forty years of noting every smallest nuance of his surroundings had made him a profoundly competent navigator. In the old days, the gold fields days, his life and the lives of his men had depended on such competence. One young robber, seeking to join his band, seeking to prove himself, had tried to substitute boldness for competence. When Joaquin next saw him, he was lying in a coffin at Hangtown. More than forty bullet holes pierced his body.

However, as the old bandit led them up the trail only a small part of his conscious mind was on this task. Most of his thoughts turned on the fear he'd seen in the young woman's eyes, fear of loss, fear for the baby loved, helpless fear beneath fate's iron hooves. It saddened him, for he'd known this fear, felt it when he was young. He knew that such fear, not the mere passing of years, ages women, bakes them until they are dry and old. The graves were invisible when they passed them.

A lantern glimmered against the hillside. Hawkins' voice sounded from shadows to the right.

"Who's there?"

"The traveler," Joaquin answered. "I have three others with me. They need shelter and help." He dismounted. Behind him, Sam helped Sarah down from her horse.

Hawkins stepped into the light. His rifle rested in the crook of his arm.

"What's the matter? It ain't raining."

Sarah lurched forward, her eyes large in the lantern light. She held out the bundle in her arms. "My child's sick, Mister. Please, let me bring her inside."

Joaquin watched Hawkins closely, saw a cord of muscle along the line of his jaw twist and knot. This rancher was an oak stump of a man, an oak scorched by life.

Hawkins' eyes rested on the boy, the girl, the baby. At last he nodded. He turned and led them into the cabin. A lantern sat on a sink made of rough planks. Its light struck gleams from a copper pan, from a bottle half-hidden in a dark cupboard. Still, though this was a small room, the light was swallowed by corner shadows.

Hawkins placed his rifle on brackets to the right of the wood stove. He struck a match, lit a kerosene lamp with a tall glass chimney. The room's shadows retreated further, but did not vanish altogether.

Sarah paused in the doorway. Her eyes, over-bright and glassy, looked left and right without seeing. She clutched her child to her. Tendons in her neck stood out with the strain of her grip. The child moaned.

Hawkins motioned with his hand, "Put her over here on the bed." Sarah stumbled across the room. She came up sharply against the bed, her shins banging against its wooden frame. She bent down and laid her child on the red wool blanket. She straightened, still gazing down, and then swayed.

Hawkins stepped across the room and grasped her arm. "Sit down, girl, before you fall down." He guided her to a crooked chair. It creaked as it took her weight.

A strangled cry came from the baby. Hawkins turned. The child's red fists clenched. Her arms stuck straight out from her body. The whites of her eyes rolled up like the bellies of dying fish.

Hawkins took a quick stride and reached the baby's side. He grasped her right arm and felt muscles twist like rawhide thongs. The baby gagged.

"Quick," he glanced at Sam, "bring me a piece of kindling from the woodbox." Sam jumped to obey. He handed the clean, white pine stick to Hawkins. "She's got fever fits. Swallowed her tongue. Got to get it out of her throat."

He pushed the pine stick between the baby's teeth, pried open her rigid jaws. Hooking his index finger, he probed deep in her throat.

"Can't clear it." His eyes bulged as he dug deeper in the child's throat. "There!"

The baby took a whooping breath. "There," he said more softly and glanced at Joaquin. "This chid is hotter than a two dollar pistol. I've seen this kind of fever before. We've got to cool her off before the fits kill her. You and the boy go outside and get the washtub. It's on the side of the cabin. Get some water in it and bring it back."

Joaquin nodded and moved toward the door. Sam followed him. The air outside was heavy with winter's black chill. Darkness pushed against them like a hand. Sam almost whispered, "I'll fetch the lantern."

Joaquin didn't answer. He felt along the rough boards of the cabin. Stars floated above the edges of his vision. His hands encountered splinters drier than coffin dust, splinters drier than the skin of a fevered child. His fingers at last touched metal, bitter smooth and burning cold.

He lifted the tub free of its nail just as Sam pushed the lantern's glow ahead of him through the door. Joaquin carried the tub to the pump. Sam put the lantern on a barrel nearby and lifted the pump handle. A stream of liquid ice gushed into the tub with a hollow, leaden clang.

After several moments, Sam looked at Joaquin, his tired eyes too dark, too shadowed. Joaquin nodded, "That should be enough. Help me. It is heavy now." They lifted the tub together. Struggling against the ungainly weight, they shuffled toward the door. Water sloshed onto the ground, onto their clothes. A slop of water plunged into Joaquin's left boot, made him gasp.

Hawkins awaited them just within the door, his eyes wide and shining. He held the baby before him. She was bent backwards like a bow. Her lips were knotted in a rictus of fever.

"Set it there," he husked in a voice that sounded like wind in trees. "Set it there, quick!"

They lowered the tub just inside the door. Water again splashed out, staining the floor with irregular leopard spots of blackness.

Hawkins motioned toward the woodstove with his head. "The kettle's full of hot water. Pour it in. Take the edge off that outside water."

Joaquin did so.

Then Hawkins knelt. He dipped his right hand into the water. His left arm held and supported the baby. He stroked water onto her feet, her arms, her face.

"There, baby, there. There, it's cold. It's cold, I know. I've got to put you in there, but slowly. I don't want your little heart to stop. There, there."

The hard man's voice dwindled to a murmur softer than hummingbirds, gentler than summer evenings.

Sam moved stiffly to Sarah's side. She remained sitting on the front edge of the chair. He touched her cheek, stroked her forehead with one finger and brushed back a wisp of stray hair.

"Good baby, that's it, not too fast. We'll get you cool. We'll get the fever out of you. Breathe easy. Your feet are in now. Now your legs."

The little girl was immersed. Hawkins' big hands cradled her in the dark water. Her eyes rolled open for a moment, blue and misted with tears. She squinted again, took a deep breath and cried.

"We'll leave you in just a moment more. Let mountain water take that fever. It will. It will."

An hour before dawn, Hawkins and Joaquin stood outside near the pump. Within, Sarah and her baby lay sleeping on Hawkins' narrow bed. Sam, head sunk on his breast, sat dozing in the chair next to them.

Hawkins chuckled, "His neck's gonna hurt like hell tomorrow."

Joaquin grinned, "Today, my friend, his neck will hurt today."

Hawkins glanced up at the sky and nodded. "Right." Then he looked down. "The fever's broke, I think. She should be okay." His eyes glanced uphill where three crosses stood invisible beneath oak shadows.

Joaquin touched his arm. "Quien sabes? But I think you are right, Mr. Hawkins."

"Course, they'll have to stay around for a few days. It'll be a bother, noise, getting' in my way, small cabin and all."

Joaquin said nothing.

"Cookin'. What'll I feed these folk? I eat beans myself. A man don't need this kind of bother at my age, I tell you."

Joaquin grinned again, "But you will make do, eh? Now I must go. There is no sleep in me this night and there is not room in your cabin. It is good for a man occasionally to ride and meet a dawn. Adios."

Joaquin mounted his horse.

"Wait, mister." Hawkins looked up. "I don't feel right about sending you off with nothin' to eat, nothin' to keep you goin'. So, here, have a drink with me before you head on down to Sonora. I ain't touched it in a long time, but whiskey don't spoil." He offered Joaquin a dusty jug.

Joaquin took the jug, pulled its crusty cork out, tilted his head back, brought it to his lips and drank. Great tongues of sun-flame and scorpion stings rolled over his tongue. He breathed deeply in and exhaled slowly. He handed the jug back to Hawkins.

Hawkins took a long, gurgling drink. Joaquin let whiskey's heat settle in his belly, run along his veins. He said, "Thank you. It's still good, very good."

Hawkins smiled.

"And, Mr. Hawkins, when I pass this way again, may I stop to see how your whiskey is aging?"

Hawkins stared at him in surprised silence for a moment and then looked quickly away. "Why, sure, sure. Stop anytime. Don't even knock. I'll be around."

"Pues, again, adios." He touched his horse's flank with his heels."

Joaquin rode to the rise above the dark grove of oaks. He reined in and lifted his canteen from the saddle horn. Whiskey before dawn gives a man thirst. He opened the canteen and drank. He had filled it from Hawkins' pump only twenty minutes before and the water was cold. The water was sweet and cold as starlight, cold enough to make an old man feel young for a moment. He straightened in the saddle, wiped stray drops from his beard with the back of his hand. He shivered, and shivered again from the cold goodness of the water.

As he shivered and watched burning, spinning stars, dawn came.

See **ROBERT WALTON'S** information on page 65.

MANIAC

Drew Davis

*(Honorable Mention 2009 Cowboy Up Contest.
Assistant Publisher Choice)*

Bryce Jardeen had to be the last person I expected to see at Forkwood Community Rodeo, but there he was. While I stood waiting to draw for my events, the shuttle bus from Crown Diamond Ranch brought a storm of Wyoming summer dust into the parking lot. He was first through the door, turning immediately to help a load of youngsters out, some nearly as tall as himself.

We had both been ranch hands there a few years back, before the owners quit working cattle and started working dudes and youth camps instead. Stubble on his chin had turned from coppery brown to gray since then, but everything else seemed the same. I'd swear he was wearing the clothes I'd last seen him in, the red and white striped shirt tucked into a well worn set of jeans, scuffed and weathered brown boots, and the tan felt cowboy hat that long ago settled into a shape all its own.

I smiled watching the familiar gait as he walked to the back of the bus, the bowlegged shuffle with a slight limp to his right leg. He opened the rear door and pulled down a loading platform, then carefully lowered a wheelchair-bound young girl to ground level. She was a cute kid in a colorful cowgirl outfit, looked to be about twelve, honey blonde hair pulled into twin pigtails bouncing on each side of her head.

Before I could holler a greeting, the registrars called me up and I said goodbye to the entry fees for my rides. Soon I was listed for calf roping, bareback and saddle bronc riding, and gave thanks that I'd been too short on pay that month to consider steer wrestling or bull riding. No need courting unnecessary breaks and bruises.

I spotted Bryce at a holding pen, having shed his young charges to the Crown Diamond counselors, and headed over, looking forward to a long overdue reunion.

"Hey, old man," I chuckled, "you always told me rodeo was a damn fool notion, calling something fun that most days is just called work."

"I hear this'un put a ranch hand in the hospital while they was loadin' him the other day," he said without acknowledging my quip. I followed his gaze to a chocolate colored Brahma with a full set of horns, dark shading across its shoulders matching the black pockets around its none-too-friendly eyes.

"So this is the bull they call Maniac," I replied. "He's done damage before. They tell me this fella was lucky to get out alive."

"I'll be lucky if that bull doesn't bankrupt me," a new voice joined the conversation. "Shoulda left him at the ranch and saved myself a bundle of headaches, not to mention medical bills."

The newcomer was quite a showpiece to be complaining about money. The black beaver-skin hat atop his wavy salt and pepper hair probably set him back over three hundred dollars and the bolo tie with inlaid turquoise on its silver clasp probably matched the hat's price. Add to those a powder gray western-cut suit with black shoulder patches sporting a longhorn skull each and a larger one in the black yoke across the back. Then, to complement the outfit, grey snakeskin boots with polished black heels still shining through a layer of fairground dust.

A long dormant cigar bounced under his bushy black mustache as he studied the bull. "They won't let me put him in the draw," he went on, "so I'm shipping, feeding, and babysitting him out of my own pocket."

"That's a shame," I replied, trying my best to actually sound sympathetic. Most stock contractors I've met were once ranch hands themselves, more at home in work clothes, ready to jump in and lend help when needed. From the manicured fingernails and the paunch expanding over his silver buckle, I got the impression this one followed a different outlook.

"Jesse McRae, Big M Rodeo Stock, new to this area and trying to hit the ground running." He smiled and offered his right hand, removing the cigar with the other. Before I could respond with my own introduction, he continued, "They did say I could place him as a challenge ride, maybe offer a cash prize at twenty bucks a try, but after the bad publicity, these part-time cowboys are too afraid to get near him."

I started to educate Mister Big M about these being actual full-time cowboys looking for a few wild rides in their little bit of spare time. The Forkwood Community Rodeo only permitted us local amateur thrill seekers to participate. Before I could unload, however, Bryce said something that made me lose all the steam I'd built up.

"I'll ride'im," he stated, never taking his eyes off the bull.

McRae worked the cigar stub once more, staring at the small, wiry man who was well into middle age and probably weighed half as much as the stockman. Finally he remarked, "That bull has pimples on his butt bigger than you."

Tension rippled his jaw muscles, but Bryce calmly said, "Keep him penned up and all the bills are yours. Let me take your challenge ride and you just might be able to stick the rodeo with some of the tab."

I could almost see the dollar signs explode in McRae's eyes as his big smile showcased a perfect set of teeth. "I'll arrange it with the announcers so they can warm up the crowd and you'll have to see the stewards about an insurance waiver," he said, then waited for that last little nugget to register. "You ain't gonna back out on me, are you?"

"Bryce," I finally found the breath to blurt, "Have you gone crazy?"

"No more'n I need to be," he replied. Bryce pulled a small wad of bills from his pocket, peeled off two tens, and held them out to McRae. "How 'bout it?"

McRae took the money and hot footed to the grandstand as fast as his shiny boots could take him. Bryce turned back to the bull and I shook my head in bewilderment as I leaned on the fence next to him.

"Bryce, there's a whole lot more to ridin' a bull than sittin' on his back and lettin' your boots hang down," I tried to reason with him. "Things like sliding up over your hand to get the center of gravity, deciding which arm to use for balance and which one to…"

"I've rode bulls before. Way before. How do you think I got this hitch in my gitalong? Bucked off, butted down and stomped on!"

"You never even went to the rodeo when I was working with you!"

"The accident kinda soured me on it," he said, his eyes focused on visions long past. "Took me a while to heal up. Thought I'd lost every chance I had to be a cowhand."

He paused a moment and I had no words to fill the gap. When he looked up, he stared me straight in the eye and continued, "That's all I ever wanted. I love every minute of it. Pulling calves out of bogs after spring rains, riding fence looking for breaks and strays, roundups and branding, even hauling feed and hay in the winter. Felt like what I was born to do. I was so glad I was able to get back to it. You're lucky, still on a working ranch."

"You coulda jumped with us when the Crown Diamond switched over."

"I meant to. Then the owners offered me the foreman job in charge of the livestock. I wasn't getting no younger and this leg did slow me down a bit. I had to take the shot. Turns out I'm not too bad at it. The adults are pains sometimes but these kids are okay."

"So why risk all that with this Maniac ride?"

"Seemed like a good idea at the time." Bryce grimaced, reaching under his hat to scratch his bald head. "You see…"

Before he could continue, the loudspeaker called all saddle bronc riders and I had to get a move on. He surprised me by holding his right hand out, thumb up. It had been a long time since I'd seen his trademark gesture, but I clapped my own hand in his and we both said, "Buckle down, buckaroo."

I drew a dandy of a saddle bronc and together we scored enough to get me into the next round. However, I might as well have watched the bareback fiasco from the stands as from the arena dirt, which became my seat right after the gate opened. The only good thing about it was the cheering of the Crown Diamond kids whenever my name was announced, no doubt spurred on by Bryce.

When it came time for his ride, I climbed his chute to offer my help and thank him for my fan club. Bryce was already aboard and suited up.

"Where'd you get the new duds?" I asked, looking at the chaps, protective vest, and riding glove that obviously belonged to someone a tad larger.

He grinned and winked just before Maniac rattled the rickety enclosure with a couple thousand pounds of bovine rage, nearly toppling me off. Bryce forced his hat tight and focused on the fidgeting bull's broad neck. Raising his free hand into the air, he leaned over the bull rope and nodded to signal he was ready.

I've always found a certain beauty to a well taken rodeo ride, whether on horse or bull, a rhythmic counterbalance of beast and man dancing on the edge of violence. One using every ounce of its being to dislodge its burden, the other using every ounce of his own to follow the lead of his dangerous partner.

Bryce and Maniac were the very image of that struggle once the gate opened: eight seconds of explosive kicks, spins, and switchbacks, matched by subtle, shifting adjustments of the rider. Spittle flew in long strands from the bull's snout while Bryce's arm waved in a ballet of balance. When the airhorn sounded to end the ride, the spectators erupted in applause and uproar almost as if they had been holding their breath for just that moment.

Then it all went wrong.

Bryce started yanking to release the bull rope but it wouldn't give. I hadn't noticed if he used the dangerous looping known as a "suicide wrap" or maybe the ill-fitting borrowed glove had simply caught in a rope and rosin snare. The bullfighters with their clown-painted faces sprang into action, some dancing in front of Maniac to draw his attention, others leaping up to help the cowboy get loose.

The bull would have none of it. He kept flinging his hind legs skyward, spinning away from his tormentors and slashing his horns with vicious jerks of his head. He caught one man behind the knees and tossed him into two others, sprawling all three. Seizing this momentary lapse, the bull took off at full speed, Bryce still astride but bouncing with a lot less grace than before.

Maniac headed straight to the bullfighter's barrel and sent it flying end over end. Momentum from charging that target carried him into the fence not far beyond. Clang! The sound exploded as he butted the reinforced junction of two sections, still in full stride.

Bryce flipped forward, his chest slamming Maniac's hump. The bull stumbled back, his hind legs buckled and with a plop he sat straight up, his forelegs pawing the air. He started to fall then, looking like his bulk would flatten Bryce. The force of the impact must have loosed the rope tangle, however, because the cowboy flung himself away and both bodies landed side by side on the arena floor.

Dirty and battered, Bryce raised himself to a knee as onrushing bullfighters, cowhands, and other helpers arrived. They pulled him to his feet and he tipped back the hat that was still jammed on his head. The dazed bull staggered up and tried to return the cowboy's stare, but lost that battle too. Maniac shook himself vigorously and snorted a slobbery, grimy dust cloud. Then he just trotted to the exit gate, throwing a halfhearted lunge at one of the riders herding him out.

Bryce limped his way through the throng, shedding his borrowed items to their rightful owners and wincing once or twice when an overenthusiastic onlooker slapped a congratulatory hand on his back. His eyes scanned the crowd until they located the girl in the wheelchair and he headed straight to her.

"You rode him!" she shouted when he knelt beside her, her wide eyes gleaming. "I thought he was gonna break you!"

Bryce smiled and reached out to tousle her pigtails. "I kept my end of the deal," he said. "No matter how scary things get, we're tough enough to ride'em out. Now it's time for you to keep yours. You brave enough?"

"Not brave as you," she replied, her smile suddenly lost in a look of concern.

"Braver!" he countered. "I could always see what I was up against. You're gonna take on something only the doctors will see. But when they finish, you'll be riding ponies in no time."

She held her hand out, thumb up. He placed his dirty, gnarled knuckles around her tiny pink fingers and they wrapped thumbs. I saw tears glisten in the old cowboy's eyes as they chanted, "Buckle down, buckaroo."

"We got a rough ride ahead," I whispered to myself, supplying the part usually left unsaid.

Jesse McRae almost knocked me over getting to the pair. The stockman took off his fancy hat, working it between his hands like a schoolboy called before the principal.

"Look, about that prize money," he said. "You're the only one who paid the entry fee, so I couldn't build a bankroll. The rodeo people are hemming and hawing about it and with all the added expense I've had…"

"Didn't do it for money, mister," Bryce threw the words over his shoulder, already pushing the little girl's wheelchair toward the shuttle bus, the setting sun glowing through its windows.

MANIAC

McRae's face contorted at what, to him, was an obviously appalling concept. He called out, "You know, cowboy, I got a feeling the real maniac ain't the one in the corral."

DREW DAVIS is a writer, playwright, and singer/songwriter in the Augusta, Georgia area. His plays have been produced in San Diego, Chicago, Atlanta, and Cheshire, England.

SHOWDOWN AT DIABLO FLATS

Michael Fishman

(Finalist 2010 Cowboy Up Contest)

Will Chandler tied his horse to the splintered hitching post outside of Shorty's Saloon. Two weeks on the trail and Chandler was tired, saddle sore and lonely for a woman's company. He'd take care of each need in time, but he had business to attend to inside the saloon first.

Will pulled his hat off and set it on top of the hitching post. Listening to the sound of the piano playing over the buzz of drunken voices coming from inside the saloon, he bent over, cupped his hands and dipped them into the water trough and splashed the gray, mucky water over his head. He rinsed his face and let some of the brackish water trickle down over his lips. Chandler shook his hands dry and ran them once again through his hair and put his hat back on.

Will stood next to the hitching post for a few minutes, clearing his head and trying to get a feel for the type of crowd inside Shorty's tonight. He took his gun belt off the saddle and buckled it around his waist. He reached down and pulled the white-handled Colt Peace Maker from the holster and checked that each of the six chambers was filled with a .45 bullet. Satisfied, Will rotated the belt on his hip and walked toward the saloon's door. A big man, Will Chandler opened the bar doors and held them momentarily, arms outstretched, standing like an avenging brown leather-clad angel under a dusty white hat in the doorframe for all to see.

Chandler scanned the room and found the man he was looking for at a poker table off to the right sitting with his back to the wall. The slight, light-haired man's hands were on the table and he absent mindedly toyed with a half-empty whiskey glass, slowly spinning the jigger around with the thumb and middle finger of his left hand, while his right hand rested atop five playing cards laying face down on the table. The whiskey bottle stood on the table in front of him. One of the saloon's working girls, a long-haired redhead with a faded blue bow in her hair that didn't quite match the sky-blue color of her eyes, sat on the man's lap with her arms wrapped around his neck. Despite the whiskey and the girl's amorous attention, Will Chandler could see the man's eyes were bright and alert and his attention shifted back and forth between the goings-on in the room and the girl who was whispering in his ear and twirling the hair hanging down the back of his neck.

Will Chandler stepped forward and paused while the saloon's doors swung closed behind him and enjoyed the rush of warm, dry air that fanned the back of his neck. Walking into the saloon, he made his way straight over to the bar on the left side of the room. With each deliberate step he took his rusty spurs tinkled a discreet counterpoint to the piano player's tuneless notes. Chandler ordered a whiskey from the bartender, turned and leaned his back against the wood; elbows back on the bar, left leg bent with a dusty, chipped boot heel on the rail. Chandler looked left toward the back of the saloon, feigning interest in the Soiled Doves gathered around the piano while keeping a sideways eye on the man at the poker table.

***

"Will Chandler, is that you?" The voice came from the front door to Chandler's right.

Will turned to look at the stranger walking toward him and his right hand, by habit, slid to his waist. As the stranger neared, a smile of recognition spread across Will's lined face. "Major Warren?" Will asked. Elias Warren had been Chandler's commander when both men served under General Hood in the 4th Texas Infantry.

"*Sheriff* Warren now, Will."

"Been a long time, Major," Will said and paused before correcting himself. "I'm sorry, sir. Sheriff."

"Just Elias now, Will. The war's over," Warren said and smiled. Both men turned to face the bar. Elias nodded as the bartender set a beer down in front of him.

"What brings you to Diablo Flats?" Warren asked.

"Lookin' for a man."

"Anyone I know?"

"Look in the mirror, Major. Man sittin' at that poker table behind us got his back up against the wall, bottle of whiskey, getting worked on by the redhead in the tight blue dress?" Will said. "Killed a lawman outside San Antonio; him and the Ketchum boys all got prices on their heads." Will turned around to look directly at the man for the first time since he entered the saloon.

"What's your interest in him, Will?"

"That price he's got on his head, that's my interest. I aim to collect it."

"So you're a bounty hunter now, huh?"

"A man's got to make a living, isn't that right, Major."

Sheriff Warren took a swallow of his beer and looked back up into the mirror. He turned toward Will and said, "Rode with the Ketchum brothers, huh? I'm guessin' you got the papers on him?"

Will pulled the creased papers out of his inside vest pocket and turned back to face Warren. He set his right elbow on the bar and placed the papers down in front of the sheriff. "Everything's right here and all in order, Major," he said.

Elias Warren picked up his beer mug and smiled, "You haven't changed a bit, have you, Sergeant?"

**

Johnny Winslow noticed Will Chandler the moment he walked into the bar. Winslow didn't know Chandler by name, but watching the way the big man carried himself told Winslow what the stranger was here for. Winslow watched the stranger talking to the sheriff, and when the big man turned and looked his way, Johnny felt a cold chill travel down his spine with the realization that only one of them was walking out of this saloon alive. Johnny Winslow didn't get where he was by being a worrisome sort and he knew with a certainty that he would be that man.

"Fast" Johnny Winslow had ridden with the Ketchum brothers for the better part of two years and times had been good. He put some money together, along with a little gold, and he finally had something worth counting. After the botched robbery in San Antonio where the brothers gunned down two bank tellers and the town sheriff in cold blood, he knew time was short for the Ketchums and their gang and he decided the time was right for him to go his own way. Aware that the Ketchums wouldn't agree to his simply leaving the gang, he waited, biding his time, until he had an opportunity outside of Tulsa to take his leave. As the gang rode north to Kansas City the next day, "Fast" Johnny rode west to Diablo Flats.

Johnny finished the last of the whiskey in his glass in one swallow. "Go on into the back room, Celeste," Johnny said.

Celeste was hesitant to leave him. "Aw, Johnny, why's I have to --"

"Go on now, hear? I'll be there shortly and we'll pick up. Now go on, darlin'."

The redhead stood up and pulled her skirts down, protecting her virtue. She smiled at Johnny and leaned over to whisper in his ear. "Don't be long now, Johnny, alright?" She kissed him on the cheek, turned and walked away. "Fast" Johnny didn't return Celeste's smile and he didn't let himself think about her perfume, or what the two of them would be doing later in the evening, he just continued to watch the sheriff and the stranger at the bar while he thought through the situation.

"You deaf all of a sudden, Johnny?" Ezra Boone said. The fat man sat with a cigar in his mouth to Johnny's left, his chubby hands laced behind his head exposing the sweat stains under his arms.

"Thinkin' is all, fat man," Johnny said.

"Well hurry up your thinkin' and get to playin'," Lee Hatfield said. "And slide that bottle over here, why don't ya."

Johnny Winslow gave Hatfield a sideways glance that made the tall, red-haired whiskey salesman shift uncomfortably in his chair. Distracted by the big man at the bar, Johnny picked up his cards and tossed them, face down, into the middle of the table and said in a low voice, "I'm out."

"I'm sorry, Johnny. I didn't mean to . . ."

Johnny slid the bottle over toward Hatfield and turned his head slightly. "I said I'm out, play your hand, Hatfield." One eye, half squinted, stared at Hatfield until the nervous man looked away. Johnny turned back toward the two men at the bar, saw the stranger staring at him, and put his thoughts together.

Johnny Winslow lived life as if every moment could be his last and he decided it was time to treat this stranger's sudden appearance like any other poker hand. It was time to force the game and see what cards, if any, the sheriff's friend was holding. Johnny stood up fast and knocked over the poker table, sending chips, cards and whiskey flying in every direction. Boone and Hatfield stood and scattered away toward opposite ends of the bar. Hatfield headed toward the piano at the back of the room and Boone slipped on the whiskey and found himself flat on his back. He rolled underneath another poker table and huddled like a fat rat, curling his head as close to his extended belly as he could. Johnny Winslow looked straight at Will Chandler and locked eyes with the big man. He unsnapped his holster and moved his hand to just inches above his gun. Ready. Shorty's went silent save for the sound of chairs scraping against the wood floors as folks turned to see what caused the noise.

"You keep lookin' over here, mister. You got a reason fer eyein' me up like you're doin'?" Johnny Winslow shouted across the room. "If you do, then maybe you wanna tell me about it, 'cuz I don't like being stared at by some biggity feller who looks like he ain't got hisself no cow sense."

Will Chandler spun toward Johnny Winslow when he heard the crash and saw the thin man stand. Instinct immediately took over and he pulled his gun.

"Easy, Will. Don't be rash," Warren said.

Johnny Winslow saw the gun pointed at his head and he raised his arms slightly. "So, you pullin' on an unarmed man, is that it?

Don't know how you was raised, stranger, but that ain't how I normally settle things."

Chandler pulled the trigger and the bullet hit the wall inches to the left of Johnny Winslow's head.

Winslow stood tall and said, "You shootin' an unarmed man, stranger, is that it?" Looking to Warren he yelled, "You seein' this, Sheriff?"

Will fired again and the second bullet hit the wall just to the right of Johnny Winslow's head.

Drawn by the noise Celeste had come back into the main hall and froze. "Johnny," she screamed. "No, baby!"

"Sheriff," Winslow said, his voice steady. "You gonna do somethin' or you gonna let this hayseed here kill me in cold blood?"

"Will, you can't do this inside," Sheriff Warren said. "You know that. Now put your gun down."

"Fast" Johnny caught the faint flicker in Chandler's eyes as the big man acknowledged the sheriff and he wasted no time in pulling his own gun and firing. Winslow's bullet hit Chandler in the right shoulder and the big man fell back against the bar. Chandler's gun flew from his ruined right arm and spun across the floor. Winslow stepped around the felled poker table, nearly tripping on Boone's shaky leg which was sticking out from his too-small sanctuary, and walked to Chandler's gun, picked it up and tucked it into his belt. Five slow, deliberate steps and Winslow stopped ten feet away from Will Chandler who was leaning back against the bar trying to slow the flow of blood from his damaged shoulder with his left hand. Winslow kept his gun sighted on Chandler's chest as blood pulsed from between his fingers to form a pool at his feet.

"Put the gun down now, mister. Let's not let this go any further, ya hear?" Sheriff Warren said.

"I didn't start this hullabaloo, Sheriff," Winslow said, never taking his eyes, or gun, off Chandler. "Just fixin' to stop what this big feller bleedin' all over the floor here started so's I can go on my way in peace with Celeste back there. That's all I want."

Chandler's eyes were squeezed tight in pain and he moaned loudly as he tried to move and stand upright.

"Not so keen on starin' at a man now that y'all bleedin' all over the floor, are ya?," Winslow said. He stepped forward and raised his gun to point at Chandler's head and a smile spread across his face.

Winslow held his gun steady and glanced briefly toward the sheriff and was just about to tell him to call for the doctor when Chandler shifted his weight and gently flicked his left hand to activate the hidden sleeve gun. The concealed derringer slid with a well-oiled hiss along the metal track strapped to Chandler's arm and landed in the palm of his hand with a satisfying, wet slap. Will Chandler raised his arm and pointed the gun straight at Johnny Winslow's head and - -

"ATTENTION JOHN WINSLOW. YOUR AMERICAN WEST OUTLAW SIMULATION HAS EXPIRED.

YOU MAY PURCHASE ADDITIONAL TIME IN THE ASTROSIMULATOR TO RESUME YOUR REENACTMENT OF THIS ERA IN AMERICAN HISTORY BY INSERTING YOUR PREPAID VOUCHER OR GLOBAL CHARGE NOW.

YOU WILL HAVE SIXTY SECONDS FROM THE END OF THIS MESSAGE TO PURCHASE MORE TIME OR THE SCENE WILL RESET.

THANK YOU FOR VISITING DRAKE TECHNOLOGY'S AMERICAN HISTORY ASTROSIMULATOR. DRAKE TECHNOLOGY, MAKING HISTORY COME ALIVE FOR YOU."

MICHAEL FISHMAN lives in Minneapolis, Minnesota. He spends much of his time thinking about things and imagining wondrous possibilities. One of the things he imagines is writing stories people will enjoy reading.

THE GESTURE

Joe Kilgore

(1ˢᵗ Place Romance Category 2010)

Dust plumed like a cock's tail behind the pickup as it rocked along. The road was unpaved and didn't take kindly to horsepower riding roughshod over it. Can't take issue with that, Hoak thought, as he rested one arm on the open window and ignored the grit swirling into the cab when he'd slow down for a pot hole or cattle guard. His right hand gripped the leather steering wheel cover he had purchased from the Navajo souvenir shop. Draw strings with turquoise and silver tips held it in place. It was the lone concession to customization Hoak had made to the 1948 Chevy Deluxe that began life white, but now looked more like a pinto due to metallic liver spots time and rust had inflicted.

Hoak shared the cab with Custer, a lop-eared, mixed-breed cur whose lineage was even more questionable than Hoak's. He stuck his head out the passenger window and let rushing air fill his flaring nostrils with the sweet smell of aspen and pine, often mixed with the pungent odor of recent road kill. It was not unusual to see the two banging along back roads or creeping up the highway at a pace guaranteed to make tourists give them a dirty look when they finally got room to pass.

The young half of the day had only recently begun when Hoak wheeled into the gravel parking lot of the Dos Pesos Diner just off U.S. 434. He was partial to the eatery because it was far enough from Taos that vacationers would pass it by on their way to the trendy mecca. He also liked it because they let him bring Custer in with him. Long as the two of them used the rear entrance, and provided the dog rest on Hoak's boots beneath the back booth. Custer seemed to take no offence to this blatant segregation, so neither did Hoak.

There was another reason Hoak was partial to the Dos Pesos. A waitress named Myrna.

Myrna looked a lot like a Shetland pony. Thick blonde hair ran down the back of her neck. She had a long, noble nose and big white teeth that Hoak bet would leave a hell of a mark on a lover's neck. Myrna had a firm, round rump and eyes blue as a New Mexico sky. Those eyes didn't miss much. They spotted Hoak's truck in the parking lot, prompting her to pause just to watch the duo disembark.

What a sight, she thought. The two of them even look alike. Custer was a lean mutt, scruffy but clean. Well, clean as a dog can be, anyway. He had grayish hair except for the black spot that covered one eye and its corresponding ear. Hoak had about as much fat on him as barbed wire. And as usual he was dressed like a man who took pride in his appearance. A well-worn Stetson topped his graying hair that used to be black. He was clean shaven save for a neatly trimmed mustache. Myna liked how it was tall in the middle then tapered toward the ends. She also liked the starched cowboy shirts Hoak wore atop stovepipe jeans. There weren't many men that could wear those without a sizable belly hanging over the belt buckle.

As she watched the two, she knew there were probably too many things she liked about that pair. Too many things for a hash slinger on the wrong side of forty.

THE GESTURE

Myrna pretended to busy herself behind the counter as Hoak and Custer came in and took their regular booth in the back. After what she felt would appear an appropriately disinterested amount of time, she took a water glass over to Hoak.

"Let me guess. Chorizo and eggs over hard, corn tortillas, large O. J. and black coffee."

"You takin' up mind readin' along with waitressin' now, Myrna?"

"No. It's just some folks I can read like a book."

"Or maybe it's because that's all I ever ordered since I been comin' in here?"

"You're consistent. I'll give you that."

"Then make it the usual."

The usual also included a side order of bacon for Custer. Myrna had brought the addition the first time they came in. Without Hoak ordering it. She was a sucker for animals. So she yelled his order, along with the bacon, to the cook, but didn't write it down. That way Hoak wouldn't have to pay for something he didn't order and Trujillo, Myrna's boss, wouldn't be the wiser. She told Hoak a customer had ordered the bacon and decided he didn't want it. Maybe the dog might like it, she offered. No charge.

Hoak had responded, "That's very kind of you, little lady."

Who the hell still talks like that, she had said to herself.

The second time it happened, Hoak realized he'd have to be dumb as a carp to think it was coincidence. Especially when it wasn't on his bill again. Here was a good looking woman going out of her way to be nice to him, or Custer. Either way, he was a bit embarrassed. So he stayed mum, accepted it and went about his business thinking a sizable tip would substitute for not acknowledging her kindness. Hoak's social antenna was not finely tuned.

As he sat sipping coffee, waiting for breakfast to arrive, his boots warmed by a lounging Custer, his eyes drifted to the only other patron, a black man sitting alone. Papers were spread on his table and a coffee cup rested on one of them. He wore a white shirt and red tie. Hoak took him to be a salesman. A productive, working man. Probably pays taxes and sends his kids to school. Good on ya', he mumbled out loud.

"Talking to yourself, Hoak?" Myrna said, putting his breakfast down. "Some of us make conversation as well as eggs, you know."

"I was talkin' to Custer."

"Well," she said, topping his coffee, "you ever want to chew the fat with someone other than that canine, just let me know."

As Myrna walked away, she thought, damn! That came out more flirty than I wanted. He's going to think I'm serving food but offering up something else.

Myrna didn't like giving the impression she was easy. Probably because she used to be. There was a time when she wasn't particularly selective. But what had that done for her? Sure, she had a good time, but one day she woke up and found more guys were talking about her than talking to her. And Hoak was one man whose conversation she coveted.

He had been coming to the diner two or three times a week, for the last couple of months. Myna took a shine to him right off. She noticed the first time she served him that he took time to read the name tag just below her shoulder without straying to her cleavage. She warmed to the way he was quiet, considerate, even respectful. She enjoyed looking at his lean hands, tanned brown by the sun and chiseled with big veins that stood out like soda straws. She took pleasure in his hazel eyes and often conjured them in her mind even when he wasn't there.

"You put a sizable dent in that breakfast," Myrna said, as she refilled Hoak's coffee.

"First-rate as always. Custer finished his too."

Myrna looked behind the counter. Not seeing Trujillo, she sat down. "I don't think you've ever mentioned how you came to name that dog Custer."

"Well, I found him when he was a pup, inside a box at the bottom of an arroyo just off the interstate."

"God, I hate people who abandon a dog."

"Dogs, plural."

"No. There were other puppies with him?"

"Parts of em'."

"Oh," Myrna managed, before putting her hand over her mouth.

"A hawk, or maybe an eagle, had gotten to em' before me. Can't blame him though. A bird of prey's a bird of prey. Only way he knows to act. But this one," he said, rubbing his dog's head, "he had tipped that box over and made it a fort to ward off the attacks. He was the last one standin' after the others had fallen."

Myrna reflected for a second. "But General Custer didn't survive. He died too."

"None of us survive in the long run. That's no reason to keep a historic name from a brave dog."

"But if Custer turned the box over on himself, how'd you know he was there in the first place?"

"Didn't. Just saw the box in the arroyo and hated the way it despoiled the countryside. I planned to throw it in the pick-up bed and cart it off."

"And by doing what you thought was right, you found a friend for life."

"Funny, ain't it? Maybe the good guys win one now and then. Better give me the tab. Custer and I need to hit the trail."

Myrna complied and began clearing the dishes. By the time she took them behind the counter and handed them to the dishwasher, Hoak had paid and taken Custer out to the truck. Myrna tried to busy herself. But as she did, something seemed to form in her chest. Some knot she felt moving slowly up into her throat. Within moments, she felt herself welling up. Tears dampened the corners of her eyes. For some reason, she couldn't let them just drive off. Not without at least trying.

Myrna yanked the dishcloth from her waistband and tossed it on the counter. She ran her hands through the sides of her hair and used her index fingers to smooth her eyebrows. Then she swept toward the front of the café passing Trujillo on the way.

"Where you go?"

"Outside. I'll be right back."

"Why? What you need?"

"I've got to look under the box," she yelled.

"Que?"

As the truck rolled toward the Dos Pesos exit, Hoak saw Myrna standing by the front door beckoning. Pulling up beside her, he asked, "Did I forget something?"

"Hoak...do you ever go out...go to eat...I mean like someplace other than here."

"I've been known to frequent places other than your establishment."

"Sure. I know that. What I really mean is, do you ever go out with anyone? Other than Custer, I mean."

Hoak had never seen Myrna nervous. At first he didn't know what to make of it. But eventually light illuminates even the foggiest places.

"Myrna…are you asking me out?"

"No. Not really. Well, yes. I guess I am. Is that horrible? If it is, just say so. I won't bother you again."

Hoak tipped his hat back. "Myrna, that's really sweet. I'm very flattered. But, I'm a little embarrassed too. I mean, shouldn't I be the one asking you out? Ain't that the way it's done?"

"I don't know how anything's done these days, Hoak. I just thought if you did want to get together and do something, or go someplace, well…"

Hoak could tell she was having trouble finishing, so he cut in. "Myna, me and Custer have to be someplace right now. Fact, we're running late for an appointment that might be somewhat important. But, I tell you what…next time we're in for breakfast, we'll continue this conversation. And I bet we'll both know exactly what to say."

A smile spread across Myrna's face wide as a two-lane blacktop. "Great. Yes, let's do that."

Looking into those bright, blue eyes, Hoak then said, "Myrna, it's to my profound regret that I haven't mentioned before that I think you're a damned fine woman." Custer barked an exclamation point. Then they pulled out of the parking lot.

Myrna stood and watched until they were out of sight.

Hoak didn't come the next day. Myrna told herself that he must be a busy man and that he'd be back soon. More days went by and Hoak didn't show. Myrna fretted something awful. She hoped he hadn't had an accident. Three more days passed and still no Hoak. Myrna began to berate herself for always screwing things up.

When a full week passed without Hoak's presence, Myrna stopped beating herself up and concluded that her judgment had simply been faulty. He obviously wasn't a nice guy after all. Or maybe when it came to women he was just a coward. Or worse. Maybe he was married. So when Hoak hadn't shown for almost two weeks, Myrna had pretty much stopped thinking about him altogether. Except when she bristled at the thought of making a fool of herself.

Then one morning a black man in a shirt and tie came into the Dos Pesos. Myrna had often seen him there. Before taking a seat, he walked over to the register and began speaking in hushed tones with Trujillo. Then he went to a booth. Trujillo motioned to her.

"That man want see you. He say it's business. Be quick. Comprende?"

Myrna walked to his table. The black man stood and said, "Myrna Collins?"

"Yes. I've waited on you before."

"Of course. Please sit down. Ms. Collins, do you know a man named Raymond Hoak?"

Myrna paused. It had never occurred to her whether his first or last name was Hoak.

"I think so. I have a customer who goes by that name."

"My name is Robert Jackson. I'm an attorney at law."

"Really? I thought you were a salesman."

"You aren't the only one. Mr. Hoak thought I was a sales person too."

That odd feeling Myrna had the last time she saw Hoak started in her chest again. But this time it felt different. And it didn't feel good. "Why are you here, Mr. Jackson? Why are you asking about Hoak?"

"I'm afraid I have some bad news."

All of a sudden, the lump in Myrna's throat almost choked her. "Please, tell me what's going on?"

"I've been retained to tell you that Mr. Hoak is dead. I'm very sorry."

Myrna heard the words. She understood them. But it seemed as if they were coming from the radio, or some other entity much farther away than the width of the booth.

"What did you say?"

"Mr Hoak is dead. He was found by the county sheriff two days ago."

Shock came first. Quickly followed by regret. Why had she been so ready to think ill of him? Confusion hovered too. What had the lawyer said?

"Found? What happened to him?"

"Mr. Hoak took his life. He called the sheriff's department Friday night and told them there had been a shooting at his ranch. When the authorities arrived it was apparent Mr. Hoak had shot himself after making the call."

Myrna felt as if a knife had pierced her heart. The pain hit her quickly, deeply. He was talking about Hoak. The man she had fantasized about sharing a future with. But now he had no future at all. And never would have.

"Why would he do such a thing?"

"Mr. Hoak had recently been diagnosed with bone cancer. The diagnosis was unequivocal. He was instructed to enter a hospice for his last few weeks. He didn't and apparently decided to end things his own way."

Myrna felt the wind go out of her. She was hearing, but still finding it hard to believe. So she just said the first thing that came to mind. "But, I only knew Mr. Hoak as a customer. Why are you here, telling *me* about this?"

"Mr Hoak was actually my client. He contacted me after learning of his terminal illness. He retained me to put his financial affairs in order and gave me instructions on what to do after his death. Now, he gave me absolutely no indication whatsoever that he planned to take his life. I simply assumed that once the inevitable happened, I would carry out his instructions."

"But I still don't understand what you're doing here with me," Myrna responded.

"Mr. Hoak had me draft a will leaving his property and all financial assets to you."

Myrna felt a weight descend on her shoulders. A weight holding her down in the booth. "But I had no connection...not really. Surely he has some relatives or..."

The lawyer cut in. "Mr. Raymond Hoak owned a hundred acres near here. His land, plus the ranch house that sits on it...in combination with the funds in his Certificates of Deposit, comes to something just over two and a half million dollars. There are no living relatives. He's left it all to you."

Myrna stared at the attorney. Virtually numb, she asked, "Did he say anything else about me?"

"No. Just that he wanted you to have it all. I'll take care of all the legal things that have to be done for you to take possession. Mr. Hoak paid in advance for that as well."

Myrna had no idea what to say. Unable to think clearly, she just sat there as a tear began to run slowly down her cheek, trailing mascara behind it.

"Mr. Hoak did have one stipulation. Your receivership of his assets is contingent upon your acceptance of responsibility for the guardianship and care of one specific member of the estate's livestock. Which, according to Mr. Hoak's requirement, can never be sold, traded or given away before the expiration of its natural life."

It was the first thing he'd said that Myrna grasped instinctively. Wiping the tear track away, she asked, "Where is Custer?"

The attorney pointed toward the back of the café. "He wouldn't come to the front door. And he also refuses to let go of those things. Just carries them around in his mouth wherever he goes."

Myrna turned and saw Custer curled beneath their booth, sprawled atop Hoak's boots. "Maybe when he goes to sleep you can hide them somewhere," the lawyer offered.

Without hesitation, Myrna replied, "No, Mr. Jackson. I don't think I'll be doing that."

Read **JOE KILGORE'S** biographical information on page 9.

COAHUILA CAPTIVE

Drew Davis

(Finalist 2010 Cowboy Up Contest)

"Torio," he said, his steel blue eyes locking onto my own, "Life is hard enough after losing my arm. I must not lose my heart."

Wiping late afternoon San Antonio sweat from my brow, I studied Lieutenant Deaghan Malloy, still in his Confederate cavalry uniform, the left sleeve fastened with a hatpin, a drab gray fold where muscle and bone used to be. He was only a decade younger than me at twenty-two, but war and other misfortunes had begun to etch their impact into his handsome face.

"It is my own loss, Dee, to have never met your *prometida* – your betrothed." Leaving Father Francis' helpers to unload the supply wagon, I strolled with my old friend to the shade of the cottonwood tree where my horse was tethered. "You make her sound like an angel."

"Heaven could only hope for such," he said with a smile, his first in the half hour since I'd entered the mission courtyard and found him waiting. "That hell of a Louisiana hospital would have finished me if not for Jessie Lynn's care."

"Why were she and her family foolish enough to try and reach Laredo on their own?"

"Some idiotic rumor General Kirby Smith was going there to continue the fight. Mr. Guillebeau, her father, gathered everything he could and took off across south Texas with Jessie

Lynn, her mother, and a few business partners. When Smith surrendered they were traveling unfamiliar territory, wandering like lost sheep, easy pickings for the Apache."

"Apache? Are you sure? Not Kiowa or Comanche?"

"One of the men lived to tell." A cloud gathered over Dee's face as he explained. "Of course, he had little scalp left, a lance point broken off between his ribs, and his tongue so swollen from lack of water you could hardly understand a word he said."

A boy at the wagon almost dropped a sack of flour, ripped a thread regaining its balance and left a thin white trail behind him as he carried it inside the mission. I waited for Dee to get control of himself. He coughed and sniffled, looking anywhere but at me and continued.

"Mr. Guillebeau pushed ahead to scout, so they were hit first. When the others saw smoke from the wagon burning, they rushed to help – smack into the middle of an ambush. Everyone was killed but Jessie Lynn and the poor fellow they left in such bad condition. Before he died he said she was carried off by an Indian with a wolf's claw painted on his left cheek."

"Ba'Cho..." The name slipped out before I could stop it.

"You know him," Dee said, hope shining in his eyes.

"Only by reputation...and not a very good one. Ba'Cho is Apache for wolf. It is also the name of a very arrogant and brutal raider from the Lipan tribe." I took a goatskin water bag from my saddle to quench my parched throat and measured my words carefully. "You know, Dee...most captives of the Apache do not last long, especially one as savage as this. You said it's been three months since the attack."

"I know, I know, but...." He removed his tan wide-brimmed hat and, still holding it, wiped his hand through his sandy brown hair. I kept silent, hoping his struggle for words would allow the futility of the situation to sink in, would make him realize the hopelessness of his quest – would prevent him from asking me to participate. It was not to be.

"She was still alive – or some blonde captive was – when I tracked them as far as Coahuila country," he continued. "I knew that you were the best one to help me there."

I offered him a swig from the bota, but even before he shook his head I knew his own thirst could not be quenched by mere water. "It has been many years since I left Mexico," I said. "I barely remember it."

"People still remember you," he said, running his hand along the Spencer repeating rifle in my saddle scabbard. "Every time I mentioned I knew the famous Victorio Cruz, they got a gleam in their eyes and called out 'El Tirador' – the marksman. From the looks of this weapon, you still know how to take care of yourself."

"With bluecoats flooding Texas now, rare treasures can be found. If your own troops had guns like that instead of muzzle-loading Enfields, you would probably still be fighting."

"Seems you also take care of others." He pointed to the empty wagon, its salt, flour, cloth, and other necessities now stowed in the mission.

"This conflict brought death, destruction and poverty with it. But also, if one has the instincts, much opportunity for trade and barter," I responded. "It's my way of thanking Father Francis for all his wonderful advice I never listened to. After all, these are my people."

"Am I your people?" he asked, locking those intense eyes on mine once more.

It took a moment for me to answer, not from hesitation, but to stem the tears that threatened to flood my cheeks. "You are, indeed. You, your father - rest his soul - your entire family took in a wild-eyed orphan and taught him how to be a man. I owe more than I can ever repay. But you knew I'd feel this way long before you came to San Antonio, didn't you?"

We spent the next several weeks crisscrossing the Rio Grande, chasing stories of captives and raids. With each familiar sight bringing unsavory memories of my misspent youth and Dee pining for Jessie Lynn, even the closest friends would chafe under the friction of futility.

One evening as we settled in, bone weary with every hope fading, he struggled to remove his ill-fitting footwear and deal with the resultant sores. I would have offered assistance, but Dee had made it very clear it was his disability alone to deal with.

"Dammit!" he grumbled. "Why did you trade my boots for these worthless things?"

"For the best meal in Piedras Negras," I reminded him tersely. "There is only so much salt pork and dried beef one can tolerate. Besides, the man had other pairs to choose from."

"None even near my size except moccasins. I refuse to wear anything that reminds me of those thieving, raiding Apaches."

"How would you have them live, mi amigo? The same way you do? The Lipan are hunters and fighters, not farmers or ranchers. Their very name means 'warriors of the mountains.' When our people invaded their world, carved up the open prairie, cut off and whittled down the buffalo herds, was it thought they would just vanish?"

"Are you defending these animals?"

"Not defending nor condoning, just explaining. Surely you learned in military service that to defeat an enemy one must attempt to understand him."

"All I need to understand is they destroyed my every hope by taking Jessie," he said. "Perhaps I was wrong in my choice of guide through this godforsaken country."

"Perhaps you have chosen one who will speak the truth, no matter what." Kneeling beside him I tugged off his offending boot, then gave him the intensity of my own eyes. "Since we started tracking you've done little else but feel the pain with your heart. If it is even possible to get Jessie Lynn back, you must make plans with your head."

***

"That's her," he said, handing me the field glasses. Except for pants with the cavalry stripe, most of his uniform was gone now, replaced by clothes more appropriate for prowling the wilderness. We had bartered the rest away, and anything else that gained food or information.

His transformation was mild, however, compared to the woman I saw. The delicate golden-haired belle of cotillions and lifesaving nurse he often described had been replaced by a bedraggled, deerskin-draped drudge with a gathering basket. She plodded amidst other women of the camp in their morning forage for firewood and the meager fruits and berries available.

We were on a bank of the Rio San Rodrigo, deep in the eastern Sierra Madre foothills of Coahuila territory, Mexico. Across the river at the base of the cliffs was a cove, nearly hidden by willow and catclaw mesquite. Scattered there were several wickiups, small dome-shaped dwellings made from bent branches, covered with hides or foliage.

"Almost missed it," I told Dee. "Tucked away like that, it makes a perfect hiding place."

"Maybe not," he replied. "Up against the hillside, there's no back way out. And they've penned their stolen livestock right under that ledge."

"Now you sound like the battler I recall from your family's roundups." I smiled as I slapped his back. "Does that devilish twinkle in your eyes still mean mischief?"

"If your shooting is as sharp as ever," he nodded. "And we'll need your water skin."

Working atop the ridge by moonlight and as quiet as death, we gathered several decent sized boulders. Leaning the lowest against my plump bota bag, we placed them in a careful counterbalance. By dawn, we were in position with Dee hidden in reeds by the river and me in shadows of the cliffside. My shot dislodging the stones would be the signal to commence.

It had been several years since my skills were so severely tested and never with this much at stake. As the sun chased the early morning shadows, my nerves jangled. I tried to be as still as possible but sweat filled my eyes and simply breathing became a monumental task.

When the women began gathering it was time. I sighted the Spencer on the water-filled skin scarcely more than sixty yards away. Exhaling as calmly as I could, I squeezed the trigger and prayed the branches surrounding me would disperse the smoke from the discharge.

The crack of the rifle immediately roused the camp, each Apache seeking the source of the shot, pointing to probable locations. Their suspicions started to swing toward my hiding place as I stared in horror at my target.

Water gushed as the bag emptied, but the keystone boulder had not budged, gravity playing an evil trick with our intentions. Then, slowly, agonizingly, it began to slide, finally tumbling as pressure from the rocks behind forced it down the hillside. A shower of debris sprayed into the encampment.

With the bucking of frightened horses added to the turmoil of cattle that bolted out of the makeshift pen, the Apaches had no choice but to restore order. Once they turned to that, I slid from my nook and scampered away.

Scrambling down the ridge, I watched for any sign the rescue attempt had been discovered. As I got closer, however, it became obvious that problems had arisen with Dee.

Squirming and pulling away, Jessie was less than cooperative. Without screaming or raising her voice she emitted a steady stream of one repeated word through her clenched teeth. "No, no, no, no, no!" she pleaded, digging her heels into the sand as Dee struggled to carry her forward, his good arm wrapped around her waist.

Suddenly she twisted away, grabbing his revolver. She pointed it straight at him and said, "You can't take me back. No! I won't go!"

"Surely you don't wish to remain here," Dee said incredulously.

"Of course not," she cried, her face contorted with grief. "They killed my parents in front of me...they beat me, abused me, shamed me. Did...did...horrid things to me. I can't go back and face my family, my friends...anyone!"

"I don't understand. What do you want?"

"If you love me…really and truly," she whimpered, turning the revolver to face herself, "end my misery here and now. I've tried, believe me I've tried. I simply cannot do it myself."

"No, Jessie!" He grabbed the gun carefully, twisted it loose and tossed it into the brush. Pulling her close, he buried his face in golden wisps of her hair. "No matter what, no matter how, we'll make it. We…broken people will pull each other through…together."

Their embrace was cut short as a half dozen Apaches rushed up. I stepped from my live oak cover and levered three shots that stopped them in their tracks. Showing the Spencer's power without turning the encounter into a bloodbath, I chose just to spray the sand at their feet.

From behind them strode one who could only be Ba'Cho. In addition to the breechcloth, buckskin leggings, and moccasins the others wore, his shirt was plundered white cotton formal wear with ruffles at the chest and cuffs. Colorful armbands encircled each bicep and long black tresses escaped his headband. His namesake's claw no longer decorated his cheek, but wolf fangs dangled from his rawhide necklace.

Standing between his raiders and the lovers, he spread his arms, palms wide. He shouted at Dee in a torrent of mixed Spanish and Apache, delivered with a sarcastic scowl.

"What is he saying?" Dee asked me, never taking his eyes off the man.

"It doesn't matter. I'll cover you while you retreat to the river."

"The rest will be here and on us before we reach the horses," he replied. "Tell me now."

"He asks what kind of man sneaks into camp to steal Ba'Cho's property," I translated, leaving out the scurrilous descriptions used. "He says if you want the woman, take her from him like he did from her people."

Dee stood in front of Jessie and said, "Gladly!"

"Don't do this, Dee!" she cried as she wrapped her arms around him. "I can't go back. Please just leave me and save your own life."

"Without you in it," he said pulling away, "I have no life."

Ba'Cho drew a knife from his waistband. He held out his hand and received a second which he tossed at Dee's feet. When Dee bent to retrieve it, Ba'Cho raced at him. Before the startled man could stand, the Apache had slapped the side of Dee's head with the knife handle and pranced away, the business end of the blade ready and pointed at his opponent. His followers shouted approval of their chieftain's bravery in "counting coup."

I watched the pair circle each other, feinting and jabbing. Dee was obviously outmatched, his cavalry officer skills useless in one-to-one knife fighting the Apache had mastered long ago. Ba'Cho was toying with him, laughing at every nick and slice that found its mark, having too much fun to land a swift and merciful strike.

Bloodied and wavering, Dee tried a desperate lunge which the Apache sidestepped. Falling past, Dee caught Ba'Cho by surprise, whipping his legs into the Indian's knees. Both men sprawled, scrambled and got to their feet, neither with their weapons.

As Ba'Cho looked for his, Dee connected a solid right to the jaw. The Apache instinctively wrapped him in a clinch and bought time to steady his senses. It was then he discovered that Dee's empty sleeve had lost its pin and was flapping wildly in the struggle.

He grabbed the dangling cloth and pulled it around his opponent's neck. With Dee's face turning a ripe plum color, Ba'Cho knelt and bent the man backward over his knee, his free hand reaching for the knife. Beaming a triumphant and devilish smile, he raised the blade skyward, an unnecessary and arrogant show for his audience.

The crack of Dee's revolver in Jessie's hands coincided with the bullet hole that appeared in Ba'Cho's chest. His lifeless body slumped and fell, a red stain curling in strange patterns through the ruffles of his shirt. Dee rolled away and crawled to his savior. Mindless of his seeping wounds, she hugged him close and tried to promise him forever between sobs.

Arrows were strung, lances hoisted and other weapons raised by the Lipan onlookers. I fired three times, got a lucky hit on an Enfield rifle that flew from its owner's grasp, but the other two shots drew blood.

"Hola, amigos," I called to the Apaches, letting the Spencer's muzzle float from one to another. "Since Ba'Cho's contest did not end in your favor, let me offer you an alternative."

I raised the rifle in my left hand. From their shuffling and whispers I knew they were aware of its reputation. "A gray-coat soldier who had the misfortune to face such a weapon described it as 'the rifle you load in the morning and fire all day.' You've just seen it in action."

Pointing my right hand to Jessie Lynn who was helping Dee to his feet, I said, "I offer it to you in exchange for the woman. Bueno?"

The Apaches took no time to dicker, lowering their weapons and nodding their heads just a few short of unison.

"Dee," I asked, leaning the Spencer against the body, "Do you have your revolver?"

"Leveled and ready," he replied hoarsely.

"Compadres," I said, drawing my own and backing toward the river, "Not that I don't trust these people – which I don't – I suggest we leave them to decide who should be the next wolf and who should possess the rifle. By the time they settle that, then realize they have no ammunition for it and little chance of finding more any time soon, we'd best be well on our way out of Coahuila."

Read **DREW DAVIS'** biographical information on page 85.

OLD OUTLAW

M. Edward Wyatt

(Finalist 2010 Cowboy Up Contest)

"Bah!" shouted the old man, fifteen minutes into the movie, his sun-baked face frowning as he scrambled to his feet.

"Where ya goin', Mr. Harper?" I whispered from my theater seat.

"Billy the Kid! Bah!" he shouted again, wobbling back up the aisle amidst a gauntlet of shushes. His form was but a thin shaky silhouette wavering from side to side against the back drop of projector lighting.

Puzzled, I was drawn to follow. So, I jumped up and ran after the old gent, catching up to him in the lobby. "Wait, Mr. Harper," I beckoned. "Didn't you like the movie?"

Stopping to catch his breath, Mr. Harper panted, "It ain't the movie, boy! It's…it's the Kid! They got 'em lookin' like some medicine show gunslinger," he growled.

Placing his Stetson on his head, he continued through the double-doors to the sidewalk under the bright lights of the marquee.

Putting my hat on, I again sided up to the small thin man. "Let's get a beer, and you can tell me about it. Whadda ya say, Mr. Harper?" The night was early; I didn't want to go back to the bunkhouse just yet. After all, since hiring on as a general hand two years ago, I only get to town once a month, other than an occasional run for supplies.

"Whadda ya say, Mr. Harper?" I asked again.

The cool night air must have countered Mr. Harper's heated response to the film's betrayal of Billy the Kid. He once again stopped and looked at me. His hat eclipsed the upper half of his face; a grin spread across the lower half, revealing a snaggletooth over-bite. "I guess I can use a cold one," he conceded.

The sound of distant music drew us down the sidewalk past our pickup truck to the corner. Crossing the street we found ourselves in front of the Rio Del Rio Bar and Grill, our faces lighting up with the glow of neon saloon lights. The Saturday night crowd of cowboys and local gals was gathering in the small Wyoming cattle-town bar. Western music blared from the jukebox in the corner as we pushed our way through the double-swinging café doors. While several patrons danced to the music, many occupied stools along the lengthy bar.

"Let's go back to that booth." I pointed to a rather remote table in the back of the bar room.

Snaking through the pool players and spectators, Mr. Harper and I met several of the drovers from the Circle J. "Hey, Hank. Hey, Junior," they bid us as we passed.

"Boys," was Mr. Harper's short response. I only nodded and tugged on the brim of my hat.

To the cowhands of the Circle J Ranch, Hank Harper was the grandfather of cowboys. He worked most of his cow-punching years at the ranch. One ranch-hand, Smokin' Smitty, said Mr. Harper was there when he hired on in 1910, some thirty-two years ago.

As we slid into the booth, a passing barmaid asked, "What can I get you boys?"

"Couple of drafts, thanks," I answered.

Our table was a good choice; it was somewhat void of busy café traffic.

Foam oozed from the top of the drafts and down the sides of our mugs as the barmaid returned with our order. After a short debate as to who would pick up the tab, I tossed four bits onto her tray, and we were finally left to talk.

"Now, tell me, just what was wrong with Robert Taylor's portrayal of Billy the Kid?" I began.

Drawing his sleeve across his mouth to wipe away beer foam, Mr. Harper grunted, "Phony!"

"Robert Taylor's a good actor," I rebutted, defending one of my favorite screen stars.

"He may be a good actor, but he don't know cow patties about Bill Bonney. . .no sir," Mr. Harper grumbled, readjusting his hat.

Risking an argument, I asked, "Why do you say that? What do you know of Billy the Kid?"

My challenge induced a strange veil of darkness over Mr. Harper's face. His eyes drew down on me. He now sat staring deep into my eyes. I felt a waft of coldness throughout – not physically, but spiritually, but only for an instant.

He leaned over and whispered coldly, "I knew *William Henry Bonney*. I knew 'im quite well."

My eyes must have been wider than dinner plates as I listened to the old man. "You knew Billy the Kid!?" I spurted out.

Motioning with his hand to keep my voice down, he scanned the crowd for anyone who may have heard my outburst. Then he continued. "If those movie folks would bother to ask some of the people who were around during the days when the Kid was pegged an outlaw, they might learn something and make a good movie."

I could see Mr. Harper's face through the bottom of his mug as he downed the last gulp of his brew. "Now, you take John Ford," he added, placing the mug back on the table.

"Who?" I asked.

"John Ford, the movie director. He made the movie about Wyatt Earp – *My Darling Clementine*. Now there was a movie. Wyatt Earp and John Ford were pals. Ford had to 've got it right– that is if Earp told it like it was."

I was stunned by the old man's knowledge of movies. However, I managed to keep the conversation on Billy the Kid. "You knew Billy the Kid?" I asked again, trying to conceal my disbelief.

"Junior, keep what I'm telling ya just between me and you. You hear?"

Like a sponge in water, my curiosity was soaking up every syllable the old cowboy was uttering. "Yeah . . .yes sir, Mr. Harper."

I wondered, *Could Mr. Harper be telling the truth, or was he just an old man with an old tale to tell?* But his intense disclosure left little room for doubt.

"Bill and I worked ranches together during the Lincoln County War."

Gulping another portion of my draft, I implored, "Tell me about him. I heard he killed forty or fifty men."

"Dangit, boy! You watch too many of those dang movies!" he barked, slamming his fist on the table. "You need to go to the library and get the facts. I suppose nobody has the exact truth of them days." His voice toned with a bit of sadness, faded off.

124

Motioning for the barmaid to bring two more, he continued. "Bill's mom died when he was fifteen, leaving him and his brother to be reared by her second husband. He was like a lot of youngsters in those days. He got into a little trouble once in a while -- nut'n serious. But his stepfather was always comin' down hard on 'im. They never got along; so he ran off, left New Mexico and began gettin' work on ranches in Arizona."

"Is that when you met the Kid?" I asked.

"Uh . . .yeah. We rode together . . . worked ranches together."

"I heard he shot his first man, just to watch him die." I knew much of Billy the Kid trivia was hyped up folklore, however, I thought, *Folklore usually starts with some truth.*

"There ya go agin, boy," he growled. "It was self defense. Frank Cahill was big, about twice Bill's size -- an Irish blacksmith. Bill was havin' an argument with him, when Cahill laid off and knocked Bill to the floor. Bill was barely conscious when Cahill started puttin' the boot to the Kid -- agin and agin."

I could see the anger growing in Mr. Harper as he witnessed to the event.

"Not a soul stepped in to stop it. So I . . ." he paused, taking another drink of his beer, then continued. "Bill pulled his gun and fired one shot, hitting Frank Cahill in the stomach."

"Where were you? Why didn't you try to stop him?" I asked.

"I don't rightly remember."

"You actually saw Billy the Kid kill his first man," I said, pondering the reality of the event.

"Cahill didn't die right away. He lived for several hours into the next day."

"What happened with Billy the Kid?"

"He was beat up pretty bad, as I recall. He crawled to a corner next to the bar and laid there a couple hours, until the saloon closed. They drug 'im out into the street and locked up."

"That's it!?" I asked, thinking, *You shoot a guy, and they just let ya go?*

"The day after Cahill died, the law found the Kid and locked 'im up. But, he escaped from Camp Grant stockade. We lit out and never looked back."

"How old was he?" I asked.

"He was about your age, maybe a little younger. How old are you?"

"Twenty-two," I said.

"Bill was eighteen, as I recollect. I grant ya, Bill wasn't no saint. He done some pretty mean things. But, most of 'em he done to mean people," offered the old man, apologetically.

"What is it about the movies that you don't like?" I asked, getting back to the old man's original grievance.

"First of all, they take those pretty-boys and dress 'em up in fancy clothes. Then they give 'em pearl-handled six-shooters and a pretty black Stetson. And, if that ain't bad enough, they distort the facts and add stuff that never, ever happened."

"How long did you know Billy the Kid?" I asked, now completely absorbed in the old man's account of one of the most notorious outlaws of the old west.

"We rode together until . . ." He paused as though he was trying to finger the next page of a book. After several seconds he continued, ". . .until Billy's death."

I had finished my beer and was watching the last of Mr. Harper's beer swirl out of the mug and into his mouth.

"Ya ready to head back to the ranch, Junior?" asked Mr. Harper.

126

"Yep." I stood and adjusted the waistline of my dungarees and realigned my Stetson.

I slowly drove back toward the ranch, while Mr. Harper kept me enthralled with more of his recollections of days with the Kid.

Western Swing blared over the radio. Knowing that what I was about to ask could provoke my elderly friend, I turned down the volume and sat quietly for a few minutes, building up my nerve. "Did you ever shoot anyone, Mr. Harper?" I asked.

Frowns, highlighted by the dashboard lights of the 1939 Chevrolet pickup, made deep wrinkles become even deeper looking on the eighty-two year old cowboy. A long silence lingered, leaving me to wonder if he'd heard me, and if I should ask him again. I chose to share the silence.

Silence stretched the minutes, leaving me to think our conversation was at an end. Had I trodden on sacred territory? With more years behind him than in front, was he ready to start placing his life on the judgment day scale? Perhaps I shouldn't have asked the elderly soul to unearth those deadly memories.

Silence ended as Mr. Harper cleared his throat and began to speak. "Ahem! Bill and I rambled around for a while, pickin' up jobs, a day or two at a time."

I glanced over at him when he again paused. He was staring off into the dark, perhaps at distant lights. An occasional bump in the road teetered his hat back and forth. Then, he continued, "We finally ended up in Lincoln County, New Mexico, right-smack-dab in the middle of a cattle grab dispute. Today, they call it the Lincoln County War. Of course Bill got off to a bad start there too -- rustling cattle for L.G. Murphy and J. J. Dolan. They were power crazy. It wasn't enough to own the largest cattle ranches in the country and all the businesses, they had to have everyone else's," he snorted, his voice growing ever so grievous.

"I thought they hung rustlers in those days."

"Oh, yeah, if ya got caught, you'd be hung," answered Mr. Harper, emphasizing the seriousness of their deeds. "But, Bill...we got out of that business when Bill met John Tunstall -- one of those English gentleman types. We went to work for 'im on his spread. He treated us . . .he treated us like we counted for somethin'."

Lights from the Circle J were beginning to show in the distance. I found Mr. Harper's account of Billy the Kid fascinating. "How long did you and Billy work for Mr. Tuns...Mr. Tun..."

"Tunstall," prompted Mr. Harper. "We worked for him until Murphy and Dolan had 'im murdered!"

Anger filled Mr. Harper's voice as he recalled how John Tunstall was like a father to the Kid. He told of how Bill was arrested, tried, convicted and sentenced to hang after he avenged John Tunstall's murder. And how he escaped, killing two deputies of Sheriff Pat Garrett.

"It was Pat Garrett who shot Billy the Kid, wasn't it?" I interjected.

"That's what Pat Garrett and everyone else thought," snickered Mr. Harper. "Ya see Garrett, knowing the reputation of the Kid, feared 'im. However, one night he got wind of Bill stayin' at a Mexican friend's house, and snuck up there to kill 'im. He went into the dark casa with his gun in hand while the rest of the posse hid outside."

Pausing, Mr. Harper stared out the window, then began again. "Someone appeared in the doorway of one of the rooms, and Pat Garrett started shootin'. The man fell to the ground dead. Garrett

128

was shakin' so hard he could barely light a match, but managed to strike one."

As Mr. Harper paused, I grew eager to hear a closure to his account. "Well? Well?" I prompted.

Dashboard lights revealed a half grin on Mr. Harper's face as he went on. "A match provides little light in the dark. Pat Garrett feared that the Kid might still have some fight in 'im. He didn't get too close, but close enough to see blood on his back. The rest of the posse remained outside until Garrett came running out yellin', 'I killed the Kid, I killed Billy the Kid.'"

"Then what happened?" I pushed for more of his recollection.

"Well, Garrett was so shook up, that he never went back in. The posse went in and lit a lantern. They found Bill's Mexican girlfriend, Deluvina Maxwell, sittin' on the floor holdin' his lifeless body against her bosom. She claimed Pat Garrett murdered Bill."

"Did he? Was he shot in the back?"

"Ain't what the law said. Oh, they had a...whadda ya call it? A..."

"An inquest?" I asked.

"Yeah. That's it, an inquest. Asked a lot of questions. But that was about it."

"Didn't they check the body?"

"Bill was quite popular among local Mexicans. They insisted on taking his body. An angry mob gathered at the casa shortly after the shootin'. Things were about to explode into a war. So the posse let 'em take the body to prepare it for a wake."

Suddenly, it dawned on me that Mr. Harper's memory was quite explicit. I asked, "Where were you when this happened?"

"The sound of gunfire woke everyone around the ranch. When word got back to me about the shootin', I grabbed my things and horse and hightailed it out of there. To this day I never went back there."

"Didn't they keep lookin' for ya?"

"Nah! It was Bill that they had it in for. Oh sure, if they'd've found me with Bill, they'd've hung us both . . .or shot us."

It was late when we finally reached the bunkhouse. The next day I was sent to the high-line to gather strays before the winter months set in. Most of the next four months I stayed in the line-rider's shack and saw little of Mr. Harper. We never spoke of Billy the Kid again.

On December 7, 1941, Pearl Harbor was attacked, and two weeks later I enlisted in the army. Mr. Harper and I exchanged letters a couple times for a year.

After basic training, I was stationed in Panama. One day, just as my troop and I returned to our tents after guard duty, we heard the Staff Sergeant yell, "Mail Call!" Mail nearly always brought a welcome relief from our duties.

"Williams!" he called. "Barton! James!"

As I stepped from my tent, I heard my name. "Shrieves!"

"Here!" I answered.

Among several pieces of mail was a letter and small package from the ranch foreman. I tossed the package onto my cot and began reading the letter: *Dear Junior, I'm sorry to have to write you about this. But Hank Harper died in April from what they called old man's friend -- pneumonia. He was eighty-four. Hank wanted you to have this old leather billfold. I don't rightly know why; there's nothing in it and it ain't much good.*

I paused, staring at the brown-paper-wrapped package tied with hemp twine, then finished the letter. *Again, I'm sorry to*

have to write you with such bad news. Keep up the good fight.
Pete Dawson, Foreman, Circle J Ranch.

I couldn't imagine why Mr. Harper would even think of sending me an old billfold, or anything else. Leaving it on my cot, I finished opening my mail and stowing my gear.

Perhaps an hour elapsed before taking the unwrapped package into my hands. With my knife I cut the twine and gently removed the brown wrap. There didn't appear to be anything outstanding about the rawhide wallet – cracked with age, bound with rawhide lace. However, as I slowly rotated it in the light, raised initials on the face of the wallet became visible and beckoned my immediate interest. They read, *W H B.*

M. EDWARD WYATT Published *1994–Lights Camera Money–Your Chance at the Silver Screen* (currently out of publication), short stories: "Hooked" for North American Fishing Club's *The Meaning of Fishing,* and "Ancient Traditions" for *Wonderful West Virginia.* A second year participant in Moonlight Mesa Associates' Cowboy Up contest, the author has written poetry, plays, video scripts (industrial/commercial) and, most recently, has finished a novel (yet to be published). Presently, Mr. Wyatt is working on his second novel, a western set in the Montana cattle country.

LLANO ESTACADO

Lane Thibodeaux

(Finalist Romance Category 2010 Cowboy Up Contest)

The cow was predictable as sunrise. She had used the same canyon draw the past couple of years for calving. Sure enough, we found them just after breakfast. Cesar was better mounted on my good horse Roany, but I knew the way. The bay I was astride was not sure footed as the roan he was riding, so it was slow. At the bottom, the cedar cleared like the Red Sea in front of Moses, but no miracle waited.

Cesar took his sweet time putting a hesitant rope on the concerned mother, while I maintained a discreet distance from her calf. I could not keep myself from thinking that the boy would have shaken out a loop and collared her first try. I took my time dismounting. If could not trust that bay mare to navigate a tricky slope, at least she would ground tie.

The calf could not get his back legs under him. His front legs were fine, but he could not get up off the ground. My guess was something went wrong during birthing. I ran my hand down his back past his hocks trying to get a reaction. Cesar glanced at me with one eye while concentrating on keeping a good dally around his saddle horn.

"Este termidado?" he asked finally.

"Yeah, afraid so." Cesar spoke to me almost exclusively in Spanish, and I always answered in English. Like an old married couple, it was just our way. The newborn was already *in extremis* and could not nurse. I looked at the sky. It had not been a good season.

Euthanizing downer cattle on the edge of the southern Llano Estacado has not changed in a hundred years. I may have been able to speak with someone halfway around the world with the cell phone in my pocket, but death came in the same caliber of rifle used in my grandfather's time. Cesar bore witness to the morbid business then griped about his wife and the cow bellowing at the end of his rope all the way home.

The SUV near the house was caked in caliche. The dark color of the behemoth matched my mood. The machine's color changed suddenly under the windows into a dull white all the way into the wheel wells. I could see she had the back open, wrestling with some type of therapy equipment as we rode past the working pens to the barn. Cesar peeled off to take the still bellowing momma cow to the pens.

"Tengo que ir a mi esposa," Cesar said before we parted. Maria had always kept the house, but had been lately impressed to service watching the boy. The therapist did not like people the boy was familiar with to be in sight when she did her work. She said it promoted distraction.

She was still lugging equipment out of the back when I walked up from the barn. She was dressed in the dull flowered smock blouse over scrub pants, required dress for home health care providers it occurred to me. I asked her how the drive was, and she said it had rained slightly as she had left Big Spring. Any rain was news and explained the caked hardpan on her SUV. She asked how the boy had responded to the new exercises since her last visit.

"You'd have to ask Maria," I said.

She stopped with some twisted up machine halfway out the hatchback of the beast of a vehicle. "No, I am asking you."

I smiled at her. I took the equipment from her and carried it into the house. The boy was in the living room. His walker was to his right, with tennis balls on the front stoppers to help with the traction and lessen the damage to the hardwood floors. He made a guttural sound that translated by anyone who knew him was of approval when he saw her.

I think he had come to look forward to her thrice weekly trips to the house. Truth be told, so had I.

"Any progress on forming words?" she asked.

"No, not really."

"Have you been talking to him? You've got to talk to him."

She went about her business, untwisting the beast of a machine I had toted in. She was gentle with the boy, but insistent.

I excused myself as she started her work. My first stop was to wash my face. My vanity got the best of me and I looked in the mirror in the mud room. I did not really like what stared back. There was a perfect circle around my head. The line of demarcation was brown and red below and white above. I stuck my hat back on and went out onto the porch to wait.

She and the boy came out after the session. "I need to show you a new exercise," she said. "I have a question. Have you taken him out to your working pens or the barn?"

"It can be dangerous down there, especially for someone with a walker. I don't want him to get hurt."

"I think it would help. He wants to improve, I know it. You have to help him help himself."

I squirmed a little. "It's just hard to take him down there. Too much history and it would only remind him of what happened."

She looked at me. "I know a little about it." She looked down slightly. "People talk, of course."

I began to tell it slowly. "It was a freak thing. Roany was, you know, probably still a bit too much horse for him. The boy was game though and he'd been able to ride anything with hide on it since before he could walk. It was at a roping in a new arena in San Angelo. He drew a soured calf that ducked into that nice new drill stem pipe fence." I stopped to explain what that meant. "When you're right handed and a calf runs along the right side of the roping pen fence, it's almost impossible to get a rope on it."

I stood up and hunched over like I was horseback and started swinging an imaginary rope. "You have to dip the tip of the rope as you're swinging it down and away from the fence." I figured I looked pretty silly squatting and pointing, but she was a good sport. "Instead of releasing the rope like a baseball, you have to release it above your head. Have to also use a smaller loop because the loop is coming down on the calf from the top, not the right side of the head. Most hands will wait for the calf to come off the fence to take their throw. It means their time will be slower, but they have a better chance of staying in the average. Not him. He shortened his loop on the fly when that calf took the fence." I paused. "He made a perfect throw."

I bowed my head. "But he got his slack too hard." I stopped and explained, "That's when you pull the excess rope back after pulling it tight on the calf's neck and throw it so you can get off your horse."

I continued, "Roany ducked off bad -- ducked away from the rope as the boy got off the horse on the right side." I paused again and took a breath. "He tried to reach around his body and grab the rein with his right hand to keep the horse straight, but he lost his balance."

136

I turned my head away from her. "The next thing I heard was this sickening thud. It was his head hitting that drill pipe fence."

Quietly she said, "It just seems so dangerous."

"Yeah, and they say it's the rough stock riders that take all the risks." I looked at her, "But there's a grace of movement when horse and the man aboard are in sync. It's balletic, really, the same kind of agility, speed and improvisation."

"Did you say 'balletic'?" she asked, a surprised expression on her face.

"You have trouble believing I appreciate ballet, the grace of movement?" I said it with a light tinge of sarcasm. "Competitive roping ties us to the land and the people who came before us. Practical ranch work still requires knowledge of a lariat. It's why I roped. That's why I showed my boy how to rope."

She turned a little crimson I thought. "Where is his mother?"

"Remarried and living in Dallas. She grew up here. I figured she knew better than anyone that cattle don't know it's Christmas, or any other holiday for that matter. But in the end she wanted something different. But she's been here every weekend to see him."

I paused and asked, "What about you? How did you get here, in this place?"

"Long story. It involves someone I was with and the oil field. Funny thing of it is I never wanted to come here in the first place but after he left, I stayed. That's the thing I have a hard time explaining to my family back east. I have told them time and space are different here and the austereness suits me. I tell them you can be lonely even with millions of people around. Archeology was my minor in school. I spend a lot of time looking for things left by the Comanche. I know that sounds a little eccentric, but it's me."

"His mother wants to move him to Dallas with her," I said suddenly. "She believes he can get more complete care there."

"And you agree?"

"There's a reason the Panateka Comanche left those artifacts you look for." I was staring at the boy. "They understood the harshness of the Llano Estacado." I stopped and glanced toward the working pen and the momma cow still bellowing for her calf. "I had to put down a day old cripple this morning. I didn't like it, but it had to be done. Dallas may be better for him now."

"Do you really believe that?"

"He can't speak, barely walk. I thought having him here with familiar surroundings would help, but I'm not sure I can do enough for him." I looked out toward the land, away from her gaze. "I had this brief window to see the man he could've become. It's hard to watch him broken down like this."

"Like that calf you put down this morning?"

"Not the same thing, but hard times mean hard decisions."

She paused. "Instead of mourning the man he could've become, what about helping me make him become the man he still could be?"

I looked at her. "Fair enough, let's give a trip to the barn a go, shall we? Be careful where you step down there." I put one hand under the boy's arm, the other under his elbow to help him down the porch steps. The three of us must have been a comic sight for Cesar and Maria -- the therapist in her scrubs, me in my hat and the boy reaching and pulling on his walker down the caliche road to the barn.

We stopped in front of Roany's stall. He was outside in his run, but sauntered back slowly, stopping to smell our scents before approaching. He lingered in front of us, wary. Suddenly he swung his big head toward the boy and stuck a tentative nose into the boy's chest and gently pushed. The boy smiled. His mouth opened and twisted into a sort of curve. I heard him say quietly but distinctly "Rooan-eee". Then again "Rooan-ee." My mouth wide open, I closed my eyes.

I felt her slip her hand into mine and squeeze. I opened my eyes and we stood, together, watching the roan horse and my son. Off in the working pens the momma cow stopped her bellowing.

LANE THIBODEAUX grew up competing in roping and cutting horse events. He has practiced law for 25 years, trying more than 100 cases to juries in Texas. He came late to writing short fiction, drawing primarily on his equine and legal experience. Thibodeaux's first work, "Cluttered Places," appeared in the online literary magazine *Southern Hum*. "Llano Estcado" is his second attempt at the form. He can be contacted through his website: http://www.thibodeauxlaw.com/

THE BARD OF STOCKMAN FLAT

Harold Miller

(Finalist Romance Category 2010 Cowboy Up Contest)

The Nevada wind was already whipping up blustery gusts and the clouds to the east were a virtual display of brilliant orange, red, white and purple. The closest mountain range was a black silhouette of mystery as the sun rose slowly up to declare its rightful place on the horizon. It was a virtual cowboy's delight as far as sunrises went.

Hank Kern stepped outside his modest log home to feed his stock and was greeted by four wagging tails. He bent down to greet each one, and as he straightened he surveyed the ten acres he called a ranch. Hank and his delightful wife Donna raised horses, a few cattle, and a brood of peacocks, besides homeless dogs and cats. Their house perched on the highest point of the land. The barn sat about sixty yards from the house and down slope a bit. The pasture had an acclivitous slope to it, flattening out at the end of the property. In the center of the parcel a cluster of pinion pines and Arizona cypress trees complimented the landscape, which otherwise consisted of sage, rabbit brush and sand. Hank loved this place and he loved his life here with his animals and his cowgirl soul mate Donna.

Hank walked into his new six-stall barn, which had tapped out the last of his savings. The horses were already in their places, pawing and letting him know they were ready for breakfast. He had five of the most beautiful horses that ever lived, he thought. All blue-papered Missouri Fox Trotters out of the old Apple Creek bloodlines, they showed it in their smooth gaits, good minds and sweet dispositions. They made good roping horses too, if worked right. Hank fed them their grass hay and stood watching them for a moment to make sure they were feeling healthy. Then he filled the water buckets. He liked feeding time; it gave him almost a spiritual high to see his horses well cared-for and happy, contentedly munching their hay. Next, Hank moved to the peacock house. The brilliantly arrayed birds squawked excitedly as he filled their feed bins. Finally, he turned his attention to his little cattle herd.

But Hank's mind was actually on something else this morning. Hank was a writer and cowboy poet, and there was a recital coming up, a big one, less than a week away. He'd been invited to compete in the 12th Annual "Cowboy Rope Off," which would include poets from all over the United States. And each one would come determined to win the honor and glory, not to mention the huge purses. The first prize for each category was $5,000 cash, a Stetson trophy hat and a two-year writing contract for a major cowboy magazine. Cowboy and cowgirl poets would be competing for the categories of funniest, most heart-wrenching, and most thought-provoking poems. Hank badly wanted to win his category. He'd worked his way up in competitions and perfected his skills until he felt nowadays he recited as good as anybody. In fact, somebody had labeled him "The Bard of Stockman Flat."

The competition would be tough. He would have to beat out Charlie Rivers, last-year's popular winner. Hank's biggest female competitor would no doubt be Dana Lou Schreiber, a poet of renown and a singer who seemed to have an advantage with the mostly male judges. Hank also had two partners who were competing for the "Funniest Poem and Poet" title: Daryl Dew, the crazy cowboy who could make an undertaker laugh, and Mark Caldwell, a scrappy little man afraid of nothing and no one. Though not a great writer, Mark seemed to cast some spell over his audiences. Poets from Wyoming and Montana, and one as far away as Maine, were also coming to the event. They were entered in different categories than Hank, which made him happy that he wouldn't have to compete against them.

The event was being held in Las Vegas; not really cowboy country, but at least it was close. Hank planned to arrive the day before and spend the night in a cheap motel. He remembered one motel he'd stayed in many years back where doors were optional and cockroaches were free. He liked to joke that he and a cockroach had a tug-of-war over the bed sheets. But that had been before he married Donna. She would not like having to fight cockroaches, he thought, and laughed to himself.

Donna, a dark-haired beauty with sexy brown eyes and beautiful skin, looked younger than her age. She was already anticipating his win and was counting the money. She had plans to look at a horse in Henderson after the competition. Hank hoped she wouldn't be disappointed.

The day arrived quickly and before Hank knew it, it was time for the drive to Las Vegas. The contest was being held in the Western Barn Theatre in North Las Vegas, a ranch-type setting that was actually a convention center for neighborhood meetings. It started at 8 a.m., and Hank had drawn the 11 a.m. slot in the "Humorous Poem" category. There were eighteen people in that grouping, too many for comfort.

Hank parked in the lot designated for poets and judges and then had a look around. People were mingling, drinking coffee, and already taking pictures. Hank recognized a few of them. His pard Daryl Dew was standing with two other people Hank didn't know, and when Daryl saw Hank and Donna he held up his cup in recognition and waved them over. He introduced them to Gary and Connie Hodman, a husband and wife poetry team from Missouri. They made small talk, but at the same time the competitors were sizing each other up. A lot of the poets were well-known and Hank knew the better known a poet was, well, naturally the judges would gravitate to giving him or her a higher score--if they didn't flub too badly.

More competitors spotted the Kerns and came over to greet them. Several seemed pleased to meet Hank and said they'd heard good reports about him. Hank started feeling more confident, almost like a celebrity. Then someone clanged a dinner bell, signaling it was time to start the rodeo. Donna took the books they'd brought to the volunteers who were handling the poets' sale items, and Hank got himself a cup of coffee. The participants took their seats. Since Hank was tall, he always sat in the back row, much to Donna's frustration. The audience was a good size, but all the performers knew it was the judges' scores that mattered.

There would be two rounds, but Hank knew he'd have to make his best impression in the first go-round; if he didn't, he might not get a second chance. Five judges would rate the poets between 0 and 10, with 10 being the best score one could get from one judge and 50 being the highest score possible. Hank's stomach churned as he waited for his turn to enter the rhyming chute.

As each poet took the stage and gave his or her best, Donna held Hank's hand and whispered things like, "Your poems are better," and "You should place easily." But Hank wasn't so sure. Then Daryl Dew walked onto the stage and in one of his impressionist voices, started reciting a familiar poem. Daryl didn't write his own stuff but he could sure do justice to other folks' lines, making them come out just right. But if a poet recited his own original poem, he received a credit of five points from the get go. Daryl received a respectable score of 37.

Next up was Mark Caldwell, outfitted in authentic old west garb: a black hat, suspenders over a white shirt, and trousers tucked into colorful cowboy boots. He cut quite a handsome figure and Hank thought he should win on his looks alone. And worse, he'd be reciting his own original poem. Mark began, and it was a good one and seemed to endear him with the crowd. His score was a 42. Just my luck, thought Hank, but at the same time he was happy for him.

Finally it was Hank's turn. The Bard of Stockman Flat knew he had to cowboy up and do his best. Donna wanted a horse and he didn't intend to let her down if he could help it. He slowly stepped onto the stage and introduced himself. "Good mornin'. I'm Hank Kern from Nevada and I'll be reciting my own poem. I call it 'Cowboy Stampede.'" He drew a deep breath, hesitated a few seconds, and then began his oration.

"The longhorn sonofaguns were getting hard to hold
as the thunder storm moved in fast and cold.
The dark black clouds were beginning to hover
as the fretful steers made a sweep for cover...."

Hank remembered to keep his southern drawl low, and used enough old west phrases in his poem to pull it off. He'd researched the scene thoroughly to give an authoritative account and make the audience believe they were really there on that hot trail drive being besieged by a powerful thunder storm.

Though the poem started out serious, it had a funny ending and the audience laughed and clapped their approval. Hank looked at Donna and smiled, then watched the scorer's board. 44 points! Hank was jubilant. That was just 6 short of the highest score possible. Wonderful, he thought to himself. Let's see if Miss Dana Lou Flirt can beat that! He hoped she couldn't.

Dana was up next and though her poem contained some near-rhymes, she did a good job of reciting. Her beautiful smile and tight-fitting jeans helped her to tie his score. Hank fairly gave her credit where credit was due.

The rest of the afternoon was filled with good and bad poems and good and bad reciters in each category. When all the scores had been tallied, the competitors who were in the short-go were announced. Four had made it to the second round in the Humorous class: Dana Lou Schreiber; an Arizona poet called Tumbleweed Jones; last year's big winner Charlie Rivers; and Hank. Donna smiled her proudest smile and gave him a big hug and kiss. The next day the semi-finalists would compete against each other. All would be in the money, but third and fourth places would just barely get enough to cover expenses. Second place would receive $2000. First place got the big prizes and the bragging rights.

The competition ended for the day and everyone went their separate ways. Daryl Dew and Mark Caldwell congratulated Hank and then departed for a casino bar, where Hank knew they would hole up for the rest of the evening. The Kerns went to a local café and enjoyed a victory dinner, then took a walk in the desert. As they skirted creosote bushes dried from the lack of rain, Hank silently practiced the poems he had in reserve for when he made the finals. He aimed to win the grand prize. When the sun finally set on the Las Vegas desert, the couple retired to their room to watch television and relax before the next day's competition.

Hank got up early to iron out any wrinkles in his western shirt and to make sure his boots were polished. He had his poems committed to memory and now he was ready for the three C's: coffee, competition and cash!

The short-go started promptly at 9 a.m.. Each poet had 15 minutes to give it his best shot. Two winners would be decided in each category. There would be a break for lunch, then the poets would go at it again. The final winner would be announced with photos and interviews following and the prizes bestowed.

The place teamed with excitement as Hank and Donna walked into the already crowded room. The pleasant aroma of brewing coffee and the talking and laughter gave the room a homey atmosphere. Then the crowd quieted as the first contestant stepped up to the microphone. Tumbleweed Jones' oration was his own poem, a humorous story of an old man's recollection about an outside bathroom. His poem was good, Hank begrudgingly admitted. The crowd applauded loudly as Tumbleweed finished his story and left the stage. He came off with a respectable score of 43. Not bad, Hank thought.

Next up was the beautiful Miss Dana. She dazzled the crowd with her slim figure and melodious voice. When the smoke had cleared she was looking at a 45 point score and first place. Of course, thought Hank, I would vote for her myself.

Hank was next, and after breathing a prayer, he stepped up to the microphone and began to recite. No use wasting time, he thought. Besides, he knew the judges liked the show to move along and he needed all the edge he could get. Hank recited like he had never recited before, making sure he spoke his poem loud, clear and flawless, and it worked. He tied Dana's score of 45! Now if he could just hold on, he and she would go head to head in the final go-round; but he knew that was a big "hold on" because last year's favorite, Charlie Rivers, was heading toward the stage with almost a smirk on his face. Hank reached over and took Donna's hand and she responded with a squeeze and a warm smile. Hank sat back and watched the show thinking, even if I lose, I'm still a winner with Donna.

Charlie did his best to repeat the performance he'd given the year before but it was not to be. He flubbed a few lines and just couldn't seem to recover. He gave it his best cowboy effort but came up short with a 41, moving into fourth place. He walked out of the room looking dejected. That's too bad, thought Hank, but then Donna and his two pards Mark and Daryl were slapping him on the back and congratulating him on making the final round. Hank was almost in shock over it all. But after a few minutes he sought out Charlie Rivers, who was standing outside the exit, and gave him a pat on the back and said, "It was a good show, Charlie." Charlie looked miserable but tried to keep up an appearance and congratulated Hank on his final bid. Then Hank left to take Donna and his two pards out to lunch to plan his strategy.

The excitement after lunch was almost more than Hank could take. Newscasters and online radio station broadcasters had arrived and they all wanted an interview with Dana and Hank. The two contestants were like boxers at opposite ends of the ring, surrounded by all their close friends but still looking each other over. Hank liked Dana alright outside the competition, but this was war and he aimed to win.

In the final go-round, Hank was scheduled first, the unluck of the draw. As the audience settled down, he stepped once again onto the stage and recited with a fervor. When his 15 minute presentation was done, he sat down, exhausted. The judges gave him a 47! Fantastic! But Dana had changed into an outfit intended to sway the judges. As she stepped up to the stage, her sleek blue jeans looked like she'd painted them on. The western-style buckskin and turquoise jacket she wore was meant to attract, and it was doing its job, and the bright silk kerchief draped around her neck completed her cowgirl-movie star look. She began her poem and never looked back. She ended up with a final score of 49, and Hank's dreams were dashed. He felt the loss, and he sympathized even more with Charlie Rivers.

The final announcement of winners in each category was made. Dana received her accolades and the reciters were paid according to where they'd placed. Hank shook hands with everyone and the crowd began to disperse. He bid his two friends a happy trip home, then he joined Donna.

Hank received a check for $2000 dollars; not bad at all for one day's work. But the horse Donna wanted was priced at $2500, and horse traders do not give credit. Hank pondered how to weasel out of taking her to look at the horse, and as he cleared his throat, Donna produced a handful of twenty-dollar bills. "Where did that come from?" he asked, surprised.

Donna grinned and said, "From your book sales -- $300 worth! We sold every one of your books!"

"Really!" he exclaimed. The book sales had completely slipped his mind, he'd been so focused on the competition.

"And," she looked up at him and paused, "I talked with the people who have that horse I want and they actually came down a few hundred bucks."

Hank looked into his happy wife's face and concluded that she had trotted her horse argument around the corral and the brand was easy to read. "Well," he said finally, as he offered her his arm, "what say we go have a look at your new horse?"

HAROLD MILLER was born in Mississippi, raised in Arizona and now lives in Stagecoach, Nevada, where he raises horses and writes short stories. Miller is a wild horse advocate and writes poems and stories about wild mustangs also. Two of his writings were used in a Documentary for PBS in 2010. Miller also works for the state of Nevada and plans on retiring soon and pursuing a full-time writing career.

THE BEST THINGS

Paula L. Silici

(Finalist Romance Category Cowboy Up Contest 2010)

Colorado, 1877

Cassie Daniels pulled her thin cotton shawl around her shoulders and peered through the batwing doors. Past nine and a Saturday night, the saloon teemed with rowdy ranch hands busting loose after a week of grinding work. Shivering, she quickly scanned the smoky room, praying Noah Ryland was here.

He was. She spotted his dark head almost immediately. It was buried in the buxom bosom of a redheaded floozy. True, she couldn't see his face, but she'd know that muscular build and the set of those broad shoulders anywhere.

A half-empty bottle of whiskey dangled from his left hand; his right fumbled beneath the woman's ruffled skirt.

She sighed. If she wasn't so desperate she'd forget this mad plan, strike out for parts unknown and pray she lived long enough to get there. Oh curse Uncle Eldon, she thought bitterly. Curse him and that prehistoric lecher crony of his, Lester Pope.

Well, she couldn't stand out here forever. If she didn't follow through with her plan, there was no telling what might become of her. Taking a deep breath, she gave the doors a firm shove.

"Um...Noah?"

The dark head slewed toward her; even darker eyes pierced her through at the moment of recognition. He didn't like her much. She'd understood that for a long time, but it never stopped her from loving him anyway. Sometimes a man just didn't know a good thing when he saw it.

She was a good thing.

"What the hell are you doing here?" he demanded, a white-hot rush of anger filling him. He clenched his jaw, as if the sight of her nauseated him.

"I need to talk to you."

She shuddered. All eyes were upon her now, causing a tide of crimson to flush her face. To her horror, the tinny piano music clunked to a halt. Furtively, she glanced around. No decent woman dared set foot in a saloon; her presence was causing a stir.

"I've gotta talk to you in private," she whispered, some of her bravado failing her. Noah's anger and sharp scrutiny made her knees tremble.

"Get the hell out of here, Cassie. Go home."

"I...c-can't." She didn't really feel like crying; she was too angry at her uncle for that. But she forced herself to concentrate until a lone tear trickled from her eye. "Can't we go and talk somewhere? It'll only take a minute."

Noah banged the bottle down on the table, causing the shot glasses to jump. Startled, his companions scooted their chairs back.

Cassie flinched.

"Whatever you've got to say, you can say it in front of my friends. Tex, Jim, Adelle..." he drawled, giving the saloon girl's breast a bawdy squeeze. "You all want to hear what Miss Daniels has to say, don't you?" The men laughed, nodding vigorously. Adelle giggled.

Cassie's stomach churned, but there was no turning back now. Bracing herself, she shrugged her shoulders as if to say, *well, I warned you.* In a trembling voice she announced loud enough for all to hear, "I'm in...in the family way, Noah Ryland...a-and you're the cause of it!"

An even deader silence settled over the barroom. For a few moments, Cassie thought Noah's heart must have stopped, he'd become so still and pale. But then, in one mighty push, he dumped a sputtering Adelle onto the floor and stood, his chair crashing behind him. Lunging after her as if to strangle her he growled, "You little lying skunk! You've made my life miserable for the last time."

Cassie panicked. She managed a slippery dodge, but just barely escaped before Tex and Jim restrained him.

"Whoa there, boss!" Tex yelled.

And then Cyrus Cutter appeared, having elbowed his way through the crowd. She'd known the kind old storekeeper forever. When she was little, Mr. Cutter gave her, a poor orphan child, oodles of her favorite peppermint drops whenever she and her uncle stopped by Cutter's Mercantile for supplies. She sighed with relief when he placed himself between her and Noah.

"Ain't no cause to harm the girl, Ryland," Cyrus panted, mopping his brow with a handkerchief. "I'm sure there's a more amiable way to get to the bottom of this."

Inside, Cassie shriveled. Noah's eyes were blazing hot, burning her to cinders. She'd expected him to be angry. After all, she just ruined his...well, sort-of-good name and reputation. But she hadn't thought he'd resort to violence. That he'd want to do her harm. No, she hadn't figured on that at all.

"Seems to me," Cyrus began, his gruff voice full of an emotion Cassie couldn't quite name, "that if what sweet little Cassie here says is true, ya ought to do the right thing by her. A real man takes responsibility for his actions, son. It's only right."

Noah struggled to free himself. "She's lying! I never touched her! Everybody knows she's been chasing after me for years. This is just another one of her ridiculous games."

Cyrus brought Cassie forward a little, turning her to face him. "Now, Cassie, this here's a right serious situation. Are you absolutely certain about all this?"

She didn't have to fake the tears now. She was terrified of Noah, her hero, the man she'd chosen to be her savior. But she couldn't back out now. She'd risked too much, come too far for that. Besides, the alternatives were too horrific to contemplate.

She swiped a hand across her eyes. In a small voice she said, "I'm sure, Mr. Cutter."

A wild whoop went up and the piano player plunked out a discordant wedding march. Men were grinning lewdly at her. They were grinning at Noah, too, but he didn't seem to notice. He was too busy incinerating her with his glare.

She swallowed hard. Noah was no longer fighting to free his arms. In all her life she'd never seen such blatant contempt and disgust on a man's face.

Drunk and grinning like a fox, Tex addressed the crowd. "Well, folks, let's get on over to Judge Jessop's place. It looks like we're gonna have ourselves a weddin'!"

***

"Noah, please don't be mad. I can explain."

The moment the judge had pronounced them husband and wife, a tight-lipped Noah took her by the scruff of the neck and hauled her off to his ranch. Not bothering to carry her over the threshold, he shoved her roughly into the house, straight toward the bedroom.

"Shut your mouth and get your clothes off, Cassie."

A full moon beyond the window drenched the room in silvery light. The rumpled, unmade bed sprawled before her like a yawning raft adrift on an angry sea.

Trembling, she forced the words past her dry throat. "Uncle Eldon was going to marry me to Lester Pope!"

That got Noah's attention, but only for a moment. Shaking his head and smiling wryly, he continued to pull off his boots. "Nice try, Cass."

He didn't believe her. Desperately, she said, "It's true. Uncle Eldon owes him a hundred dollars. Pope said he'd forgive the debt if my uncle agreed to let him marry me."

"Cassie, you've always been a whopping liar, but this tears it. Lester Pope is old enough to be your grandfather."

"Exactly!"

Noah narrowed his eyes. Mocking her, he said, "Look. Thanks to you, some lucky son of a bitch--who isn't me--is sporting Adelle right about now. I've got a big discomfort that needs tending. I told you to get your clothes off, *wife*. Do it quick and get over here so I can exercise my conjugal rights."

Cassie gasped, backing up until her bottom bumped the wall.

"Oh, come on, Cass. You told that entire barroom you've got a brat in your belly. This is no time to play the shy virgin."

"Noah, I swear I'm telling you the truth. Uncle Eldon was going to give me to that decrepit lecher, Pope. I was desperate. You're the only man I've ever truly c-cared f-for. I know you think I'm a pain in the...arse. You've told me that a m-million

155

times. But...but...well, when I sneaked out of the house tonight, all I could think about was that I love only you and...and...."

He was naked now and coming after her. Horrified, she pressed her shoulders against the wall, praying the wood would swallow her.

It didn't. His arms swallowed her instead.

"Since you love me so much, *wife*, let's get to consummating."

In one, screaming tear, he parted her dress from neck to hem. Too shocked to move, she stood numb and mute as her camisole and drawers came off next. In the next instant he dumped her, sprawling, onto the bed.

She did cry out then, but it was a pitiful croak of misery and defeat. Shielding her breasts with her hands, she looked up at his angry face through a film of tears.

In a rush she said, "I never meant to hurt you, Noah. I'll be a good wife to you, you'll see. You're lonely, just like me, even though you try to hide it. We'll be good for each other--"

"Hush," he ordered harshly, yanking the pins from her hair and flinging them across the room. Slowly, he finger-combed her chestnut tresses until they formed a halo around her head. "Let me make myself clear, Cassie. First, I won't be hornswoggled because your lover let you down. Second, if you were telling the truth about Pope and your uncle, which I very much doubt you were, it's just too bad because I'm taking you straight back home in the morning." He paused, the set of his jaw hard and bitter. "After that, I'll be riding to Denver to see about an annulment."

Crestfallen, she stared up at his handsome face, trying to hold back a floodtide. If only she could make him understand how much she loved him and wanted to belong to him. His brutal rejection hurt her more than she could bear.

He clasped her hands, settling them firmly at her sides. The next time he spoke, his voice was raw and low. "I'll say this for you, though, Cass, I sure never figured such treasures were hidden under those rags you wear all the time. It's almost enough to make a man think twice about...things."

He bent his head and kissed her then, slow and deep, hot and searing, as if branding her with his lips. Cassie loved him so much, it never occurred to her to object. He was her husband now. This was her Noah, the man who was and always had been the heart and soul of her fantasies.

"You taste...sweet," he murmured against her lips. He sounded surprised, as if he'd just nipped a bite of Eden's fruit and couldn't wait to treat himself to more. He devoured her lips again, breathing hard and groaning deep in his throat. Soon his large hands were everywhere, touching, stroking, exploring her at will.

The pleasant scent of his whiskey-tinged breath filled her. Of their own volition, her small hands explored him, too, trailing a path across the hills and valleys of his perfect, male body.

"I love you, Noah," she whispered against his skin. And when he stilled, she said it again.

"Don't," he murmured curtly, shoving his knee between her thighs. And then he was inside her, pushing against her virginity, tearing it asunder just as he had torn her clothes. He did it angrily, without thought, without gentleness or concern for her feelings.

His body trembled, then stilled. A long moment passed.

"Cassie." Her name tore from his throat.

He rose slightly, cupping her face between his hands. For the first time, his gaze held a glimmer of warmth instead of cold disdain.

"I...I made it up about the baby," she whispered tremulously. "I've never been with anybody else. I told you, Noah, he was gonna give me to Lester Pope."

He smoothed a wisp of hair from her glistening cheek. "I hurt you just now," he said, his voice tinged with sadness. And maybe a touch of regret, too? She couldn't be certain, but she hoped so.

"It doesn't matter."

"Yes, it does."

His lips pressed hers tenderly this time, the kiss gentle and probing as he began to move inside her again. She melted like spring snow beneath his touch, and as he moved inside her she allowed her mind to drift and her body to soar to heights she'd never dared imagine before now. True joy and happiness began to overtake her for the first time in her life. And then her body exploded into thousands of shards of light, the pleasure so exquisite she never wanted to regain her senses. *Oh, Noah. My dearest Noah. How I love you so!*

***

An hour before dawn, Cassie eased from the bed. She was tired and a little sore, but so pleased and happy she could barely contain her joy. Noah had loved her in so many ways during the long night, she couldn't begin to count them all. He cared for her, her heart sang. Finally, she truly belonged, body and soul, to Noah Ryland.

Since her clothes lie at the foot of the bed in tatters, she slipped into Noah's shirt and pants, rolling up cuffs and cinching the jeans with his belt. Silently snatching up her shoes, she left the room.

An hour later, Noah entered the kitchen, an uneasy frown crowding his face. Noticing the fried ham, potatoes, and the

158

platter of biscuits and gravy spread out on the kitchen table, he turned to her warily.

"Hi," Cassie said, trying to mask her nervousness. "Your breakfast is ready."

"The cows need milking," he said, that familiar edge of anger in his tone.

"Already done," she said. "I fed the chickens, too."

"Already done?"

"Yes. Eat your breakfast before it gets cold."

She turned to the stove, attempting to look busy, trying to shove away the hurt. How she'd hoped for a good morning kiss! Hoped for a smile and some kind word to show he'd forgiven her deception. Well, he'd given her nothing of the sort. Did that mean he meant to keep his word, then, and take her back to her uncle?

She heard the scrape of the chair, heard his sigh as he settled in. Quickly, she grabbed the coffee pot and filled his cup. As she poured, her hip brushed his arm.

"Do you take cream and sugar?" she asked, her hands trembling so much she almost missed the cup.

"Sometimes," he said, his lips curving into a small smile. "Nice duds, Cassie."

The comment embarrassed her, as she was sure he knew it would. As she turned away, blushing furiously, he grabbed her arm.

"Next time I'm in town I'll buy you a new dress."

That wasn't what she wanted to hear. She'd hoped he'd tell her they'd be going out to Uncle Eldon's place to pack up her belongings. But he didn't say that, and a lump of sorrow knotted her throat.

Noah had just swallowed a last mouthful of coffee when they heard horses approaching.

"The ranch hands slithering back from their night on the town?" she asked, unable to keep the bitterness from her tone.

"Maybe," Noah said.

He got up, grabbed his Winchester, and peeled back the window curtain. "Nope," he said. "It's your Uncle Eldon. And that sorry sidewinder, Pope."

Cassie paled. Noah looked angry with her again and she withered inside. He was going to give her back to them. She just knew it.

"Come on, Cass. Buck up." He strode to the door, opening it wide.

Spotting her immediately, her portly uncle blustered in like he owned the place. Before she realized what was coming, before she could duck, he raised his heavy arm and backhanded her hard. She reeled, crying out, stumbling to her knees.

At once Noah lifted the Winchester. Cocking it, he spat angrily, "You ever hit her again, Daniels, and it'll be the last thing you ever do with that hand. Back off!"

Noah helped her to her feet. "You okay?" he asked, putting an arm around her waist to steady her.

She nodded, so confused she could barely stand. Had Noah just defended her?

"Look here, Ryland," Uncle Eldon blustered. "I've come to take Cassie back. The deceitful, disobedient little chit ran away last night! Pope and me spent the whole night tracking her down."

For a long moment her uncle glared at her, trying to shrivel her where she stood. "Some boys in town told us a tall tale about her trappin' you into marriage. Did we hear right?"

Pope suddenly came alive. His screechy voice, like fingernails raking a schoolroom slate, sent shivers down Cassie's spine. "Did you go and marry my *fee-an-see*?" he squawked at Noah, clenching his gnarled fists. "Or was that story we got over at the saloon just a trough of hogwash from a bunch of drunks?"

Noah leveled the rifle at the old man's chest. "It's true," he answered evenly. "Cassie and I were married last night."

Uncle Eldon swore. "Aw hell," he groaned. "You've gone and ruined me, Cassie! I'll whip your ungrateful hide for this, damn if I won't. Get over here, girl. Now. You're comin' with us." He looked at Pope, a sick grin splitting his thick lips. "I'll fix this somehow, Lester. She's still yours. We'll get the law on our side. When this mess is all cleared up, I'll give her to ya just like I promised."

Cassie swayed against Noah's arm.

"That's enough!" Noah snarled, jerking the rifle up and squeezing the trigger. Wood splintered above their heads, showering the two elderly men with stinging chaff. They jumped, Pope baying like a wounded wolf.

"Cassie's my wife, Daniels. There isn't a lawman in the territory who'd side with you on this. We've got papers and plenty of witnesses to prove our claim. Judge Jessop did the marrying himself."

Crimson with anger, Pope raised an arthritic fist, shaking it like a madman. "You stole my *fee-an-see*," he yowled, lacerating the word a second time. "She was mine and you stole her from me!"

To Cassie's surprise, Noah ignored the outburst. "There's something else you ought to know, Daniels," he said, pulling her close. "Cassie's in the family way." His voice was steady, deadly calm when he added, "And make no mistake. I'm the cause of her condition."

Pope and Daniels gasped in harmony. Daniels flexed his fingers, scowling murderously at his niece. Cassie couldn't believe her ears.

"Give it up, gentlemen," Noah warned. "Cassie's mine. You two ever involve her in your sick schemes again, I'll make sure you both live to regret it."

"Well! We'll just see about that," Uncle Eldon sputtered, his face mottled with rage. "I'll have you--"

Noah aimed the rifle at the ceiling again, but before he could pull off another shot, the two men, grumbling and swearing, scrambled out.

Noah sat Cassie down, doused a towel in cold water and gently pressed it to her bruised cheek.

"That bastard," he said angrily when she flinched. "Does it hurt bad?"

"No." Cassie brushed the tears from her eyes. Her cheek hurt like crazy, but that wasn't why she was crying.

"Then how come you're crying?"

"Because y-you blew a h-hole in your roof, defending me."

His hand stilled. "The roof's fixable."

"And...b-because you called me your w-wife."

Noah shrugged, not meeting her eyes. "Well, you *are* my wife."

"Truly?" The tears were coming harder now.

"Don't cry, Cass."

"B-but you h-hate me. You've hated me since we were kids. I've always been your pain in the arse."

He chuckled, tracing a finger along the arch of her brow. "You are that," he agreed. "But you're such a pretty pain. Strange, I hadn't really noticed that before."

He studied her a moment, his features softening. "Those were mighty fine vittles you fixed." He cleared his throat, obviously uncomfortable. "And for the first time in years I didn't have to milk the cows or feed the chickens. A fellow could get used to having a wife around, I think."

She blushed and he pulled her close so that her uninjured cheek rested against his belly. "Of course, there's other nice things about having a wife."

She sniffed. "There are? Like what?"

"The best things."

"The best things?"

He kissed the tip of her nose. "It's Sunday. Everybody takes Sundays off around here." He threaded his fingers through her hair. "We could go back to bed if we want."

"And do what?" she teased shyly, looking up at him with wonder in her eyes.

"Those best things," he said.

PAULA SILICI is an award-winning author and editor whose works of fiction, nonfiction, and poetry have appeared in both regional and national publications. She is currently associate editor for the online literary magazine, TalkingWritng.com.

EIGHT SECONDS

Melissa Embry

(3rd Place Winner 2010 Cowboy Up Contest)

The obituary came in an envelope with no return address, just a Dallas postmark from a zip code near the Intertribal Center. I thought at first it was a plea for funds – "$20 puts food on the table for hungry Indians" – that kind of thing. I usually give a hundred. A hundred bucks isn't much to me now and it quiets my conscience a little. I ripped it open, feeling inside for a return envelope to put my contribution in, but there was only the piece of newsprint, and I read, remembering what had happened to Jimmy Kotay.

Big Jimmy and Little Jimmy, they called us, but we were the same height and build, Little Jimmy maybe a shade slimmer. He had walked, late, into my class at Vista College. That was my second try at physiology, and if I failed again, Ma could pack away the dream she had of me being anything but a cowboy or a drunk.

Little Jimmy was way past the five minutes the lecturer Samuels allowed everybody to finish a cigarette, take a leak, and grab a cup of sludge from the pot in the school secretary's office, before sliding into their desks.

Samuels shoved his glasses to the top of his head to give Little Jimmy the full effect of his pale-eyed stare. "You must be

Ghulam Jilani," he said, looking from the newcomer to the class roll.

"Just Jilani," Little Jimmy said.

In his tweeds and tie, Little Jimmy seemed to have wandered into the wrong class. Except for Samuels in his stained lab coat, the rest of us looked like starving students -- clothing ripped and faded, hair long and greasy, the men three days from a shave. Little Jimmy thought we were refugees, he told me later, and he wondered what disaster had made us flee to a small town in Texas. He sat by me, maybe because I looked the least unshaven. Not that I was a stickler for grooming -- us Kiowas just aren't much in the beard department.

"Why the hell are you so late?" I whispered.

He pursed his lips reprovingly. "I was deciding which tie to wear. I wanted to make a good impression."

Except being a clotheshorse wasn't the only reason for his lateness. Being late was as much a habit for Little Jimmy as being hung over was for me.

But I learned that later. That first day, he looked so neat and prim, his mustache barbered within an inch of its life, I choked on my coffee when he told me his dream. We were sitting over vending machine cups in the student center where he'd followed me. He talked and I tried to ignore him while the TV blared the theme to a rerun of *Bonanza*.

"My mother always wanted me to be a doctor," he said.

"Yeah. Mine too." I pulled out papers and a tobacco pouch to roll a smoke.

"Of course, I won't be able to break the news to her until I'm famous, but I'd like to do so before she hears about my exploits in the news."

"Your exploits?"

166

"My exploits as a cowboy."

"You gotta be kidding. You want to be a cowboy? Like me?"

"I thought you were an Indian."

"I'm a cowboy and an Indian. I can play both parts in the Westerns. But if you got to pick sides, yeah, be a cowboy. At least cowboying earns a few bucks when somebody needs an extra hand. There's no pay in being an Indian."

I tossed my cigarette butt in the last inch of cold coffee. Little Jimmy sat, very straight and quiet in his tweeds.

"You need money?" I asked. "You could try out for the school rodeo team. They give scholarships. That's the only thing that's keeping me here."

"I have a scholarship from my country." He turned back to *Bonanza*. I could tell he was sore about being laughed at.

"I can teach you, Jilani."

"Teach me what?"

"To be a cowboy."

He turned to look at me again and his face lit up like Christmas when he saw I wasn't stringing him along.

He held out his hand. "Call me Jimmy."

***

I did roping, mostly, on the team, and some bronc riding. A few afternoons showed me Little Jimmy wouldn't learn to rope that semester, maybe not that lifetime. But as a beginning bronc rider, he wasn't bad. He was stronger than you'd think for a skinny kid and he had a natural rhythm for the ride. I tried him out in a few local rodeos. He insisted on using what he called his alias, although I couldn't for the life of me figure out how his mother would ever hear about it.

"Try not to talk any more than you have to," I told him. "That accent of yours is bad enough, but if this crowd thinks you're a Muslim, they'll go crazy. If anyone talks to you, say '*no hablo ingles.*'"

"What if they talk to me in Spanish?"

"There was a cowboy on the circuit once from a town called Iraan." I said it the right way -- Ira-ann. "When he was announced, they nearly booed him out of the arena. Thought he was Iranian."

"I certainly do not want anyone to think I am Iranian," Little Jimmy said.

He went by Jimmy from Karachi. Pakistan wasn't in the news much then and nobody knew where Karachi was. The unfamiliar name and his brown skin and me hanging out with him made everyone think he was Indian, too, in spite of the hair on his upper lip. With a kidnapped white girl or two in my family tree, even I sported a stringy mustache.

In a quiet way, Little Jimmy was popular at the rodeos -- a polite, nice-looking kid who kept to himself. Always sober. The day he stayed on a bronc for seven seconds, everybody applauded. They knew applause was all he'd get. It takes eight seconds to win.

***

The Sunday morning things started to go bad, I had slipped out of church craving some hair of the dog. I should have realized the church door had opened when I heard the swell of the hymn.

He wore a purple robe,
He wore a purple robe,
My Lord wore a purple robe.

168

EIGHT SECONDS

Then the door shut and Ma yanked the flask from my mouth and smashed it against the cracked dirt of the yard.

Coach washed his hands of me that afternoon.

"You're a bright kid, Jimmy. I'd hate to see you have to slink back to the rez. But if I smell whiskey on your breath at a meet again, you're off the team. And you can kiss your scholarship goodbye."

I took a gulp for luck from a fresh bottle as soon as he turned his back.

By the time they called my event, I couldn't find my gloves, but I was past worrying about a few rope burns. I pulled on my black hat with the feather in its band and swaggered out for team roping. I was the header. My sorrel parked himself next to the chute where a white-faced steer snorted, ready to jump as fast as the gate opened. The heeler was already in place. He gave me a measuring look across the steer's back.

The steer broke from the chute, the sorrel close to his shoulder, the heeler's horse at his flank. A loop blossomed at the end of my rope, hanging in the air for an instant. Through the loop, like a frame, I saw Ma's face in the stands.

The loop dropped over the steer's horns, the rope's free end hissing through my fingers. I dallied up, throwing the rope around the saddle horn. My eyes never left the steer. I didn't even feel the rope burn. The big whiteface stopped with a jerk, my saddle creaking as he hit the rope end. The next instant, the heeler's loop caught the steer's back hooves as they left the dirt. I glanced at the board, loosening my rope to let the steer up. We'd made great time, nearly a second faster than our closest competition. The heeler flashed me a grin and raised his hand for a high-five.

I thought at first my fist must be cramped from the speed of the dallying, because I couldn't see all the fingers. From the stands, somebody screamed and I wondered why Ma was crying when I'd done so well. Then I saw what she saw -- no, understood what I'd seen but hadn't believed.

Where two of my fingers should have been there was only spikes of bone poking from blue-white stumps. The rope loop I'd dallied so fast was still twisted tight into my skin, the loop that had popped off my fingers with all the weight of the steer thrown against it. I couldn't look away from the sight of that hand, even when I heard Ma and Little Jimmy beside me. I tried to dismount, wedging the heel of my numbed hand against the saddle, leaning on Little Jimmy. And then I fell into Ma's arms.

***

A couple of weeks later Little Jimmy sat watching me determined to roll a smoke. My bandages had just come off and the stitched-down flaps of skin on the missing finger ends had healed over, pink and shiny. They itched like crazy.

Little Jimmy had searched the arena for my lost fingers, thinking they could be sewn back on. But the sorrel had trampled them with backing up to keep the rope tight, and by the time Little Jimmy picked the fingers out of the dirt, they were too far gone to be reattached, even if the doctor had been willing.

Fingers or not, if I couldn't qualify for another event soon, I was off the team with my scholarship forfeited.

"Let me ride for you," Little Jimmy said.

I thought I hadn't heard right.

"Not roping," he said. "Bronc riding."

I licked the edge of a cigarette paper, considering. It was crazy. But we were the same size, and with my feathered hat pulled down to his mustache and with the right horse. . .

***

Sunny was seventeen hands tall, and heavy, the biggest bronc in the college's string. His ears flattened and he twisted his rear end toward me. But he was only a bad actor because he was old and hurt so bad, a worn-out riding stable horse. Being on the bronc string was his last stop before *adios* to a Mexican slaughterhouse. The best riders hated drawing him. With his arthritis, he could hardly give much of a show. I didn't expect him to have too much fight for Little Jimmy to deal with. And nobody would be surprised about me riding Sunny, thinking I needed an easy qualifier while my hand healed.

I led Sunny and the sorrel who'd be my pick up horse to the arena the night we practiced. I put on Sunny's rigging, pissed that Little Jimmy wasn't there to help, loaded the old bronc in the chute and took a snort to stop the ghosts of my lost fingers from howling. I'd switched to vodka -- less smell on the breath -- after Coach's tirade. The drink and the pain pills from the school clinic made me dopey as I leaned over the chute, looking at Sunny. He stood a hand and a half taller than my sorrel and weighed three hundred pounds more. He looked as big as an elephant.

"What took you so long?" I asked when Little Jimmy showed up.

He ignored me, climbing onto Sunny and fussing with his rigging.

"What the hell are you doing?" He wasn't just rosining his glove. He was tying the glove to the rigging -- a suicide wrap.

"That shit's just for crazy bull riders."

In the moonlight, Little Jimmy looked pale for a kid with a brown face. "I'm not coming off this horse until my eight seconds are up."

"It's your funeral." Then I threw the gate open, my stopwatch ticking, and scrambled onto the sorrel.

Little Jimmy made a beautiful ride -- laying back on Sunny, his spurs raking the old bronc high and handsome, one hand in the rigging, the other waving to God. He was still on top eight seconds later.

I reined the sorrel close for the pickup. Little Jimmy clapped his free hand onto the rigging and tried to jerk his other hand from its hold. Horror spread over his face.

"Pull out of the glove!" I leaned back to undo Sunny's flank strap.

Little Jimmy panicked and jumped for me, still tied to Sunny like he was. He fell, pulling the rigging loose. It slipped halfway down Sunny's side. Little Jimmy held out his hand for me and I reached out to catch him, touching the fingertips of his glove, feeling them slip through my three-fingered hand. I couldn't look in his eyes. Then he dropped between my horse and Sunny.

Sunny screamed in fear at the swaying weight dragging on his side, at Little Jimmy's leg flailing against his flank. I grabbed Sunny's neck rope, but he wasn't thinking like a tired old bronc, glad to get his chore over with. He was twelve hundred pounds of mindless terror.

I heard a crack as Sunny's hooves hit Little Jimmy and I screamed with Sunny, but Little Jimmy was past screaming.

Somebody flipped the lights on. The arena was full of people running. A shot echoed and Sunny collapsed onto the sorrel and me, and onto Little Jimmy.

Eight Seconds

"Where am I?" was the first thing I said. And when some stranger's voice said the hospital, "Oh, God, where's Little Jimmy?"

"Your friend?" a nurse asked.

She wore a starched white cap, and she was young, too green to know how to give bad news.

"I'm afraid your friend is dead." There was blood everywhere, even on the nurse. Underneath, her face was the color of her cap.

"I got to see him -- I got to tell him -- " I grabbed the neck of her uniform, seeing my hand, the stitches torn open and oozing blood again, like it belonged to somebody else.

Her mouth worked. "You don't want to see him. It's not -- there's not --" And then she puked all over the gurney.

A man stepped up and hauled her away.

"Your name?" He flipped through a clipboard.

"I'm Jimmy." I stopped, thinking of Little Jimmy's scholarship, and the one I'd lost. "Jilani Farouk, that is. Jimmy's my nickname. My full name is Ghulam Jilani Farouk. I'm a student at Vista College."

***

Everybody at the college understood how I felt. They handled the paperwork for my transfer through the mail, knowing I didn't want to see anybody while I recovered from my grief and the injuries I'd got trying to save the life of my friend Jimmy Kotay. In spite of the rumors that ran wild after the accident, the autopsy on Big Jimmy didn't show a drop of alcohol in his blood. Lucky the coroner didn't know the body he looked at should have been short a couple of fingers.

I hated that they put Sunny down. But it was for the best. He hurt so bad. And I told myself it was for the best that I'd changed places with Little Jimmy. His scholarship put me through college and medical school.

I felt bad for Ma, but worse for Little Jimmy's mother. At least Ma's dream had come true, even if she didn't know it. And she was sure her son was safe in the arms of Jesus and that he hadn't died drunk. But Mrs. Farouk . . . I wire her money anonymously every year, like I do for Ma. Lately I've thought Mrs. Farouk must be getting pretty old. Maybe she's even dead and someone else takes the money in her name. I can't afford to ask.

I stood in the front hall with the obituary clipping in my hand. The next thing I knew, my wife -- my nice, blonde-haired wife -- leaned over my shoulder, smelling like Chanel and the spearmint gum she chews since she broke her cigarette habit.

"What is it, honey? Is that the family of your Indian friend, the one from college? And they remembered you after all this time? How sweet."

I couldn't say anything, but it wasn't just from shock at reading the news of Ma's death. It was from seeing the secret I'd never told anyone, the secret I'd left everybody I loved for, set down in black and white.

Somewhere in this big city I'd fled to, someone had learned the truth. Somebody I'd passed on the street, somebody in the crowd smoking by the stairwell after an AA meeting, knew me. Or somebody in the stream of patients at the county hospital where I worked had seen that the name on my ID badge didn't match my Kiowa face. Somebody had dug deep enough to find that pauper's grave in Vista with its ten-fingered skeleton. And next to the printed list of Ma's family on the obituary, they'd penciled in the name of another survivor -- Jimmy Kotay.

MELISSA EMBRY is a former small-town journalist now living in Dallas, Texas. Her short fiction has appeared or is scheduled to appear in *Mystic Signals*, *Pulp Empire*, and *Short-story.me*. She thanks ex-rodeo cowboy Lynn Yaklin for sharing his knowledge of suicide wraps and dallying (in the rodeo sense) but any errors are purely her own damn fault. When not writing, she volunteers at Equest, a nonprofit stable that provides therapy through horsemanship to disabled children and adults.

THE MYSTERY OF FIRE OPAL MINE

R.L. Coffield

(First Printed in the Award-Winning Map of Murder, *published by Red Coyote Press, 2007)*

Tom sat astride his horse studying the bloated carcass before him. The dead body stunk and Who-Dat, Tom's mount, clearly did not like the smell of death.

"Easy boy. Take it easy." Tom dismounted, held Who-Dat's reins tightly, and squatted to get a better look at the man on the ground. Though swollen almost beyond recognition, Tom could still identify the corpse as Henry Blackwell, a prospector and drifter from the Wickenburg area who, by the looks of it, was caught in the current of death. There was an oddity about the corpse, however, and it took Tom a moment to recognize the horror of it. Henry Blackwell's eyes were missing. Not pecked out by buzzards. Not eaten out by ants. They were neatly excised as though a surgeon had removed both of the old man's rheumy orbs.

"I'll be," was all Tom commented as he straightened and reluctantly set about stacking stones on the body. He had no shovel to dig Blackwell a regular grave, but this would help protect the man from predators…at least for awhile. Tom would mark the grave and report the death to the authorities in Wickenburg when he got there. It wasn't a proper Christian burial, but Tom figured it was the least he could do for the harmless, homeless old prospector.

Tom's meeting with the sheriff two days later did not bode well. "That's about the fifth or sixth body this last coupla' years that's been reported," growled Sheriff Ben Branson. Stern by nature, and now irritated about the report he knew he was going to have to make, Branson tried to dismiss Tom with a curt nod.

"It's getting out of hand!" The deputy muttered as Tom stood up to leave. "We oughta go out there and just shut that mine down!"

Tom stopped. "What mine are you talking about?"

"The old Hickman mine," the deputy gabbed on despite the sheriff's warning look.

"What's wrong with it?" Tom queried.

"You got a personal interest in it, mister?" Ben Branson demanded.

"You could say that. My partner just won that mine in a poker game in Tombstone. I'm headin' out there to take supplies. I'm supposed to meet him there."

Both the sheriff and deputy exchanged knowing glances. Neither spoke for a few seconds. Branson studied Tom over his half-rim glasses, leaned back in his chair, and stretched his long legs. "Hmmph."

"If there's a problem, I'd like to know. I'd like to be prepared."

"Don't rightly know. For sure anyway. All I know is that there's a record of dead, eyeless bodies that goes back a good thirty years or more. Ever since Hickman bought the rights to that mine forty some years ago there's been trouble...beginning with him."

"So...you're saying what exactly?"

"I ain't sayin' nothing for certain. All I'm sayin' is dead, blind bodies show up now and then. Be careful is all I'm sayin'."

Tom ambled down the dusty Wickenburg street, anxiously hoping to hear the unmistakable sound of his partner's voice from behind every establishment's saloon doors. He knew there was more to this saga than the sheriff was letting on, for he'd heard stories on his trip north, stories about the Fire Opal Mine and its previous owners found dead in the Arizona desert, all of them missing their eyes, stories that made him regret his agreement to meet up his long time partner, Jake Starr. It was unsettling, plain and simple, so Tom stopped at the Old Miner Saloon to have a beer or two to distract himself from his worrisome ways. He entered, still hoping he'd see Jake sitting there telling his tall tales to anyone who was within ear shot, but he was disappointed.

"Damn you, Starr. Where are you?" Tom mumbled to himself as he downed his first brew. Maybe he's at the mine already, he absently thought. "I'll head that way tomorrow. Early." Whether he left early or late made no difference, he decided, as he downed his fifth beer. It was still going to be a three-day, hard, hot ride.

***

The old man sat cross legged in front of his fire staring into its orange-red depths. He hummed in a shaky voice, repeating the same three note melody endlessly. His face, lined with decades of solitary desert living, was dour and stern. Twenty feet away, squirming against the leather straps binding him, the new and currently regretful owner of the Fire Opal Mine struggled. Jake had won the mine in a poker hand, and now he was forswearing his gambling days. Even at the time it had bothered him how readily his opponent had laid the deed to his newly inherited mine on the green felt table. Jake now fully loathed his poker playing habit and promised himself if he got out of this alive he'd mend his ways. Jake had mended regularly throughout his life, but never had he been so earnest about it.

The straps binding him seemed to grow tighter the more he struggled. Damn it all, he was in a fine mess, he thought to himself as he characteristically tried to downplay the seriousness of his situation. Where the hell was Tom? Tom was his only chance over this lunatic who'd been singing the same damn tune for two days now.

"Hey! Do you speak?" Jake demanded during a hopeful lull in the old man's humming. "Hello? You know, I think we got off on the wrong foot here. I'm sorry if I intruded, but I do own the deed to this here mine."

Jake could tell the old buzzard understood, yet the miner refused to respond. Instead the aged coot began to slowly rotate a knife on a whetstone, his humming growing momentarily louder each time the revolutions of the knife came full circle.

"Come on, Tom. I don't have all day!" Jake gritted through clenched teeth.

The miner went by the name of Gunner. He couldn't truthfully recall his last name. He'd just been called Gunner ever since he could remember. He'd been working the mine now for nigh on to forty-seven years. It belonged to him, and damned if he was gonna let these upstarts come in and take what was rightfully his. As he sharpened the knife to cut out Jake Starr's eyes, he began a low cackle and chant. "Gotta blind 'em. Gotta blind 'em so they can't find their way back. They'd all tell if they could. Not my fault they die. Desert does that. Not my fault. Not my fault. I only blind 'em." He continued his little incantation for some time, lost in reverie and the fire's warmth. How many men had he blinded and set loose in the desert over the years? Hmmmm. Many. Many came and tried to chase him off, claiming the mine was theirs, but the mine belonged to him. The gold and silver were his. Especially the fire opals were his.

And now, this struggling man would be the next to be blinded and led into the desert. Gunner noted that the stranger acted a bit differently than the others . He wasn't begging and pleading for his life. Yet. They all did in the end though. They all acted almost thankful after he cut their eyes out, put them on the mule, and took them into the desert. Thankful, that is, until he pushed them out of the saddle and they heard him leading the mule away. They always screamed, cursed, and cried. "Not my fault. Not my fault," he quietly crooned.

***

Jake could not quit squirming even though the leather cords felt tighter. He had to do something. He was a good talker who'd talked his way out of a peck of trouble in his time. He'd give it another try.

"Hey, mister. I see you got a patch on your eye. What happened? I'm an eye doc, you know. Maybe I could fix it for ya." Jake grimaced at the blatant lameness of his ridiculous fib.

Gunner smiled maliciously, showing the decaying, yellowed three teeth remaining in his grizzled head. He slowly turned, his one good eye alert and excited. He carefully stood and hobbled over to the tied man. "Wanna see?" With that he raised the patch, and Jake found himself staring at the reddest bulging object imaginable.

"What the hell!" he exclaimed as he tried to pull himself away from the monstrous looking, fiery red eyeball.

Gunner cackled again, clearly enjoying the response. "It's an opal. A fire opal. I put it in there after I lost my eye in the fight." He began to hobble away but turned suddenly and added, "I can see the future, you know. Fire opals do that, and your future don't look none too good right now." He laughed again as he touched the stone with the point of his knife. "See? It don't hurt at all. Yours won't either. After a while."

***

It was a long, hot ride to the mine. Tom Corcoran found himself thinking of Oregon where he'd been born and reared 'til he was seventeen, and found himself wishing he was back in the tall, cool fir forests. He wasn't quite sure how Starr had talked him into this, but in for a dime -- in for a dollar. Something like that. Somehow the years had passed and he and Jake were still riding the west, driving cattle here, mining there, all in all just pretty much drifting through the decades. This was going to be his last stake, Tom vowed silently. He'd seen a lot of land north of Wickenburg that had reminded him a bit of home. Tall pines towered only two days away. He'd head there and become a rancher. Maybe he could find that little Becky girl he'd seen that day in the mercantile, marry her and have a family.

He also could not stop thinking about the stories he'd heard around town about the dead men found in the desert with their eyes missing. Most people began the story the same, but the endings and explanations were varied. Everyone agreed that Joshua Hickman had arrived about forty-five to fifty years ago and filed a claim for a mine northwest of town. He and a tagalong named Gunner had gone out. Nobody thought about them until two bodies were found pretty well scavenged. One was identifiable as Joshua Hickman, and the other was assumed to have been his partner, Gunner.

From this point on, everybody's theories diverged. Some said renegade Indians were doing the killing, especially an old Indian named Eyes of Fire who'd lost his whole family in the area at the hands of gold rushers. Others said the men got scared into the desert by ghosts screaming through the canyons, caves and gullies, that what they saw scared them so much they tore their own eyes out. A few thought the miners had gone mad from drinking bad cactus water and desecrated themselves. But no one wanted to venture out to the mine to find out. The ride was hard, hot, and long. They were scared, too.

Distracted by his thoughts, it was some minutes before Tom realized he was almost on top of the mine and hearing someone calling to him. "Tom! Tom!" The distinctly weak voice trailed off. What he saw next startled him badly.

An old derelict stood motionless in front of a dead fire with a brilliant red eye bulging obscenely and a bloody knife in his open hand. Quickly Tom glanced around for Jake, knowing well the owner of the voice he'd heard, even in its weakness. Twenty feet away Jake sat, his head lolling forward, arms tightly secured around a stake behind him.

"Hey, Buddy, you okay?" Tom called. Both Jake and the old man remained dead still.

"You just get on down off that horse, mister. Real slow. Don't try no fancy stuff 'cause I'm good with a knife. Ask yer friend there."

Every fiber in Tom's body screamed at him to turn tail and run, but he found himself frozen, and so he continued to sit mutely on top of Who-Dat.

"When you people gonna git it through your damn heads? This is my mine. Don't make no difference you come here with paper and all sayin' it's yourn. It's mine. Now I got t'deal with you too. Come on, now. Dismount."

Tom had an advantage here, he kept telling himself. He was mounted, he was far enough away that he doubted the old man could lunge and grab him, and he was substantially younger.

"Who are you?" Tom found himself demanding.

"Name's Gunner."

"Gunner?" Tom paused, his eyes widening in surprise. "*Gunner?* I thought you died a long time ago. You and Mr. Hickman. In the desert."

"Nah. That weren't me. That was some fancy man come ridin' in. Hickman told me the stranger was gonna take my place. Had capital, Hickman said. The bastard knifed me in the eye when we got into a fight. I fixed 'em though." Gunner began snickering. "Fixed 'em good, didn't I?"

"Gunner, you got to let this man go. He's not going to hurt you. He's gonna leave you alone. He's gotta go with me."

"Oh, he's goin' alright. Just like the others. I'm gonna lead him into the desert and let him find his own way. Not gonna hurt him anymore." Gunner paused, "You feelin' a bit better now, Jake?" He glanced towards the bound man, then he turned back to Tom. "You git on down now, like I told you."

"That's not going to happen, Gunner. I'm going to ride on over and untie that man. I'm going to take him with me. We're going away. You just stand still, Gunner. I don't want to hurt you." Tom deeply regretted that his gun was, as usual, in his saddlebag. He'd have to kick his own ass for this after Jake kicked it for him first.

"What about him?" Gunner asked, nodding.

184

"He's not going to hurt you either, Gunner. I'm going to take him with me. He doesn't want your mine. He just made a mistake."

"No. I mean him…the guy behind you," Gunner now shifted his good eye and looked beyond Tom and the pack horse.

Involuntarily Tom whirled Who-Dat about. There was no one there, only an excruciating pain in the middle of his back where the knife imbedded.

"Not my fault. Not my fault."

BECKY'S information is on page 56.

HOSTAGE TO FORTUNE

Simon Lake

(Finalist 2009 Cowboy Up Contest)

Bunk Tatum woke to the sound of footsteps. He blinked open his eyes and found the muzzle of a six-shooter pointed at his head.

"Steady now. Don't go making no sudden moves."

Bunk tried to focus. His head throbbed and his vision was blurred. The wound in his side felt like someone was poking him with a branding iron.

"Don't reckon I'm up to doing anything sudden," he croaked.

The stranger knelt beside Bunk, peering into his face. He holstered the gun and took a silver dollar from his pocket. It glinted in the dim light of the cave. He spun the coin and then nodded at Bunk.

"Okay, wait here."

Bunk struggled to remain conscious. The events of the morning came back to him in flashes. The ambush of his men; outnumbered, gunned down or forced to flee. Cattle lost. His own attempts to fight back. If he closed his eyes he could still see the face of his attacker. Sunburnt skin but pale eyes. A crooked nose and a scar on his left cheek. Bunk hadn't even had time to draw his gun before the other man had been on top of him.

The rest, his escape into the mountains and the shelter of the cave, had the blurred quality of a dream.

The stranger returned with a canteen of water and placed it to

Bunk's lips, raising his head so the liquid would go down more easily. "Here. Reckon you need some of this."

Bunk swallowed, almost choked and then gratefully allowed himself to drink some more.

"Thanks," he said at last when he'd taken all he could.

"You ain't looking too good."

"Neither would you if you'd been shot."

The stranger pointed to a patch of dried blood below Bunk's ribs. "I'm gonna take that shirt off and get a better look."

He nodded reluctantly. For a moment he thought he would pass out from the pain. He felt a hand touch his side, gently probing around the edge of the wound.

"How's it looking?"

"I got good news for you. That's a clean wound you got there. Seems the bullet only grazed the side of your chest."

The stranger ripped a piece from Bunk's shirt, soaked it in water and then worked at cleaning out the wound. Bunk winced, holding his breath and then letting it out slowly.

"Easy now. You'll heal just fine. I guess you got lucky."

"Yeah, sure. I'm feeling real lucky today."

The stranger backed away into the corner of the cave. For the first time, Bunk studied him more closely. He was tall and thin, rangy, unshaven, and with a mess of straggly black hair. Take away that stubble and he probably wouldn't look much more than eighteen. Maybe younger. There was something odd about the coin he carried too, the way he kept fingering it like it was some kind of charm.

"What's that?" Bunk asked.

"Huh?" The other man stared down at the coin, as if surprised to find it there. "My lucky piece. When I spun it earlier the liberty side was showing. The coin told me I ought to help you."

188

"And if you'd got the eagle?"

"I probably would've shot you." His voice betrayed no emotion. "There's a lot of dangerous men in these parts. Showing mercy can sometimes land you in big trouble."

Bunk shook his head. *How could you decide whether to trust a man on the toss of a coin?* "What's your name, stranger?"

"Ash."

"I'm Bunk. Bunk Tatum. I head up the Bar Q."

He told Ash how he'd been ambushed on the trail back to Alta. "I lost four good men and a couple thousand head of cattle."

The younger man nodded. "It's like I told you, there's a lot of dangerous men in these parts."

Bunk looked around the cave. There wasn't much to see. A blanket roll. Some basic cooking implements. "You been living here long?"

"A while."

"Seems a strange life for a young man."

"I do alright for myself."

"Things must be pretty basic out here."

"The less you own, the less you have to lose."

Bunk supposed there might be something in that. He'd lost a lot today, that was for sure. Not everything though. He wondered what had happened to his horse. He tried getting up. The pain in his gut made him wince and he had to sit back down again.

"You should take it easy for a while."

"I need to check on my horse. Without her I might never get home."

Ash smiled. "She's fine. I got her tied up for you. Found her some food to keep her happy."

"I guess I owe you."

"It's okay. You don't owe me anything."

"If you fancy a job, I could use a hand down at the Bar Q. Especially on account of the men I lost today."

"That's very good of you, but I'm happy with the life I got here."

Bunk looked hard into the other's face. It didn't seem like much of a life, but maybe he was laying low for a reason. Plenty of people fell foul of the law in these parts and chose to stay out of sight. Yet Ash struck him as a regular fellow, apart from this strange obsession with the coin.

"Tell me about that lucky piece. How come you depend on it so much?"

Ash fingered the coin. "I got it from a storekeeper in Utah. Stole it, I suppose I ought to say. You see, I was orphaned at a young age and life was pretty hard. I fell in with a bad crowd. These two brothers, Jack and Rye Bolas, took me on to work for them. They were con men. I'd scout out places or act as a decoy when they wanted to pull off a job. There's a lot you can get away with when you're small.

"They looked after me though, and that's the truth. I guess when I got older these things didn't always sit right, but that was pretty much the only life I'd known."

For a moment Ash was silent. "That storekeeper, he'd have done okay if he'd let them take what they came for. Maybe he figured if he toughed it out things would work out better. The brothers weren't much to look at, but Rye could be mean when he needed to. The storekeeper exchanged a few words and then he moved on Jack. The way I saw it, he may have been packing a weapon or maybe not. Rye wasn't taking no chances though and he gunned him down on the spot. The crazy thing is, for all the man's actions, there weren't nothing in the register to protect but a single silver dollar."

He studied the coin, looked up again. "Well the heat was on after that killing and Jack and Rye were fixing to make their escape across the border to Mexico. I didn't know whether to follow 'em or head out on my own. In the end I got so tied up over what to do, I decided to throw the coin and let it choose for me. That's how I ended up traveling west. Later I heard the Bolas brothers got gunned down by rangers outside Winslow. Seems like my luck changed from that day. Now I just--"

Ash stopped abruptly. Bunk could hear something moving outside.

"What's that?"

"Shh." Ash put a finger to his lips. He moved to the side of the cave, keeping himself hidden in the shadows. Bunk crawled across to join him. Two men came past on horseback. He couldn't see the first one, but he got a clear view of the second. Dark hair. Crooked nose. Scar on the left cheek.

"I know that man," Bunk whispered, his gun drawn.

"Wait." Ash pushed him back from the cave entrance. Bunk winced at the pain. He crouched down until he could get his breath back. Ash seemed more interested in his coin than in watching the outlaws. He tossed it, caught it and flipped it over in one practiced motion.

Bunk made another move for the entrance, but Ash was there to stop him. "Let them go."

"Like hell I will," he hissed. "They took my cattle. Killed my men."

Ash knocked the gun from his hand. "Let them go. The coin says to."

Bunk looked at him in disbelief. "You're crazy."

"There's nothing crazy about wanting to stay alive."

"There was two of 'em and two of us and we had the element of surprise. I'd take those odds any day of the week."

"It's getting dark out there. You're injured and I've got no horse. There's probably others following on behind those two. I'd say that's some gamble."

"I won't let those men get away. They're thieves and murderers."

"They'll get what they deserve, if not today then tomorrow or sometime soon enough."

Bunk spat at the ground in frustration. "Is that your philosophy? Sounds to me like the kind of hokum you get from a frontier preacher."

Ash did not appear to take offence at the remark. "I'm just telling you how these things are."

He laughed sourly. "You're too young. You still got a lot to learn."

"I do alright for myself."

Bunk grabbed the silver dollar from his hand. "Maybe you just got lucky so far." He tossed the coin, caught it, smiled. "One day your luck's likely to run out."

Ash snatched back the coin. "That piece ain't ever let me down."

"It put you in this cave in the middle of nowhere. If it wants to, maybe it can keep you here the rest of your life. Is that what you really want?"

Ash remained silent.

"I might die tomorrow, but at least I know I'm living the life I chose to. People headed out west because they wanted the freedom to forge their own destiny. Why'd you want some other man telling you how to live your life, let alone a stupid piece of metal?"

Ash looked at him, hurt showing in his eyes. When he spoke again his voice had lost some of its earlier defiance.

"I'm bunking down for the night. Don't let me stop you if you want to go hunting for revenge out there in the dark."

Bunk went to pick up his gun. He was almost mad enough to try it, but not quite.

**

He must've slept the best part of twelve hours. When he woke, his body was stiff and sore but he felt stronger than he had the night before. Sunlight slanted in at the edges of the cave. He looked for Ash. The cave appeared to be empty. The blanket roll and the cooking pot were gone. He kicked around the spot where they'd been, but no trace of anything remained.

How d'you like that? The kid just lit out on me.

Bunk walked outside to find his horse. The important thing was to make it back to the Bar Q in daylight. He stopped to take a last look at the cave. Something glinted in the sunlight, catching his eye. He bent down to get a closer look. It was the silver dollar. He grinned. *Figure I did the kid a favor. He's smart enough to make a life for himself without any piece of metal telling him what to do.*

Bunk made to get on his horse and then went back to scoop up the coin. Surely it wouldn't do any harm to carry a bit of luck on his side for a while?

SIMON LAKE lives in the wild, wild west of Cornwall, England! *Hostage to Fortune* is his first published Western story, but he has had other short fiction featured in *Cadenza* magazine and *Pulp.net* as well as in the Leaf Books' anthology *The Better Craftsmen*. Aside from being a writer, he is also a musician and presenter of the weekly online music show *Radio of the Second Dimension.*

ALL THE WATER YOU WANT

Jerry Guin

(Finalist 2010 Cowboy Up Short Story Contest)

The sun had just dipped below the desert horizon. Nocturnal creatures, under the cloak of coming darkness, would now leave the safety of their dens to scour for food and water. For humans, it was the time of day to open doors and windows, an invitation for the coolness of the evening to invade every corner and chase away the stifling heat of the day. It was a time for rest and reflection of the day's activities.

The hacienda that Colonel Benjamin Buffington had just moved into was situated a few miles outside Lordsburg in the shadow of the Pyramid Mountains. He had purchased the place from Avery Studdard, the lawyer and executor of the estate of the late Don Diego Santos. It was a well-built adobe with walls eight inches thick, purposely engineered so one could enjoy the cavern-like interior in relative comfort, despite the intolerable heat of a summer day.

Everything remained just the way Don Diego had left it before his untimely demise. Don Diego, a solitary man of about sixty, had no known relatives, so the place had sat dormant. That is until Avery Studdard mentioned it to Colonel Buffington at a luncheon in Las Cruces. Avery Studdard knew the colonel was a land speculator and had the money to pay if a deal could be struck. The lawyer, eager to sell the little rancho and collect his commissions, made quick talk telling Colonel Buffington how Don Diego Santos had died as the result of injuries received in a carriage accident. He soon turned the conversation to the assets of the property, and the Colonel became intrigued when Avery said there was water available year round on the premises. Water in the desert is an invaluable commodity to a land speculator.

"With water being there, one might consider locating a way station for travelers," Avery had suggested.

The following week, Colonel Buffington journeyed to Lordsburg to meet with Studdard. The lawyer had made arrangements for the Colonel and himself to survey the property the next morning. They rode out to the vacated rancho on a mild August morning, before the heat of the day began. Avery Studdard guided the team past the adobe hacienda, then tugged at the reins to stop the carriage next to the well. Studdard knew the sale depended on the water. He drew a full bucket from the well's depths then gleefully handed Colonel Buffington a gourd dipper that hung nearby. "Didn't I tell you so?" Avery gleamed.

Colonel Buffington drank his fill then handed the dipper back to Avery. "I'd like to see the house and barn now," he said. They soon struck a deal and Colonel Buffington moved in for a temporary stay.

"I want to get a feel for the place and to see what else it has to offer besides water," Colonel Buffington stated.

***

The Colonel was enjoying a cool drink and looking over some of Don Diego's papers in the study when a knock sounded at the front door. At first it was a light knock, almost inaudible, then it intensified. Colonel Buffington looked up from his reading. He wondered why Maria, his newly hired housekeeper, had not answered the knocking.

"Maria!" he called in a tone of irritation. He leaned his head to one side in an effort to listen for her reply over the now incessant pounding at the door.

Maria appeared in the doorway of the study. "I am sorry, Señor Buffington. I was upstairs opening the windows." Maria hurried toward the front of the adobe. It had only been a day since Colonel Buffington had moved in and hired Maria to handle the household chores. When he'd interviewed her for the job, he had instructed her to address him as Colonel. He mentally noted that he would need to remind her of his title…again.

Benjamin Buffington, a short, cocky man of about fifty with thinning, gray-streaked hair, always dressed in a suit and tie whenever he ventured into the public eye. At all times he kept his back straight in an air of authority. Though he had no military background, he had adopted the title of Colonel at the close of the Civil War because he felt it gave him greater stature. Overbearing and used to giving orders and having those orders carried out without argument, he was cold and indifferent, ready to make a fuss over any incidental trifle in order to get things done the way he wanted. He'd never married. No woman, at least the few that knew him, had ever moved him to that kind of relationship.

The noise out front ceased. In its place muffled voices were barely audible. Soon Maria returned to the doorway. She stood quietly until the Colonel acknowledged her presence. Colonel Buffington did not look up, but merely said, "Yes?"

"It is Juanita Morales, Señor Buff- Colonel," she quickly corrected. "She wishes to speak to you."

Colonel Buffington glanced up. "About what?" he asked.

Maria nervously wrung her hands while talking. "She would like some water."

Colonel Buffington stared at Maria with a look of incredulity. "So give her a drink," he said in a matter-of-fact tone.

Maria shifted her stance as if to be ready to move quickly, for she feared her new employer and his demanding, gruff way. "She wishes for much water for her animals, Señor Colonel," Maria blurted.

Colonel Buffington rose to his feet and said, "That is out of the question, but I will speak to her." He strode past Maria and headed to the front door, figuring to set this person straight before it went any further. The availability of water was the reason he had bought the place, and he intended to preserve the precious liquid.

The well was actually an underground spring. From above ground, the outside casing, rounded and roofed, looked like any other well. Inside the casing was a hole about four feet in diameter. A few feet down, the hole opened into a larger cavern with solid rock walls. Seventy-five feet down water pooled, fed by an underground spring that seeped from the mountains a few miles away.

Don Diego Santos had discovered an oasis to build his estate on. He'd built his hacienda nearby and had positioned the barn and corral near the well.

Maria stood in the hallway, a few feet behind the colonel. She listened as Juanita introduced herself.

"My name is Juanita Morales. I live at the next rancho a few miles distance." She pointed in the direction where the sun had set. "I came for water, like I always do, and found that someone has removed the rope and bucket from the well," she said.

Colonel Buffington listened to the woman and could see behind her a team of four mules, attached to an open wagon loaded with four barrels.

"I removed the bucket," he said. "I saw the tracks of someone near the well. I figured that they had been helping themselves, so I took the rope and bucket away." Juanita stood silently listening. The Colonel continued, "It's been said that a man can live without food for forty days, but he can only live a few days, perhaps mere hours, without water. Out here," he paused and swung his arm around the horizon, "the water is too precious to waste."

Juanita Morales was visibly taken aback. "Señor, the water would not be wasted. It is for my thirsty goats and mules. They will die without water," she implored. When she did not get an immediate response to her plea, she continued, "I have been getting the water from the well for many years, but only in the season of the hot sun. Señor, Don Diego Santos allowed me to freely take the water that I needed. He only asked that I wait a few days for the pool to refill before taking more, and I have always done that. Don Diego has been gone for a long time and I still only take the amount that my animals require."

Colonel Buffington waited until he was sure the woman had finished before he spoke. "Things have changed since Don Diego Santos lived here. I own the property now, so you cannot have all the water you want. I was told that Don Diego had only two horses and a milk cow. I intend to have more animals than that. As many animals as the well will allow. So you see, I will need all the water for myself."

Juanita stood listening intently. Perhaps another chance to persuade would come.

The colonel continued, "A thirsty horse or cow will drink twenty gallons of water every day if you allow them the luxury." He paused briefly then spoke again. "Those same animals can get by nicely on five gallons a day if properly trained and not worked hard in the heat."

It seemed he was finished and Juanita was about to say something when the Colonel said in finality, "You may fill one barrel -- that should do you for a long time. Maria will accompany you to the well."

Astounded, Juanita Morales spoke quickly, "That will not do, Señor! I have to have more than that!"

The Colonel, not used to anyone talking back to him, grew instantly infuriated. His brow furrowed and his jaws clenched. When he turned to face Juanita, she could see the contempt in his flushed face and eyes. Intimidated, she reacted by taking a step backwards.

Colonel Buffington pointed an index finger at Juanita and commanded in a low voice, "Madam, you need to train your animals to use less water, then find another source to provide your needs!" he exclaimed.

"My husband will not be pleased!" Juanita flamed.

Colonel Buffington retorted, "Well, pleased or not, you send him to me and I'll see to it that he understands!"

Colonel Buffington turned his back to Juanita Morales then strode past Maria to the study. Maria waited until the door to the study closed before she went to assist Juanita Morales.

The two women struggled, in lantern light, to lean over the well casing and re-thread the rope in the pulley. It took the better part of an hour for Juanita and Maria to draw the water up the

200

well, one bucket at a time, and fill one barrel. When they had finished, they put the rope and bucket back in the barn and Juanita mounted the wagon seat to leave. She spoke more to herself than to Maria, "My animals will need more water than this. They will die if they don't get more in a day or so."

Maria tried to console her. "I will speak to the Colonel."

When Maria returned to the adobe, Colonel Buffington summoned her. "If you see anyone around that well, be sure you let me know immediately. Do you understand?"

Maria nodded, "Yes, yes of course, Señor Colonel. Juanita wishes for only enough water to preserve her animals through the hot season."

"I have given her a barrel full. That's all she gets," the Colonel replied. "Things are not what they used to be. She could have bought the place long before I even knew it was for sale. Then she could have had all the water to herself."

"She is a poor woman, Señor," Maria said.

"Why didn't her husband come along?" Colonel Buffington asked. "He's not much of a man if he has to send a woman to do the work."

Maria stared at him incredulously, then spoke, "Her husband is Pedro Morales."

When she saw that the name of Pedro Morales had no effect on the Colonel, she attempted to explain. "Pedro Morales is a much feared bandito. They say that he was responsible for the death of Don Diego Santos."

The colonel looked up, "But I thought Don Diego Santos died in an unfortunate accident."

"It is true, what you say, Señor, but others say Pedro Morales argued much with Don Diego Santos. They say that Don Diego told the lawyer in town that Pedro had threatened him after he told Pedro that he could no longer get so much water."

"So you think that this Pedro Morales killed Don Diego Santos so that he could take the water?" Colonel Buffington asked.

"Possibly for the water, but they say it was because Don Diego insulted Juanita," Maria said.

"How did he do that?" the Colonel asked.

"Don Diego say to the cantina keeper that Juanita should not have children with Pedro Morales," Maria said. "He say the children would all be worthless, like their father."

"Sounds like a job for the sheriff," the Colonel quipped.

"Pedro has not been seen since the discovery of Don Diego's body. They say Pedro went back to Mexico. The sheriff cannot locate him," Maria said.

Colonel Buffington looked at Maria and said, "She knows where he is. She said that her husband would not be pleased about the water. So I'm sure she'll go running straight to him tonight, wherever he hides from the eyes of daylight and the law. I think, perhaps, that the sheriff would be interested in this. I'll pay him a visit tomorrow."

Maria bid to excuse herself. "It is late. I must go to my family, Señor Colonel. I will return in time to fix breakfast in the morning."

"Very well, Maria. I would like my breakfast at seven," the Colonel said.

He watched from the front door as Maria rode away.

Later that night Colonel Buffington thought he heard a noise outside. Armed with a pistol, he stepped outside and walked a few paces from the adobo. The rancho was cloaked in semi-darkness under a quarter-moon, but the stars could be seen clearly. He looked skyward and gazed aloft for a short time.

Maybe it was the darkness along with the clear, cooling night, but it seemed to the Colonel that there was no cause for alarm. He felt very pleased with his new rancho and its quiet surroundings. Only the howl of a distant coyote broke the silence. A stealthy, shadow moved near the barn, but he presumed the movement to be that of another coyote and figured to leave the creature to consort with others of its own kind. Colonel Buffington entered the adobe to retire for the evening.

Mid-morning the next day, Maria Gonzales entered the office of Sheriff Arles Grooms. The sheriff was sitting at his desk and looked up when Maria entered. "What can I do for you, Maria?" he asked.

Maria stood before the sheriff. "I have been working for Señor Colonel Buffington and I cannot locate him," she said. "I checked the hacienda and he was not there. I looked in the barn and he was not there, but his horse is in the corral."

"Well, you couldn't have worked for him very long because he just now moved into Santos' old place."

"That is true, señor. Yesterday was my first day."

"Maybe he went to sleep in some nook in the adobe that you don't know of," the sheriff said. "When did you see him last?"

"He was there, in the doorway of the hacienda, when I rode away last night, but he was not in the hacienda this morning. I was to fix his breakfast at seven, but he did not answer when I called his name. I think, maybe, that he fell into the well. I called to him, but there was no answer."

Sheriff Grooms stood, "Why would you think that he fell into the well, Maria?"

"Señor Buffington kept the rope and bucket in the barn so that no one could take water without him knowing it. When I looked in the barn, the rope and bucket were not there, señor."

"That doesn't mean that he fell in," Grooms replied.

"The rope is very difficult to attach to the pulley. Señor Colonel Buffington is short like me, and without help, he would have to climb up on the well to attach the rope. I fear he has fallen in," Maria concluded.

At first the Sheriff thought Maria's explanation the exaggeration of an excitable woman, for he had been acquainted with her for many years. Since, however, she had reported the Colonel missing, he would do his duty and ride out to see for himself. He fully expected to find the Colonel sitting in the hacienda, awaiting Maria's return.

"I'll have to get some rope and lower a lantern down that well," the Sheriff said. "I'm going to need some help. Maybe I can get Harlan to come along. In the meantime, Maria, I want you to go on back out there and wait for us," he said as he buckled on a six-gun and holster.

Maria nodded her understanding.

As Sheriff Grooms finished tying the nose of the holster to his leg he asked, "By the way, Maria, have you seen your brother-in-law, Pedro, lately?"

Maria replied, "Oh no, Señor Sheriff. Pedro went back to Mexico, I think."

***

Later that day, Sheriff Grooms wrote in his log book: *Pulled Colonel Benjamin Buffington from well. Death due to falling into well and drowning.*

Much later, in the moonlight, the quietness at the hacienda was broken only by the sound of water being poured from bucket to barrel.

JERRY GUIN is a veteran of the U.S. Navy and a former lumber trader and propane gas distribution manager. A nature lover, he wrote *Matsutake Mushroom* in 1997, a guidebook published by Naturegraph Publishers. Then he turned his abilities to writing western fiction and had short stories appear in *Western Digest*, *The Shootist*, *Roundup Magazine* and *Great Western Fiction Magazine*. Jerry became an Associate Member of The Western Writers of America in 1999. "Likker Money" appeared in the short story anthology, *White Hats*, edited by Robert J. Randisi, 2002. Jerry's book, *Trail Dust, 12 Western Short Stories*, was published by Publish America in 2007, ISBN 1-4241-04404-03.

LOST LETTERS

Barbara Marshak

(Finalist 2010 Cowboy Up Contest)

Marsha lugged the bulky clothesbasket into her bedroom, hip-hugger blue jeans spilling over the side. The summer of 1975 was about to unfold on the western edge of Minnesota and the air already smelled of the hot, dusty days ahead. She dropped the basket onto the slate blue carpeting as a warm wind from the Dakotas surged through the open window.

"It's good to be home," she whispered. Marsha turned in a slow circle, her dark eyes scanning the familiar room. An aura of happy childhood memories greeted her, wrapping around her like a cozy quilt.

She sank onto the princess style bed her parents had bought for her eighth birthday, tears threatening like a sudden spring rain. Her freshman year at the University of Minnesota had been a struggle from start to finish and she was dangerously close to failing. How could she muster the courage to tell her folks she had no intention of going back. As an only child with older parents, Walter and Betty Browne were sometimes hard to relate to.

"Goodness, what do you have in here? More rocks?" asked Betty, carrying another box. The pale mauve in her paisley print pantsuit accented her rosy cheeks.

Marsha blinked back the tears and giggled. "C'mon, I haven't done that since I was twelve."

"Remember our vacation to Yellowstone? That old station wagon we had was so loaded the bottom was scraping the highway!" With striking blue eyes and a contagious smile, Betty's rounded face always lit up a room. "Oh, it's so good to have my baby girl home! Dinner's almost ready."

Marsha rolled onto her side. "Mom?"

"Yeah?"

"I don't...want to go back."

"What?" A distressed look crossed Betty's face, clouding her bright eyes. "Oh, my, don't let your father hear you say that."

"I'm serious, Mom."

"Oh dear, there goes my buzzer," she said, patting Marsha's forearm. "I made all your favorites tonight, sweetie. Let's wait a bit before we talk about this." Betty kissed the top of Marsha's head and hurried to the kitchen.

Marsha opened her satchel and thumbed through the canvas sheets of colorful artwork. Second semester she had taken a painting class in order to fill her credits. To her surprise, dabbling with pastel watercolors and bold acrylics had become a soul saver.

She held up "Sunset on the Mississippi," her most recent, and pinned it on the wall next to Robert Redford's portrayal of the Sundance Kid. The popular movie poster from the modern version of *Butch Cassidy and the Sundance Kid* had hung above her desk since ninth grade. She reached for a pin...maybe it was time to take the poster down.

Something about Redford's rugged cowboy image still intrigued her. His cowboy hat sat low, mysterious eyes staring back at her; head cocked to one side, thick, reddish brown hair touching her collar. She pushed the pin back into the wall. "Okay Sundance, you can stay."

"Dinner's ready!" Betty called.

Marsha walked to the dining room, her bare feet leaving indents in the freshly raked shag carpeting. Smells of baked chicken permeated their contemporary ranch style house. "Mmm, this looks delicious!"

"You'll love this potato casserole." Betty placed the steaming hot roaster on the center of the table. "The ladies at church raved about it at our luncheon. Walt-er Brow-nnne!" she scolded as Walt reached for a plump chicken breast. "We say grace in this family."

Walt sighed while Betty recited a quick prayer, his glasses slipping down his narrow nose. He filled his plate and cut a piece of the tender meat. "The ladies are ready for you to come back," Walt said, pushing up his wire frames. "No more receptionist for my college girl. I set it up so you can work with Elaine in loans. Before you know it, you'll have your degree in finance and can help run the whole bank."

Marsha pushed back her plate. "I'm...not going back to school."

A deep frown creased Walt's forehead and he stifled a low growl. "What kind of nonsense is that?"

"I'm failing, Dad...maybe college isn't for me." The words poured out in a flood.

Walt pounded a fist on the table. "I won't hear you talk like that! Do you hear me?"

"Walt, there's no need to raise your voice." Betty's expression saddened as she glanced from husband to daughter. "It's Marsha's first night home. For the love of the Apostle Paul, let's have a nice dinner together." She gave a half smile and squeezed Walt's hand. "Like the old days."

Marsha inhaled a deep breath. "Dad, I'm serious. I'll help out at the bank for the summer, but don't make me go back to college."

Walt's eyes narrowed to slivers of dark green and he ran a finger along the collar of his dress shirt. "You need to apply yourself. You're not trying hard enough," he said with authority.

"You're not listening! I hate school, I hate it!" she said, and ran to her room in tears. Within minutes a soft tap sounded and Betty joined her on the bed. "Why won't Daddy listen?" Marsha asked between sobs.

Betty brushed Marsha's honey brown hair back in tender strokes. "He only wants the best for you. It's been our dream to send you to college ever since we brought you home and called you our own. We want to give you chances you might not have otherwise had."

"I know that, but why is Daddy so moody lately?"

"Oh, sweet Jesus…" Betty mouthed a prayer heavenward in earnest.

"What is it?"

Betty dabbed her eyes with a tissue. "Wait here…"

Marsha didn't want to hurt her parents, but why couldn't they understand her side. Unable to have children of their own, they had adopted her in 1956 when Marsha was three months old. With Walt's job at the bank, Marsha had grown up lacking nothing. Their small prairie town offered an idyllic life—family vacations every summer, ski trips to Colorado, a comfortable rambler on the nice side of town. The only thing Marsha didn't have growing up was a brother or sister, but she didn't know life any different.

Mom was right—Dad only wanted the best for her. They both did. So why did college feel so wrong?

Betty returned with three envelopes, creased and yellowed. "These came for you two weeks ago." She brushed back a tear, her voice catching. "It's upset your father to no end. He doesn't want to lose you."

"Why would he lose me?" Marsha asked, sitting up.

Betty pressed the faded letters into Marsha's hand. "They came with a note explaining the letters had been lost, left in a desk drawer for years. They're from your..." she paused, "your *mo-ther.*" Betty enunciated the word as though it pained her to say it.

"My *mother*?"

"Go ahead, read them. We can talk when you finish."

Marsha never expected to hear from the woman who had given birth to her. Yes, there were times she wondered and had questions, but *her* mom and dad were Walt and Betty Browne, president of Wentworth Bank, and president of the ladies circle at the Methodist Church. Together they defined the young woman Marsha had grown up to be and she loved them too much to think about the woman who had abandoned her at birth without another thought.

Marsha fingered the worn envelopes, postmarked Mission, South Dakota, 1960.

*   *   *

To my sweet Josette Rioux Sandolz,

Josette...what an unusual name.

A day will come, when you will have questions and there will be no one to give you answers. I am writing with the hopes this letter finds you. Not a moment has passed since the day you were born that I haven't sent a thought to the Creator and asked the Great Spirit to guide and protect you.

Marsha held her breath, her heart pounding deeper into her chest. Creator? Great Spirit? Who used words like that?

You are a special child, Josette, half Lakota, half Wyoming, the best of each. When I was a young girl my sisters and I went to the boarding school for Indians. It was hard—I missed my folks but they told us it was important to get an education so we could adapt to the white world, that life would be better for us than it was for them.

My father, your lala, was a soldier in the great world war and gave his life to our country in 1945 when I was ten. He always called me Josie Girl. Our mother did her best to raise us three girls. The electric lines didn't come far enough out to reach our tiny one-room house. We had a rusty wood burning stove in one corner. It was our job to go out behind the house and pull long weeds to use as fire starter. We had to be careful and listen for the rattlesnakes hiding in the grass.

When Mother was a young girl she was beat in school for talking our Lakota language. Mother wanted better for us girls, so she instructed us to do what we were told, be like the whites, speak the English words. My older sister ran away from the school; she thought Mother didn't love her. I told her she was wrong, that Mother loved us so much she sacrificed being with us. I finished high school to honor my mother's wish and graduated second in my class in 1953. My mother, your unci, was so proud!

Being Indian it was hard to find a job. I moved to Rapid City and started waitressing at a café. I kept my hair curled in a short bob just like the other girls, but it wasn't so easy to hide my brown skin or high cheekbones.

One summer day in 1955 two cowboys strolled in and took a seat at the counter. The first one, stout like a workhorse, said, "You're a squaw, ain't ya. I don't take my supper from a squaw." He said it like it was a dirty word.

The other cowboy shoved him clean off the stool. My boss heard the commotion and came running. Altora was larger than life; she had a deep voice with a booming laugh, yet pretty green eyes that sparkled like jewels. She ordered them out and warned them not to come back.

The next evening I noticed the silhouette of the tall one in the doorway. I remember it like it was yesterday...he had on buckskin chaps with fringed edges and nickel spots. His belt sat loose on his hips and he walked with a purpose. He held his cowboy hat in his hand, exposing his white forehead in stark contrast to his suntanned cheeks.

Altora snapped her gum and stepped around the table to block his path, her legs planted in front of him like fence posts. He held up a hand. "I'm not here to cause trouble, I swear." He glanced at Altora and then his blue eyes locked on mine. "I came to apologize for yesterday...if I may."

Altora sized up his scuffed boots and stained hat. "You damn well better. This girl here's a sweet one. If you know what's good for your skinny backside, you best not mess with her or you'll be messin' with me later."

"Yes, ma'am." He tipped his hat to Altora and turned to me. "My name's Trent Sandolz and I am sorry for yesterday. Ol' Buck can be a real idiot sometimes. We're not real friends, he works on our ranch."

He told us he was from Lusk, Wyoming, a small town about a hundred fifty miles from Rapid. He'd come to Rapid to pick up a stock trailer, but the hitch broke so he was stuck in town until it was fixed. A soft smile formed on Altora's face and she nodded in approval.

Trent Sandolz had the prettiest blue eyes I'd ever seen, and when he smiled there was a hint of a dimple in his chin. He ordered the roast beef special and blueberry pie and by closing time he was the only customer in the café.

Trent offered to give me a ride home. A thick layer of dust covered the dash of his Chevy pickup and the floorboards smelled of ranchland and cattle. We drove through the quiet streets and talked the night away. The next day, there he was, waiting for me at the café.

Altora fell for his charming smile and polite manner. That afternoon she gave me the keys to her brother's cabin in the hills. "Go on," she said with a wink. "You deserve some fun." I was lucky to have Altora for my boss; she looked out for me.

It was difficult, ashamed at times of being Indian, like it was a bad thing. Trent came along and took away those feelings. He made me feel beautiful. We drove up into the hills; I'd never seen them close up. See Josette, the hills are special to my people, your people; sacred even. It is where the Great Spirit talks to His people through the vision quest. My unci, grandmother, told me this, for my parents lived the white man way and didn't talk about the Indian way.

We walked to a meadow behind the cabin and I spread a quilt on a pink patch of clover. Sunlight filtered through the tall pines, casting lace patterns all around us. We lay on our backs, gazing at wildflowers every color of the rainbow, as though sprinkled from heaven.

214

We shared our dreams, wrapped in each other's arms amid a perfume of sweet clover and pine. Trent talked about his family's ranch. His father had gotten hurt and went blind. As the only son, Trent felt it was his duty to help run the ranch. He didn't get along well with his mom...and I sensed he felt more trapped than obligated.

For three wonderful days Trent was free from all of that, free to love me. When he held me close that night I knew I wanted to spend the rest of my life with him. He asked if I could live on a ranch in Wyoming and I told him I could live anywhere, as long as it was with him. So our love had taken root and began to grow.

Two months passed before he came back, for a cousin's wedding. Trent brought me to the wedding to meet his family. His father was soft spoken and easy going, like Trent. His mother was petite and stoic, her face weathered like a rancher's wife. As we got closer, I saw her smile fade, her back stiffen. Trent hadn't told them I was Indian.

His mom took me aside. She told me in a harsh tone I wasn't right for Trent. She said his daddy would never let an Indian live on his land. I knew in my heart it wasn't his daddy who felt that way. And as the evening progressed it became clear that neither father nor son would ever stand up to her rigid ways. I told Trent I was sick and needed to go home, too scared to tell him what his mother said.

A month later I realized I was pregnant. Altora told me to write to Trent, that he would do the right thing. So I wrote a letter, and then another, and a third. My broken heart wants to believe his mother destroyed my letters before he ever saw them.

I went back to the reservation to live with Unci to wait for your birth. I'd seen firsthand how mixed bloods were treated, not fully Indian, not fully white, not accepted by either side. I didn't want that kind of pain for you. So I gave you up for adoption, praying that you would have a good home, one that I couldn't give you.

Three years later the cancer came and it was then I could see the Creator's plan unfolding. Unci told me about the Seventh Direction, how it is the truest direction of all. There is north, south, east, and west, the four directions of Mother Earth. There is above and below. And there is the Seventh Direction, which is from within, for it is the truest of all. Listen to the Seventh Direction, Josie Girl, and you will never regret it. I wish I had known it sooner, I would have told Trent about you. I know he would have loved you too.

Now the sickness is ravaging my body. I have only a short time left in this world and I ask the Creator to bring my letters and my love to you.

Josephine Rioux,
Of the Rosebud Nation

***

Marsha slipped on a corduroy blazer over her white turtleneck with her favorite blue jeans. The mountain air surrounding Spearfish already carried an autumn crispness. The pristine hills, visible from her second story dorm window, offered a peaceful and protective presence. Since switching to Black Hills State College, her days had been a flurry of transferring credits, orientations, and getting settled. She was registered for a major in Art and a minor in American Indian Studies…and so far it felt more right than anything she'd ever done.

She read Josephine's letters several times. It was hard to think of Josephine as her *mother*, but it warmed her heart to know they shared the same nickname.

Her *mom* had offered some good advice too. "Pray about it, honey," Betty said, "and when the time is right your father and I will go with you to the Rosebud Reservation, and maybe Lusk as well."

"Daddy too?"

"Yes, Daddy too."

Marsha picked up her satchel. The late afternoon sun angled through the single window, shining onto Redford's poster above her bed. She smiled, imagining a handsome cowboy and a beautiful Indian girl falling in love. What a beautiful painting that would make.

BARBARA MARSHAK is the author of *Hidden Heritage...The Story of Paul LaRoche,* the inspiring biography of the Native American recording artist, Brulé. *Hidden Heritage* earned Finalist in the Biography category of the National Indie Excellence Awards (2007), and the USA Best Book Awards (2006). Barbara also co-writes for *Hidden Heritage,* a documentary-style television series based on the book and hosted by Paul LaRoche on RFD-TV. In 2008 Barbara won the Bearlodge Writers Residency at the Devils Tower National Monument, Wyoming. She is also a freelance writer with over one hundred published stories and articles.

THE DIFFERENCE BETWEEN COWBOYS AND CLOWNS

Loree Westron

(Finalist 2009 Cowboy Up Contest)

More than anything, Dakota Styrone wanted to be the Tri-State Barrel Racing Champion, for this, she was certain, would win the attention and affection of Lyle Crabtree, *All Round Cowboy of the Year* for three years running. She had been in love with Lyle Crabtree since their paths had crossed -- or rather their horses' paths had crossed -- during the opening parade at the Tinkerton Roundup, the year Lyle won his first silver buckle. One by one, the participants in that weekend rodeo had entered the arena as the announcer called out their names. It was traditional for barrel racers to race round the ring at speed, showing off their equestrian skills while mechanically saluting the crowd. New to the circuit, and nervous amid so many pro-rodeo riders, Dakota did something she had seldom done before. She made an impression. Unfortunately for her, it was not the sort of impression she had wanted to make.

As she adjusted her neon-pink straw Stetson, Dakota's mount, an excitable young quarter horse called Rainbow, darted into the arena in pursuit of the previous rider. With reins dangling, Dakota had been unable to regain control of her horse, and half-way round, the startled animal rose up on hind legs and sent her tumbling, unceremoniously, to the ground. She had landed on her back, flattening her hundred-dollar hat, and for a moment had lain in the dirt listening to the laughter and jeers of the crowd. "And this, ladies and gentlemen," the announcer had said, "is a young lady I'm sure you're going to remember." It was Lyle Crabtree, the next rider to enter the ring, who reached down from his saddle and helped her to her feet. As he took her hand, she had hoped he would pull her up onto his horse and gallop away with her, away from the glare of the floodlights and out into the night. Instead, he simply let go of her hand and left her to make her exit on foot.

It had been the briefest of encounters, but as his hand touched hers, Dakota was certain that their futures would be inextricably linked. Dakota Styrone and Lyle Crabtree were destined to be together.

In the three years since that first meeting, Lyle had proved to be the perfect gentleman. Not once had he reminded her of that humiliating introduction; not once had he questioned her horsemanship or her headwear. His silence on the matter showed that he was a man of honor. The fact that he had not spoken to her whatsoever, had little consequence: he had not sought to add to her humiliation, as others had, and in Dakota's eyes, that proved he was worthy of her love.

Although she admired the circumspect way he approached romance, and his restraint from taking advantage (and seeking recompense for his gallantry as other cowboys might have done), Dakota had grown impatient. She had to get his attention.

"And the next contestant through the gates is last year's runner-up, Miss Dakota Styrone."

Dakota tore into the arena, crossing the start line at full gallop as she headed for the first of the fifty-five gallon drums. Rainbow thundered beneath her, churning up the dark, loamy soil.

"That is one fine-looking filly," the announcer called as Dakota pulled her horse into a tight turn, doubling-back towards the second barrel. Legs flapping like the wings of an earthbound bird, Dakota leaned forward in the saddle, urging her horse into the second turn.

"It's going to be a mighty close race." The voice boomed around the arena, but Dakota did not hear a word as she focused on the final barrel. Pressing her right leg into Rainbow's side, she kept a straight line as they approached the apex of the clover-leaf. Dakota gripped the saddle horn as they plunged into the final left-hand turn and slid round the barrel. She felt her inside leg brush the steel drum, and from the corner of her eye saw it tip to the side. Grabbing the whip, she lashed Rainbow straight down the middle of the arena and back through the gates.

"What a shame," the announcer said. "That five-second penalty has knocked Dakota into third place, just behind our next rider -- last year's Tri-State Barrel Racing Champion, Jo-Jo Wheelan."

"Tough luck, Styrone," Jo-Jo sniffed as Dakota jumped down from her horse. "Let me show you how it's done." Jo-Jo blew a kiss to Lyle on the other side of the fence, then sped into the arena to the cheers of the crowd. As Dakota watched, Jo-Jo's horse made a clean pirouette around the first barrel.

"Don't worry about it, girl," Smithy said from the top rail of the corral where he waited for the bull riding to start. "You'll get her back in the next round."

Smithy always knew how to cheer her up. "When you gonna get yourself a decent pair of jeans and a proper belt?" she teased, nodding at his oversized Wranglers and the frayed hemp rope which held them in place. "You look like an old fool, Clown."

Before he could respond, Dakota's eyes drifted through the railings of the fence to where Lyle warmed up for the next event, the denim clinging to his long, lean thighs as he stretched and loosened his knotted muscles.

Smithy cleared his throat to regain her attention. "We prefer to be called *bullfighters* these days," he said with mock self-importance. "And why do you gals always have to judge a man by the clothes he wears? Pretty packages don't necessarily hold pretty things." Smithy's mouth continued smiling even when his eyes had turned serious.

"I better get out of here," she said as the crowd broke into another cheer. "Jo-Jo's coming through."

"Thirteen point nine five-five seconds," announced the voice in the loud speaker. "That puts Jo-Jo Wheelan back into first place."

Horse and rider sped into the enclosure, pulling up sharply, inches from where Dakota stood. Jo-Jo glared at Dakota, then snapped at Smithy, "Haven't you got something to do besides lech over second-rate barrel racers?"

As Jo-Jo led her horse away, Smithy sneered through his painted smile and climbed off the fence. "I better get back to work," he said, hitching up his jeans. "But don't be so hard on yourself. You're as good a rider as she is. Better even."

Lyle Crabtree was in position to take the All Round Tri-State Cowboy of the Year four years in a row, and for four years in a row Dakota dreamt of joining him on the podium on the last night of the championships. They'd make the ideal couple in their matching Stetsons (she had long since adopted his more sedate stone-colored style of hat): Cowboy and Cowgirl of the Year. In the bedside drawer in her tiny RV, Dakota kept a color photograph, clipped from the *Lewiston Morning Tribune* at the end of last season's Roundup. It captured Lyle at his manly best – stoically bearing up under the pain of having been stepped on by a red roan bull in the final round of the bull riding, his championship silver buckle gleaming at his waist. Every night before turning in she looked at that photo, and every night her eyes welled up at the thought of one day being Mrs. Dakota Crabtree. After three years on the circuit, however, traipsing from one rodeo to the next, Lyle Crabtree still didn't know she existed. This year, though, was going to be different. This year, Dakota Styrone was going to knock Jo-Jo Wheelan off the podium.

"Next rider to come out of the chutes is Toby Wyatt."

The gate swung open and the bull erupted into the arena, hind legs kicking out, and flinging the lean boy rider into the dirt before the bull had time to make a second lunge.

"There goes two-thousand pounds of unadulterated *meanness*," the announcer called as Smithy lured the bull from the fallen rider and chased it out of the ring. "Good try there, Toby. Next up is Lyle Crabtree and a bull they call Hurricane."

From where she sat in the first row of the bleacher seats just to the side of the chute, Dakota could see Lyle easing down onto the back of the silver-white bull. He pulled the bull rope tight around the gloved fingers of his left hand, roping himself – literally – to the back of the beast, hesitated a moment as if in prayer, then gave a quick nod for the chute to open. Dakota held her breath as the bull plunged into the arena twisting in mid-air and spinning tight little circles as it tried to dislodge the rider. A stream of snot arced away as the bull swung its heavy head to the side.

Lyle moved in time with the bucking beast, his free hand held high above his head, swinging forward and back, forward and back. He held the animal firmly between his thighs, his weight centered behind the meaty hump of its shoulders. Dakota held her breath. Eight seconds and a good ride was all it would take. She'd seen cowboys battered before, stepped on and gored, cowboys who forever walked with a limp. And those were the lucky ones. Eight seconds felt like forever. She prayed he'd be okay, prayed as well that he'd get the points he needed, that the bull would keep bucking, that Lyle's free hand would resist the temptation to grab hold.

As Smithy waved his arms above his head and danced around the ring, the bull went into its trademark spin. If Lyle could hang on, this could be a winning ride. Then suddenly the bull changed direction, lunging to the right and throwing Lyle off balance. Dakota saw his purchase waver as his body whipped back against the haunches of the animal and began to slide. She knew he couldn't recover his seat. The ride was over.

"Looks like the boy's in trouble," the announcer said.

As he slid off the side of the bull, Lyle's hand remained held in place by the bull rope, and he dangled helplessly as the animal trotted around the ring. With each shake of the bull's great head, each turn and shift and swerve of its bulk, Lyle's body flailed wildly in the air.

Dakota jumped to her feet.

Immediately, Smithy and the other bullfighters went to Lyle's aid. Smithy threw himself at the bull and loosened the rope, and as the bull swung round to face him, Lyle's hand came free. The cowboy fell to his knees, and Smithy dove between him and the bull, buying the cowboy time to find his feet. Cradling his injured arm, Lyle ran to the edge of the arena while the contest between Smithy and the bull continued.

Dakota was still on her feet, but for the first time since their first -- and in truth their *only* encounter -- her attention was not on the cowboy.

"You better watch yourself, young Mr. Smith," the announcer said as Smithy and the bull eyed each other, each of them pawing a patch of ground. "Hurricane might mistake that for a mating dance if you're not careful."

Smithy turned to the crowd and with an exaggerated nod of his head shouted up at the announcer's booth, "It is!" then darted off to the side as the bull charged towards him. Smithy and the bull spun round in unison, breathing heavily and facing each other once more. As the bull lowered its head, Smithy plunged forward, tapping it beneath the boss of its horns. This was Smithy's chance to shine.

"Is the idiot trying to get himself killed?" Lyle and Jo-Jo stood at Dakota's side, neither of them noticing her presence.

"What do I care?" Lyle said, spitting a string of tobacco juice between the fence rails into the ring. "The sonofabitch cost me my title. He deserves whatever he gets."

"Hey, Smithy," the announcer called, "Hurricane doesn't seem very impressed with your wooing. In fact, I think you might be making him mad."

Smithy played to the crowd, turning briefly away from the bull, and wiggled his hips.

During the eternity in which Smithy was suspended mid-air, Dakota Styrone's world changed forever. She had wasted the last three years in love with a photograph, in love with a man who wasn't worth loving. Watching Smithy as he cartwheeled through the air, she knew that he was the real hero and it was him, not Lyle that she loved.

***

"What a shame," the announcer said as Jo-Jo left the arena. "These young ladies live and breathe their sport, so I know she's going to be mighty disappointed with that ride."

"Tough luck, Wheelan," Dakota said as Jo-Jo reined her horse to a stop. Dakota smiled her broadest smile and looked up at Smithy, perched, as ever, on the top rail next to the gate. "Fingers crossed," she said.

"The next rider will be Dakota Styrone. Dakota has placed second in the women's barrel racing for the past two years and is currently lying in third. The ride she needs to beat is thirteen point five-nine six seconds." The announcer's voice could be heard.

Dakota spurred Rainbow into the arena and veered off to the right to take the first barrel. She cut in close, but they took the turn smooth and sure, then took aim at the second.

"That's two-tenths of a second faster than last year's winning ride by Wheelan."

Dakota grabbed the saddle horn and steered Rainbow into a left-hand turn, pivoting around the second barrel. Dakota felt the crowd's sharp intake of breath as the barrel wobbled briefly then righted itself. One barrel to go.

"This girl is itching for that top spot. It's going to be awfully close."

Approaching the third barrel, Dakota had two choices. She could sacrifice time by taking a slightly wider arc to make sure they got round the turn safely, or they could cut in close and risk upsetting the barrel for another penalty. If the barrel went over, she'd lose the race; if it stayed upright, they were sure to win.

Dakota clutched the saddle horn and kneed Rainbow close to the barrel, reining round to the left. She felt the barrel brush past her leg as they spun out of the turn, then kicked and kicked as they raced back down to the finishing line.

"That's thirteen point five-nine two, ladies and gentlemen. Dakota Styrone is this year's Tri-State Champion."

"I knew all along you could do it," Smithy said, jumping down from the fence to welcome her over the line.

As she slid from her saddle into Smithy's arms, Dakota knew her race was finally over. At last she could tell the difference between cowboys and clowns.

LOREE WESTRON grew up in Idaho but now lives in the UK where she is working towards a PhD in Creative Writing. Her research involves questions of landscape and identity in the literature of the American West. Her short fiction has been highly-placed for a number of awards, and published in journals and anthologies in the UK and United States. She is on the editorial board for the journal *Short Fiction in Theory and Practice* and administrator of *Thresholds, the international postgraduate short story forum.* Secretly, she has always wanted to be a cowboy.

THE BANKER'S WIFE

T.A. Uner

(Finalist Romance Category 2010 Cowboy Up Contest)

It was another dry, hot summer in Tucson, Arizona, 1877, and "Skull" Johnstone sat inside his sweltering shack shining the barrel of his Navy Colt. Inspecting the smooth finish of his weapon, he smiled and holstered it before taking a seat behind his desk. His black Labrador retriever, Sabretooth, lay curled up next to the foot of the desk.

Skull was in the business of killing people. But lately business had been slow and he needed lady luck to turn his fortune around. No matter. Perhaps he could get one of his past customers to ask about and find him work if he got really desperate. After all, the majority of people Skull killed were either cattle rustlers, horse thieves, or murderers that someone wanted dead; and killing those types of people made Skull a well-respected man.

A knock at the door stirred Sabretooth from his sleep. Skull swung his feet off the desk and straightened himself. He wasn't expecting anyone at this hour and wondered who it could be.

"Come on in, it's open," Skull hollered gruffly.

A well-dressed man in a three-piece suit shuffled into Skull's makeshift office. The man wore a bowler hat above circular, silver-rimmed glasses which highlighted icy blue eyes and a weasel-like face.

"Are you Skull Johnstone?" he asked.

"What if I was?" Skull replied as he took off his hat and scratched the back of his head.

"I hear that you're good at taking care of problems," the man said.

"I reckon."

"Well sir, I am in need of your services. Allow me to introduce myself. I'm James Bartleby, of the Bartleby family."

Skull nodded and placed his hat back on his head. "You related to the same Bartlebys that own all those banks up in Phoenix?"

Bartleby smiled. "Yes, that would be us. I am here because I want someone eliminated, Mr. Johnstone. I assure you that I will pay quite handsomely for your services." He handed Skull a small, worn, black and white photograph of a Mexican woman. Skull studied the picture for a few moments before handing it back.

"I suppose you want this woman killed?" Skull asked.

"Yes. Immediately!" Bartleby replied excitedly.

"Who is she?"

"My wife," Bartleby said as he took out a handkerchief and wiped the sweat from his forehead, "or should I say, my soon-to-be ex-wife, Magdalena."

Skull laughed. "If you're looking to get divorced, mister, I reckon you need a lawyer, not an old confederate gunslinger like myself. Besides, I only kill ne'er-do-wells, not innocent young women."

Bartleby scoffed. "Innocent? Dear sir, do not let her feminine charms beguile your judgment. I assure you she is quite the devious vixen. After our whirlwind romance I quite unexpectedly found myself married to her. Of course, my family was most unhappy with my decision to marry and induced her to leave town by offering her a large sum of money; but now, she is refusing to divorce me, no doubt in an attempt to extort more funds from my family."

"And if she dies unexpectedly that would make you a widower and solve all your problems real quick, right mister?"

Bartleby's eyes glimmered malevolently behind the lenses of his eyeglasses. "I knew you were the right man for the job, Mr. Johnstone."

Skull picked up a newspaper from the desktop and began reading. "But it's like I told you, mister, I only kill ne'er-do-wells."

"Would the sum of three thousand dollars convince you to take the job, Mr. Johnstone?"

Skull's eyes nearly popped from their sockets. Sabretooth noticed this and began barking loudly. Bartleby smiled, looking very pleased with himself.

"You just hired yourself a gunslinger, Mr. Bartleby," Skull said happily.

"Excellent. Here is a map that will give you directions to the small ranch where she lives. It's outside Tucson -- on the outskirts of Sahuarita." Bartleby pulled a yellow parchment from inside his jacket and handed it to Skull who studied it intently.

"I know where that town is. If I get started at sunrise, I can be there by late morning.

Bartleby placed Magdalena's photo on the desk and pulled out a roll of money. "Here's a third of the money, Mr. Johnstone: one thousand dollars. Cash. You'll get the rest when you bring me proof of her death. I would also like you to bring me her wedding ring, as well."

"I reckon I can take care of that. How's about I bring it to you along with her severed hand?" Skull asked.

"That would be acceptable; I'll be back in three days, Mr. Johnstone. I bid you good day."

After Bartleby left, Skull downed a shot of whiskey from a bottle he saved for just such special occasions. Today lady luck had not abandoned him.

***

The next morning Skull left Tucson and headed for Sahuarita, using the directions from Bartleby's map. He could not help but admire the salmon-colored, dawn sky as it gave birth to a crimson sun that began its ascent above the majestic desert skyline. After riding for over an hour Skull reined his horse, Lucky Lady, to a stop and secured the animal to a gnarled, dead mesquite.

The spectacular sunrise and ride had ushered in the memory of his late wife. On the weekends he and his beloved wife used to picnic at a nearby spot. Looking back, those had been the happiest days of his life and he wondered if he would ever again experience those emotions. He took a flask of whiskey from his saddlebag and downed a large gulp, the warm liquid cascading down his chest before settling in his stomach. Capping the flask, Skull forced himself to think about the job ahead.

The money he'd make from this killing would set him up real good, he mused. Maybe he could even become a rancher -- anything would be better than the assassin's life he'd embarked upon shortly after his wife's death. Being a woman of strong faith, he knew his wife would've condemned his current lifestyle. But there were few opportunities for a former confederate soldier from Texas who'd migrated to Arizona twelve years ago.

Skull sighed and stared at a large saguaro cactus that stubbornly stuck out of the rocky desert ground. Its lethal green arms reminded him of porcupine quills. He took another gulp of whiskey and then remounted.

"C'mon, Lucky," Skull muttered. "Let's get this over with."

***

An hour later Skull reached the outskirts of the ranch where Magdalena Bartleby lived. The compound sat surrounded by a serpentine rail fence that wrapped around a cluster of wooden cabins of various shapes nestled at the base of a sloping ridge. Skull dismounted and took out a worn spy glass. Searching the grounds of the ranch he espied a Mexican woman hanging laundry on a clothes line behind one of the wooden cabins. The woman's description readily matched the picture Bartleby had shown him. This is too easy, Skull thought. He decided to wait till sundown before killing the banker's wife.

Hours later the clear afternoon sky settled into a dark violet glow as the moon slowly announced its presence behind a patch of evening clouds. Skull walked swiftly toward the ranch and climbed over the rickety fence. He approached the wooden cabin and peeked in the window. Inside he saw Magdalena Bartleby sitting in front of a dresser mirror combing her long black hair. He noticed that she wore a handsome red corset over a grey skirt. Skull stared at the woman's light brown skin and womanly curves, and fought off the image of his wife. He took a deep breath, drew his revolver, and used its grip to shatter the window.

***

Magdalena Bartleby was preparing for bed when she heard a loud crash behind her. It sounded like a shotgun blast as pieces of glass fell to the floor. Startled, she jumped from her chair and stood frozen as a strange man climbed effortlessly through the window, glass crackling under the heels of his boots.

"Who are you?" she asked, her heart racing like a frightened mare.

"Your husband sent me," the intruder said as he leveled his revolver at her.

"So this is what it has come to?" Magdalena said sadly. She knew her husband was a devious man, but she never dreamed he'd hire an assassin.

"I'm afraid so, ma'am," the gunman replied as he cocked the revolver's hammer.

"Can you at least tell me your name, sir? I would like to know the name of my killer before I die."

"I reckon I can tell you that much, ma'am. My name is Skull."

"Skull? Is that what your mother named you?" Magdalena asked, looking surprised.

"My Christian name is William; Skull is my nickname."

"And why would anyone want to nickname you Skull?"

"I suppose because I kill people for a living, ma'am."

Magdalena Bartleby inched closer toward the assassin. The man's lined forehead highlighted a sad, somber face. She sensed hesitation in the gunman. She should've been dead by now. Why hadn't he pulled the trigger already? Perplexed by the killer's apparent vacillation, Magdalena decided she would try approaching him.

"So, why do you kill people for a living, William?"

"Because wealthy folks pay nicely to have their problems fixed."

"I'm not a problem, William. I am simply a woman married to a selfish man who thinks only of money," she said, inching toward him. "He works all day and never even touches me anymore. Do you know what that's like, William? Not to feel loved anymore? Have you ever been in love, William?" she asked mournfully as she stood before him.

"Yes, ma'am, I was married once. But my wife, she, she passed on over a year ago."

Magdalena Bartleby shook her head sadly. "I see. So you must know how I feel?" she asked as she leaned against him and planted a soft kiss on Skull's dry lips. Skull quickly holstered his revolver as he grasped Magdalena's soft, bare shoulders and drew her tightly to him.

***

Two days later James Bartleby walked through the door of Skull's office. The gunman was sitting behind his desk again, shining the new leather boots he'd bought with the money Bartleby had advanced him.

Skull glanced up at the banker. "Hello, Mister Bartleby," he said before spitting tobacco juice into a bucket.

"Did you take care of our little business arrangement, Mr. Johnstone?" Bartleby asked nervously, removing his bowler hat as Skull pulled on his boots.

"Mister, I must say that you haven't been completely honest with me."

"What on earth are you talking about?" Bartleby looked confounded.

Skull arose and smiled. "You never told me that your wife stood to inherit a vast sum in the event of your death."

"What does that have to do with our arrangement?" Bartleby asked, looking confused.

"You see, Mister Bartleby, I require honesty in any business relationship, and after talking with your wife, she made me a better offer, so I'm afraid I'm going to have to cancel our little business arrangement."

Bartleby's eyes narrowed to furious little slits. "Now listen here, you barbarian. I hired you to do a job for me!"

Skull drew his revolver and shot Bartleby in the kneecap. The Banker howled in agony as he fell, blood spurting onto the wooden floor.

Skull stood over the angst-ridden face of Bartleby and smiled. "You were right about your wife, mister. She does have some *real* feminine charms. You probably didn't know that I lost my wife a while back. She got sick from cholera and died. Since then, ol' Skull here's been pretty lonely. So you can imagine when a beautiful woman walks into my life and makes me a darned good offer, well, I'd have to be a fool to turn her down."

"You'll never get away with this! The Sheriff will come after you! You're a dead man!" Bartleby said as he took out a handkerchief and pressed it against his knee to stem the blood flow.

Skull laughed. "I seriously doubt that. Like I said to you when you first came to see me, mister, I only kill ne'er do wells; and any man, however rich or powerful, has got to be lower than dirt to have his wife killed for money. I do believe you're a ne'er-do-well, Mr. Bartleby."

A single shot rang out, silencing the banker, making the banker's wife a very wealthy woman indeed.

T.A. UNER was born in New York and graduated from George Mason University with a degree in Speech Communication and a minor in History. An avid traveler, his love for history has taken him across America and to various countries around the globe. He lives in Virginia.

BULL PEN

Paul Conn

(Finalist 2009 Cowboy Up Contest)

We had finished our breakfast and decided to have a smoke with our last cup of coffee before we left the Elk Antler Café in Walden when one of the largest men I have ever seen in my life charged through the front door.

He had to be on the upper side of a half a foot over six feet tall and if he didn't weigh all of two-eighty, well, I'd walk over there and eat his hat, which would have been a hell of a chore at the moment because I was stuffed.

The pretty waitress, Missy was her name as I recollect, turned abruptly and fled to the kitchen.

Johnny Marlow, my pard, leaned in my direction and whispered under his breath. "It's a good thing we done et. That rascal could finish off all the grub in this joint and then use one of these table legs for a toothpick." I just nodded my head and went back to rolling my smoke.

That big fellow seemed in a raw mood as well. After slamming the door, he turned and ambled up to the bar. The owner of the establishment, Will Stamps, a dandy cook I might add, eased up to the bar wringing his hands on his apron. "Can I help you, Ike?" he said.

"Just a cup of coffee," the big man snapped. "I'm in a hurry this morning. Has Smitty been in here yet?"

"I ain't seen him or none of your sidekicks this morning," Stamps stated, as he set a cup of steaming coffee in front of the man.

"Sidekicks my ass!" Ike bellowed, as he came up off of the stool. "You would be wise to watch your manners around me, old man." And with that said, the behemoth turned and stormed back through the door of the cafe.

By the time the dust had settled, Johnny and I had finished our smokes so we strolled up to the counter to pay for our breakfast. Johnny was a little short on spending money, as he called it, so I had graciously told him that I would pay…again!

Mr. Stamps saw us approaching and met us at the counter. He had a beleaguered look on his face, so I thought to cheer him up a little. "Who was that raging bull what left without paying for his coffee?" I said.

Stamps gave us a halfhearted smile.

"That bull moose is none other than Mister Ike Fletcher. He seems to think he has got everyone pretty much buffaloed around here. And I guess he does to some degree. I have never seen him do harm to another man, physically mind you, but he has two or three saddle tramps that I suspect does his dirty work for him. There is one man in this park though, that has not, and will not, take any guff from him. His name is Clyde Sweeney, but I seldom see him up this way. He has a nice spread down at the south end of the park near Rand."

Johnny and I exchanged glances.

"What's the tally for our breakfast, Mr. Stamps? Throw in the price for that cup of coffee settin' there gettin' cold as well."

"Why? Are you men friends of Ike Fletcher?"

"No sir. Clyde Sweeney is my uncle. Thanks for the lowdown."

Will Stamps' face lit up with a smile and he extended his hand to the both of us. "It's a pleasure to meet any kin of Clyde's. Tell me y'all's names again. I'm gettin' to where I can't remember nothin'."

Johnny grabbed Stamps' hand and gave it a good pumping. "Mr. Stamps, the name is Johnny Marlow and I'm not rightly kin to Mr. Sweeney but I'm pard to his nephew here."

I extended my hand and shook. "I'm Coley Parnell, late of Benavides, Texas."

***

The year was 1883, just past the peak of the cattle drives, and Johnny and I had left south Texas for what I knew would be the last dust-choking, thunderbolt-dodging, stampeding and bean-eating time. We were both getting a little long in the tooth for this line of work and I was ready to do something else. I didn't know about Johnny, but he said he was along for the ride.

A month before we left I had received a letter at the post office in Kingsville from my Uncle Clyde. It was postmarked Rand, Colorado. In the letter he stated that he longed to see me and he thought that I might like a change of scenery. That was all the kick in the pants that I needed. Before I left Kingsville I penned him a letter in return stating the fact. One last drive to Ogallala and from that point I was Rocky Mountain bound!

I still had that letter from my uncle in my pocket as Johnny and I rode out of Walden and more or less followed the shallow Illinois River south through the most spectacular country these eyes had ever seen.

We stopped to water our horses after we were a couple of hours out of town and Johnny had been smilin' like a possum the entire way. "This place is grand," he said. I was glad that he had come with me.

Uncle Clyde was a sight for sore eyes. "He looks just like a mountain man," declared Johnny. My uncle just chuckled as he embraced me in his arms. "I've missed you, son." Before the both of us got misty eyed, he fixed his gaze on Johnny. "Hell, I reckon I am a mountain man, John. Get your skinny ass over here and let me see if I can squeeze them dust caked lungs of yours past your gizzard!" Johnny got the first hug of his life from a man, and I'll be damned if he didn't blush.

Uncle Clyde had been meticulous in his planning and building over the past seven years and he had a place any man would be envious of. As we were all making our way toward his cabin the front door opened and out walked an…an Indian. He stopped on the porch before reaching the stoop, raised his right hand, and said, "How!"

Out of the corner of my eye, I saw Johnny's Adam's apple bob three times. I swear it!

"How Hell!" Uncle Clyde laughed. "Grassy Knee, get your goofy ass off that porch and meet my nephew, Coley Parnell, and his friend, Johnny Marlow."

Grassy Knee could speak the white man's word as well as any of us, and he regaled us with stories around the fireplace well into the night and early morning. It was a grand time. Johnny was laughing and spinning his own yarns. Uncle Clyde and I were just happy to be together once again.

We all slept in the next morning, with the exception of Grassy Knee. Johnny didn't budge until almost noon. We sat on the porch until the early evening and just enjoyed each other's company.

"Let's saddle up, boys," Uncle Clyde chirped, as he rose from his rocker. "I want to show you men what I've been up to all these years."

***

Uncle Clyde laid claim to sixteen hundred acres in a place that could best be described as Heaven. As we rode across his spread, he enlightened us about the land.

We had just ridden upon a small rise when Uncle Clyde stopped his horse and dismounted. We followed his lead and dismounted as well. "This entire area is known as North Park," he said. "As far as you can see until the mountains rein it in. There was so many buffalo in here at one time that Grassy Knee's Ute tribe called this place the Bull Pen."

"There was a heap of antelope and deer in this place with the buffalo," Grassy Knee added. "That was many winters gone. I was ready to go with them until that old man found me. He gave me a new home. He is my brother now. I will wait some more winters before I rest."

A moment of tranquility followed as each one of us, in silence, paid homage to a land that none of us rightly deserved. But we were all, every man jack of us, tickled as hell that we had been blessed enough to stand upon the ground where others had been so blessed as well.

As the moment waned, I rolled a smoke and tossed the makings to Johnny. "You say they called this place the Bull Pen. That reminds me of a big fellow Johnny and I saw yesterday morning up to Walden as we were finishin' our breakfast."

"Ike Fletcher?" Uncle Clyde asked.

"That was the handle Mr. Stamps said he carried. Also said you didn't take to the man and his ways. Is he serious trouble?"

"Did you or Johnny have words with Fletcher?"

"No sir."

"That white man is a heap of dung," spat Grassy Knee.

"He's trouble alright," Uncle Clyde finished. "Just don't know when it will come to a head."

Uncle Clyde continued by telling us that Ike Fletcher had been coming out to his place about once a month for the past year wanting him to sell out. He stated that the conversations had been cordial, although annoying, at the beginning, but that they had deteriorated during his last visit.

"I told the sumbitch not to set foot or hoof on my land again," said Uncle Clyde. "And I damned well meant it."

We saddled up and traversed the rest of my uncle's land. This was a handsome place. As we made our way back to the cabin along the western banks of the Illinois, we could see the Medicine Bow Mountains to our east and the Rabbit Ears Range and Never Summer Mountains to the south. A robber jay scolded us from a nearby tree as the sun crept behind the low hanging clouds bordering the Park Range.

***

Johnny and I had finished the supper dishes and were heading out to the front porch when I noticed riders approaching. The big one in the middle looked damned familiar. We both grabbed for our gun belts and slipped out the back to make our way around to each side of the cabin. The riders came within twenty feet of the porch before halting, and Johnny and I were in place and waiting.

244

"First time you brought any company with you, Ike," said Clyde, still sitting in his rocker. "Are introductions in order or are we just wasting our time?"

Ike Fletcher was flanked by Jack "Smitty" Smith and Charlie Hogan, and all three men sat quietly atop their horses with hands draped across the saddle horns.

A nod from Fletcher and the two outlaws turned their horses, walked them out about ten paces, and then turned them again so they would be back in line with their leader.

"There is no need for introductions," Fletcher bellowed. "This will be our last conversation. You will write out a bill of sale for what I have offered you and payment will be made right here on the spot. Then you and that old Indian can pack your shit and leave. The alternative is to repeat your previous statements and be pumped full of lead where you sit. Either way, this place will be mine before the sun goes behind them mountains."

Uncle Clyde and Grassy Knee rose as one, the arms of each man raised in unison, thus showing their antagonists that they were unarmed. Each man came to rest upon singular lodgepole columns that supported the entrance onto the porch.

I could hear a coyote off in the distance serenading the sun as its rays blistered the tops of the ridges miles away. And I could hear Johnny, not literally, but nonetheless I still heard him, taking a calming breath as he placed the sight of his .36 Navy Colt upon the left coat pocket of a man named Charlie Hogan. A man he had never seen before this day.

And I was hearing myself as well, and with the coyote's plaintive cry expiring with the sun's final burst of flame, I took my calming breath and waited for my uncle to start the parade.

"That was a pretty sunset," Clyde spoke softly. "I wish you fellows could have seen it. But here we are waiting on me to make up my mind about what I should say to Mr. Fletcher's fine offer."

Smitty and Hogan eased their guns from their holsters. Fletcher had a rifle seated in his scabbard but he left it there. He would not dirty his hands with what was to come.

"What's your final word, Clyde? I want it now!" Fletcher roared.

"Go to Hell!"

Uncle Clyde and Grassy Knee both let loose with matching Greeners and Ike Fletcher, or what was left of him, hit the ground dead. At the moment the shotgun blasts found Fletcher, Johnny and I were emptying the saddles of Smitty and Hogan. Three men were dead in a matter of seconds, and as the acrid smell of burnt powder filled the air the sun found its place behind the mountains.

"Where in the hell did those shotguns come from?" I asked, as I stepped around the corner of the cabin. Johnny and I were checking the men we had just shot for any signs of life when Uncle Clyde answered my question. Both men were dead. There was no need to check on Fletcher.

"You boys come here and we'll show you," Uncle Clyde replied.

Johnny and I climbed the steps as the two men stepped back and pointed to the backsides of the lodgepole columns. Both columns were exposed to show the slide away compartments that had housed the deadly weapons. Johnny and I stared in disbelief as Grassy Knee stepped forward and slid the rounded door back into place on one of the columns. Once closed it was undetectable to the naked eye.

"I'll be damned," Johnny said.

"Not tonight you won't," Uncle Clyde stated. "Don't know if I can say the same for them fellows, though."

***

A week later as we watched the sun setting over the Park Range from the front porch, I asked my uncle why it was that some men thought they had the right to hold dominion over their fellow man.

"I don't rightly know the answer to that question, son," he replied. "And I doubt that I'm the man that you need to be asking."

Grassy Knee rose silently from his chair and walked slowly into the cabin.

PAUL CONN is a native of Salem, Oregon, who has resided in rural Cullman County, Alabama, for more than forty years. Previous stints in the Alabama Army National Guard, as a writer and photographer for *The Cullman Times*, and as a supervisor in the production of pistol ammunition have provided a wide range of experiences to draw upon. His wife of more than thirty years, Dana, is a preschool teacher and they have two sons. Joshua resides in Cullman with wife Carolina and daughter Jazmin. Lance resides in Nashville with wife Debra.

GRABBING THE REINS

Arthur Kerns

(Finalist 2010 Cowboy Up Contest)

Pa just sat balanced on the corral rail and stared at that nag he got stuck with. The brim of his beat-up gray hat was pulled down almost to his nose to keep the late afternoon sun out of his eyes. I looked at that round white mark on the back pocket of his jeans. It came from holding his can of tobacco chew and matched the faded circles on the backsides of most ranchers up here in north Arizona. Wished he paid more attention to our money problems instead of trying to keep the ranch the way Grandpa ran it. I decided to see if he was in the mood for listening to me about those pothunters.

I climbed up next to him and pointed at the quarter horse in the corral. "Pa, think he's worth breaking?"

"He's already broken, Scott," Pa answered, chewing his tobacco plug slow. "Just needs some training."

Yeah, I got the point. Just like me, I needed some training. I tapped out a cigarette from a fresh pack. Pa's hair used to be light sandy in color, like mine. Now it had gray hairs mixed in.

"Done anymore thinking about the proposition from them diggers?" I continued.

His shoulders stiffened and I regretted bringing the topic up again, especially right before suppertime. He just stared ahead at the quarter horse that was pawing the dirt. It was useless to try and persuade him. Pa, when he set his mind, he was like a rock. Period. He would have nothing to do with those *grave robbers*, as he called them. He said that the pottery and old stuff in those mounds scattered on our land should stay there, especially the bones. Still, maybe I hoped he would bend a little bit.

"We discussed this matter, time and time again," Pa said, taking his time, saying each word distinctly. "We don't lease our land to pothunters." He gave me that look he always gave me, as if I had a hard time understanding anything.

However, I understood a lot, like our ranch barely broke even what with the price of cattle being what it was. I also knew we had valuable Indian pots on our land and we could dig them up legally. That pothunter told me that this was the time to sell. The collector's market wanted Indian stuff and if we didn't act, maybe in a year nobody would be interested. Right now we could get good prices.

"Come on Pa, it's not as if we don't pick up a pot or two, now and then." I tried to see if his eyes showed any kind of compromise. "What about all that Indian stuff hanging around the house?"

"Those we found on our land, without digging."

The rail creaked when Pa shifted himself, but he wasn't budging an inch on the pothunters. Stubborn as that mule we once owned and which Pa found me hitting with a board because it wouldn't move. Pa had yanked the board from my hands and walloped me on the butt with it, yelling something about God's creatures and how we shouldn't mistreat them. Then he whispered something in that mule's ear and both of them just walked off. He liked animals as much as he liked those Indian burial mounds.

"Grandpa used to dig and he sold to that store in Scottsdale for years," I reminded him.

Now that was the truth and Pa knew it. In the ranch house, we had a room full of pottery, wooden sticks with old feathers, baskets, you name it. Just laying there in the bookcases, up on the walls. Next to the barn was a shed full of the stuff in boxes collected by grandpa and great-grandpa. Pa himself had brought back some of that stuff when he had been out working the range.

Then Pa took a deep breath and said, "Scott, can't you see the difference?"

I expected a sermon about acting on principles coming up, but all he did was take a big spit of tobacco and look at me in a disgusted way. Then Ma came to the corral.

"The family can use the money," I said, looking in Ma's direction. "We could get a new truck and, Ma, you could get some new appliances."

Well, she had put on that haughty attitude of hers. She had been hanging around with some of the rancher wives who had leased out their land to the pothunters and had some extra money to spend. The women wore fancy clothes from Phoenix, and I knew she envied them. I guess that's why she had bought herself a big pair of sunglasses, which she wore on top of her head, like those rich gals in the magazines. She murmured, "I'm getting more than just some washer and dryer." Her answer did not sit well with Pa. That really made me feel uncomfortable. No one said anything for a few minutes, so I started to ramble a bit.

"I'd like to get some cash and try out Phoenix for a while," I said, and Ma's mouth opened the same way it had when my brother announced he was heading for San Francisco. Quickly I added, "And maybe enroll in some business courses at Arizona State."

This, of course, was a load of bull, which I'm sure neither of them believed, especially Pa. All I wanted was to get out of northern Arizona and live a while in Phoenix, work in a bar, meet women, and generally enjoy myself. Ranch life took up a lot of time, and I'd just turned twenty years old.

Pa looked at me and Ma, then started in on what our Indian friend, Quentin, would say if we sold out to those pothunters. "What about Quentin's ancestors laying there in those mounds?" he almost shouted.

I told Pa we were not selling the bones, just the artifacts. We would respect the bones. Hell, I liked that old Hopi, Quentin. I liked him a lot. When I was a kid, he used to take me out on the range exploring. He'd showed me where fresh springs were, showed me places and things even Pa didn't know about. He took me to see the petroglyphs over in the east section of the ranch, the ones chopped off by thieves a few years later. But there was no way of reasoning with Pa, so Ma and I strolled back to the ranch house.

On the way back she whispered she had something important to tell me. "Just listen," she said, "until I'm finished what I have to say." We walked into the kitchen and she sat in a chair and looked me in the eye. The room was warm and smelled good from the roasted chicken in the oven.

"I'm getting a divorce from your father. I'm tired of all this and I'm getting older. I want a change and something brighter in life."

I turned away and looked out the window toward the corral. Pa had gotten off the rail and was wandering around picking up tack. Ma didn't say anything else. Behind me, I heard her get up and start setting the supper table. I remember my throat being so dry I had to walk over to the sink and get a glass of water.

"I guess you'll come down to Phoenix with me," she said, scooping the mashed potatoes into the red bowl her mother gave her the year before grandma died.

"I was looking forward to going on my own for a spell. Know what I mean?" From the silence, I knew it wasn't the answer she wanted. "I'll wash up," I added.

When I returned to the dining room, Pa was seated at the head of the table and had just finished saying the blessing he always gave before meals. Then he helped himself to the potatoes. Ma pretended to be concerned with filling her own plate. I had no appetite, except that the chicken smelled pretty good.

Pa broke the silence. "One way to bring in some extra money would be to sell some of the Indian collection we have laying around here. Some of this pottery is valuable. That store in Scottsdale would take it, I'm sure."

Ma said nothing. Since I had been the one talking to him about dealing with the pothunters, I thought it was my place to say something.

"That's a great idea, Pa," I said, and turning to Ma, "Don't you think so?"

She just sort of threw her fork onto her plate. "Too little, too late. That money will get me down to Phoenix."

I never saw Pa look the way he looked. The look didn't come all at once, just sort of grew from one stage to another, from not understanding what she was saying, to coming around and knowing full well that she intended to leave him and the ranch. Damn, he was about to cry. I knew I had to do something.

"*Mother*. That money will help pay for you to spend a few months down there in Phoenix this winter. You can be a snowbird like all those people from the Midwest."

"Scott, I think you should let your father and me talk alone."

Damn. She was going to make the big announcement, although Pa, I figured, knew what she was going to say. Also, I felt partly to blame in that I'd pestered the old man all this time about the money we'd make, and how I could go to Phoenix and raise hell. All that probably had put the bug in Ma's ear to move out, and besides, I knew what divorce meant to ranchers, just like what had happened to the Judsons over near Winslow. They couldn't get a mortgage to buy the other spouse out, so what did they do? Divided up the land. Most of the ranch got taken by some gentlemen ranchers from California, and what remained of the ranch old man Judson couldn't make go.

"No. I am staying and being part of this." I surprised myself. Pa looked at me as if I was speaking Navajo or some other strange language. His eyes were watery and sort of bouncing around in his face, like what happens when someone falls off a horse hard.

"Scott. Please do go, and tend to the animals." Ma sounded snottier than I had ever heard her.

"No, *Mother*. Our temporary money problems are solved. Father just solved them."

"Jonathan," Ma stuck her face in Pa's direction, "I am leaving you and this ranch for good." Ma tossed her napkin on the table.

Pa just lowered his head. He looked old. He had a quick mind and I was sure he knew what it meant for the ranch. That was when I mouthed off.

"So where will this divorce leave me," I shouted. "The son who stayed home and worked the spread to help the family keep

254

on going, when my big brother got to be a lawyer and live in Sausalito?" I banged the table with my fist. "That leaves me screwed!"

They both looked at me as if they were looking at some stranger who had just walked in the door. Neither one said a word. It was as if I scared them.

"And another thing," I said, grabbing a chicken leg, "This family ain't leasing out to any damn pothunters. Period."

ARTHUR KERNS and his wife Donna, a noted watercolorist, moved to Scottsdale, Arizona, nine years ago from Northern Virginia after he retired from the FBI. Since his first recognition in high school, he has pursued the dream of putting words to paper (now onto the computer screen). Recently, he won first place for a short story in the Cave Creek Film & Arts Festival and has published articles in national golf magazines. In addition to an espionage thriller set on the French Riviera, he has completed a mystery based on an unsolved 1929 murder of an FBI agent in Phoenix.

STATE OF GRACE

Becky Coffield

(Honorable Mention 2007 Arizona Authors Literary Contest)

Grace Niece was a familiar sight as she ambled the beach each morning, stooping often to gather interesting sticks, shells, and what she called her "magic rocks". Slung over her bony shoulder was a large canvas tote that she carefully carried her treasures in. Often her decrepit thirty-eight year old horse, Count-On-Me, joined her. The horse wore neither halter nor lead rope, but dutifully accompanied Grace, stopping when she did, moving on at her behest. There was a time when horse and woman were one, and Count-On-Me had carried Grace swiftly down the sandy beach, into the hills and up the Elysium River. Now the two shuffled along shoulder to shoulder.

Tall for her years, still ramrod straight, and terribly thin, one could tell Grace had always been slender, but now fragile better described her. Her curly gray hair peeped from under an old stocking cap she had knit years before, and her large hazel eyes, although slowly becoming dulled by cataracts, were still expressive and alert. She had once been very stylish, but in her older age she dressed only in denim and colorful layers of shirts and sweaters, half of which ended up tied around her waist when she got too hot.

Three decades ago Grace had come to Gold Rock, a small town on the southern Oregon coast. Despite her longevity there, no one really knew her, and as the small coastal town exploded in growth, even fewer yet came to know her name or anything about her – only that she owned over 350 feet of river front property and a ridiculously large house, which many had, in vain, tried to buy. Early on Grace had the thirty-seven acres well fenced. Count-On-Me, Mr. Nibbles (her pet goat and the Count's close friend) her dogs, cats, and chickens roamed the acreage freely, even up to her back porch. She loved to sit on her back veranda in good weather and hold court with her small cluster of devotees. Mr. Nibbles and Count-On-Me did a wonderful job of keeping the lawn and wild foliage under control. Grace kept her vegetable plants and flowers in pots on the back porch in exchange for the free weeding and yard service the animals performed.

Of the half a dozen people who knew Grace, Carol Davis, the long-time local postmistress, knew her better than most, as postmasters often know their clients by their mail – or lack thereof. Twice weekly for thirty years Grace had walked to the post office, some two miles from her home, to look for letters from her son. There were never any personal letters for Grace, but Carol made sure there was always some kind of mail in Grace's postbox – flyers sent randomly to "Postal Patron," or months-old magazines belonging to people who'd long since moved that she tore the address labels off.

"Today's the day, Carol. I know I have a letter today. I dreamed it last night!"

As always Carol feigned a search. "Hmmm. I don't think so. Not today, Grace. Maybe next time, hon."

"Well, my Matthew will be coming any day now. Any day he'll be here."

"I'm sure he will, Grace. You be sure to bring him on by so I can meet him," Carol's response was always the same as she watched the older woman look forlornly out the post office windows, square her shoulders, then leave on her trek.

Slowly Grace would retrace her steps home, make a cup of tea, then proceed to muck out any horse droppings that were within fifty feet of the house.

"Hey, there, Mister Count," she always addressed the horse thusly, "what are you doing droppin' your apples by my porch?"

The horse gravitated to her like a tired, old lover, and she stroked his long muzzle and whispered in his ear. "Matthew is coming any day, Mister Count. I've got to be ready. Keep an eye out for me."

Dinner hour was usually early for Grace and it, like her other meals, was simple, but her table was always elegantly arrayed with extra place settings lest Matthew and a friend should drop in unexpectedly. She still put out seasonal table decorations, especially at Halloween and Christmas, Matthew's two favorite holidays. She carved a pumpkin every year and bought a bag of Halloween candy, which she would eat over the course of many months.

Nights were hard for Grace. Never a television watcher, she usually read or worked on her poetry or books until she had to prop her head up. Sometimes she sorted through the treasures she had gathered from the beach. She kept all her precious sticks, shells and rocks in boxes in the bedroom she had set aside for Matthew, each box labeled with her son's name scrawled across its side.

For the last two years she had been making an inventory of sorts of her achievements – and her shortcomings and failures.

She had labeled the slim notebook: My Reckoning. Grace counted on dying when she turned 76. "People go to hell in their 80's," she told me, her veterinarian, the only person in town who really knew her. But 76 passed – then 77. She was 78 and ready to go. She would die, she resolved, as soon as she saw Matthew again. "The 80's seem too wicked to have to live through. Best to go with some dignity," she dispassionately reasoned. She wrote out her Will in her little notebook, leaving her animals, property and monies to Matthew…and, so I later found out, to me.

I called monthly on Grace and her little menagerie. She was the only customer that I didn't charge for a house call, for she'd been my first client thirty-odd years ago when she'd moved to Gold Rock as a recently widowed, handsome woman. I'd opened my practice only a few weeks earlier when she presented me with Count-On-Me who was in need of hoof trimming. Desperately seeking customers, I gladly accepted her and her little idiosyncrasies and growing menagerie.

For three decades I called upon her, sometimes only checking to make certain everything was okay. I ministered to Mister Count, Mr. Nibbles, the dogs she had over the years, and the various cats who took up residence at her abode. Now it was Count-On-Me who increasingly worried me. The horse, though lovingly cared and provided for, was failing, and I feared the horse's death would be a fatal blow to Grace.

"Grace, we need to talk about Mister Count."

"Now, now, Jered, you musn't worry so much. He's doing fine. We all have our little down days."

"Grace," I began again.

"Did I tell you my son is coming? No? Well, he is. Anytime really."

"That's good, Grace." I'd wondered where the hell this thoughtless, irresponsible son was. I'd have a few words to say to him if I ever got to meet him.

"I'd like to meet him." I forced a smile.

"Oh! What a splendid idea! You look so much like him, you know. I'll have a large dinner and invite everyone in Gold Rock!" Childlike, she clapped her hands.

I nodded encouragingly as I closed up the back of my truck. To date no one, including myself, had ever seen the inside of Grace's house. "That will be good, Grace." Then I could not help but add, as I always did, "Grace, you have everything you need now, don't you? You'll tell me if you need something?"

"Of course, dear. Don't you worry yourself about me. I've got Mister Count, Nibbles, and Nestle," she smiled warmly, her eyes tearing slightly.

Grace was adamant that she'd seen Matthew two summers ago. She'd been at a crosswalk when he had turned his car across her path. She called out in a shocked, weak voice, but the car had continued on. Every day that week she walked the highway, praying for another sighting. She looked like a pathetic bag lady to the tourists who sped up and down that stretch of road, her large eyes frantically searching the occupants of each passing vehicle. Locals just shook their heads in pity.

"Something has got to be done for that woman. She's getting too old to live alone like that. Look at her, poor thing. She looks like a good wind will blow her away. What does she need all that property for anyway?" And grumble, grumble, grumble.

Standing in line at McKay's grocery late Sunday afternoon, buying a bottle of water, she saw her son exit the store. She called and frantically waved her skinny arms, but he did not hear her over the store's summer hubbub, and she could not push through the crowded line. "Wait your turn, you old bitch," growled a fat man in a loud Hawaiian shirt three people ahead of her.

"Matthew! Matt! Wait! Please wait!" By the time she made it to the parking lot he was nowhere to be seen. Devastated, she paid to have her groceries delivered from then on. For three entire weeks she did not journey to the post office. She went out only to feed Mister Count, Nibbles, Nestle and the other citizens of her backyard.

"He saw me, Mister Count. I'm sure of it. But he walked away. Why would he do that? He's all grown up now, Mister Count. So handsome, too." She cried as the old horse breathed softly in her hair. "Why would my Matthew do that? Perhaps he didn't see me, that's all." He just hadn't seen her, she decided. But she continued to have her groceries delivered.

Several outbuildings, slowly losing their battle with ferocious winter storms and lack of maintenance, miraculously managed to stay erect on Grace's property. A woodshed and a small barn stood exhausted. The barn, kept clean and warm, served as headquarters for her menagerie, and was filled with a cacophony of animal talk. In the decaying woodshed set further back on the heavily treed property, under a heavy, rat-chewed tarp, a demolished, old sports car rotted away. She had not looked upon the car in thirty years. The settlement Grace received from the insurance company had been unimaginably large, but not large enough to mend the hole in her heart as two caskets had been lowered into the ground. Aimless for many years, she had finally moved to Gold Rock and purchased the property to be near the site of her husband's fondest memories, to see him fishing in the Elysium River, to hear him laughing in the breakers on the beach.

"Mister Count's not looking so well this afternoon, Jered. Can you stop by? He hasn't eaten in two days. He won't even touch his grain."

"I'll be there first thing in the morning, Grace," I promised.

She spent the evening with Count-On-Me, gently brushing him and quietly singing his favorite songs. The aged horse groaned in appreciation and looked on Grace with love-filled rheumy old eyes. "Now, darlin', you'll be feeling better tomorrow, I promise. We'll go for a short stroll. It'll be sunny, you'll see," she said softly as rain pelted the metal roof almost drowning out her voice. "The doc will come and fix you up. You want to feel good when Matthew comes now. You remember him, don't you?" Mister Count feebly switched his tail as if in reply.

Midnight had tolled when Grace returned to the barn, her heart heavy. Count-On-Me lay on his side, his breathing slow and labored. Grace put a ruffled pillow under the horse's head and covered the stiffening body with a comforter. Tears stung her eyes and a hard lump formed in her throat. She sat on her knees studying and gently stroking the dying horse, humming Matthew's favorite lullaby, and as she gazed upon Count-on-Me, she saw not her decrepit, old horse. Thirty years of blindness fell away as the horse gazed lovingly upon her. In crushing pain she realized she could not possibly have seen her boy at the store. She saw Matthew as he lay next to his father, deep in the dark, cold earth. She had put his mangled six-year old body there. Slowly she lowered her head and let out a piteous groan of agony. In an instant she knew there would never be letters or visits. Her long wait was over. "Mr. Count, I have been a very foolish old woman," she cried.

She laid down under the comforter with Count-On-Me, resting her head on his shoulder. She could hear his heart painfully laboring and his breath becoming shallower.

Soon the two breathed as one. Their hearts, beating slowly in unison, finally faltered to a stop. Only the light breathing of Nibbles and Nestle filled the barn as the two small animals gathered in vigilance and mourning. Grace and Count-On-Me had made their last passage together. I found them early in the morning, both under the pink flowered comforter, Mister Count's head resting comfortably on a frilly sham, Grace's curly hair peeping from under her wool knit cap.

BECKY'S information can be found on page 56.

OTHER TITLES BY MOONLIGHT MESA ASSOCIATES, INC.

Western Titles:

Stoney Greywolf Bowers, *Reflections from the Wilderness*,
Cowboy Poetry, 2009.

Jere D. James, *Saving Tom Black* A Jake Silver Adventure,
Book I, 2009

Jere D. James, *Apache,* A Jake Silver Adventure, Book II,
2010

Jere D. James, *Canyon of Death*, A Jake Silver Adventure
Book III, Forthcoming 2011

Rusty Richards, *Casey Tibbs – Born to Ride*, Biography, 2010

J.R. Sanders, *The Littlest Wrangler*, Award-winning Young Reader
Book, 2010

J.R. Sanders, *Some Gave All*, Western Nonfiction, Forthcoming 2011

Paula L. Silici, *A Way in the Wilderness*, Western Romance, 2011

Other Titles:

R. L. Coffield, *The Ben Thomas Trilogy: Northern Escape, Northern
Conspiracy (The Thomas Bay Murders)* and *Death in the Desert.* Award-
winning Suspense, 2005, 2009, 2011

Becky Coffield, *Life Was A Cabaret: A Tale of Two Fools, A Boat, and a
Big-A** Ocean,* Award-winning Humorous Memoir/Travel Adventure.

Breinigsville, PA USA
28 March 2011
258645BV00004B/39/P